W9-BUF-832

"The point being," Xanthy went on, "it has nothing to do with us, or with this place. Shirley. Shirley! You don't seem at all relieved!"

"I'm not," she replied. "I mean I am, but . . . but we still don't know who she is."

Though at the moment she couldn't say why that should matter to them. She'd never really known the woman. J.Q. had made the reservation. Alberta had cleaned the house. Others had seen her, spoken to her. Shirley herself hadn't laid eyes on her until she was dying. Perhaps that was it. To die among strangers seemed a horrid fate. Not to have people around whom one knew. Not to have one's last breath listened for, one's last words . . . What had her last words been? *Ahmiss macuhly.* A mumble. Barely articulate. The brain, even then, being taken over, destroyed. Identity fading. Though, in this case, identity was just plain missing.

"I still want to know who she was," Shirley said stubbornly.

By B. J. Oliphant
Published by Fawcett Books:

DEAD IN THE SCRUB
THE UNEXPECTED CORPSE
DESERVEDLY DEAD
DEATH AND THE DELINQUENT
DEATH SERVED UP COLD

DEATH
SERVED UP
COLD

B. J. Oliphant

FAWCETT GOLD MEDAL • NEW YORK

Sale of this book without a front cover may be unauthorized. If this book is coverless, it may have been reported to the publisher as "unsold or destroyed" and neither the author nor the publisher may have received payment for it.

A Fawcett Gold Medal Book
Published by Ballantine Books
Copyright © 1994 by B. J. Oliphant

All rights reserved under International and Pan-American Copyright Conventions. Published in the United States of America by Ballantine Books, a division of Random House, Inc., New York, and simultaneously in Canada by Random House of Canada Limited, Toronto.

Library of Congress Catalog Card Number: 94-94396

ISBN 0-449-14896-3

Manufactured in the United States of America

First Edition: December 1994

10 9 8 7 6 5

Prologue

In southern Colorado the high, jagged spine of the Rocky Mountains splits at the southern end of the Sawach Range into the San Juans on the west, the Sangre de Cristos on the east, two rugged legs bestriding the vast reaches of the San Luis Valley. From these surrounding mountains, snow-fed creeks wander across the wide basin to join the upper waters of the Rio Grande. East from Del Norte and Conejos and Romeo, southwest from Saguache, west from San Luis the crooked rivers run, joining, melding, plunging at the border into a narrow gorge cut below the surface of the desert, where mile stretches upon empty mile of chamisa and cactus, and distance is limited only by the far-off crumple of blue mountains.

The gorge goes deep, cleaving northern New Mexico in two, the gleam of its tumbling waters both tantalizing and unapproachable from above. Infrequent tributaries cut the looming walls, but they are only seasonal gushers, muddy torrents from the melt-off in spring, or spills from the frequent cloudbursts that enliven late summer. At other times they are only dry and plunging arroyos, dotted blue lines on a thirsty map.

North of Taos, joining the east and west sides of the severed land, a bridge spans the gorge to create an awesome photo opp, as attractive to tourists as sugar to ants. There travelers point their cameras over the bridge railings at rafters floating far below: at black boats bobbing on white water in the spring or yellow dots placidly floating on the inky surface of late summer, dwarfed by depth, deep in the somber shadow that a thousand firefly flashbulbs cannot illuminate.

At the town of Taos, as self-consciously arty a settlement as any in the Western world, the north-south highway approaches the river, running parallel while the mountains draw in on either side. Here little rivers spill down once more, from the Jemez in the west, from the narrowing end of the Sangre de Cristos in the east, sometimes silt-laden, sometimes clear, draining the cloud-capped, snow-topped heights. From these tributary streams a skein of ditches unwinds, centuries-old acequias that veer from gates upstream to wander along miles of carefully sloped canals, crossing arroyos in wooden flumes, dipping below streams in grated siphons, flowing into a stutter of bright orchards, a thousand corn and squash patches, a greening of narrow alfalfa fields and grass pastures beneath the welcome shade of thick-boled trees.

The trees dig in their feet along the ditches, beside the little rivers, driving their toes deep into sands that remain moist even when the desert winds have dried the stream to nothing, deep enough to hold the trees erect through the squalls and surges loosed by monstrous thunderheads of summer, flash floods that wash through the arid land, leaving a sodden ruin in their wake. Most often, however, the braided sands of the floodplains bask dryly beneath a silver-green tremble of cottonwood and willow, an emerald fur of tamarisk, a gray-green fluff of Russian olive—an exotic tree, imported long ago and now become as native as the

2

Anglos, as the Spanish, as the Navajos, as the Pueblos, who were all, at one time or another, invaders, too.

These sinuous riverine woodlands are, collectively, the bosque, prowled by raccoon and snake and skunk, nested by the crow and the magpie, home to the woodpecker and the owl. Here children go exploring, local folk go riding, and fireflies blink lavalieres upon the trees at dusk. Here woodcarvers find fallen cottonwoods with hard and twining roots from which kachina figures can be made. Here cows wander, some who have broken their fences, some who have been let out to save the cost of hay. Here abandoned dogs make uneasy alliances with the local coyotes to win a precarious living.

And, like beads strung upon the bosque, here are the little farms with their orchards of peach and apricot, apple and plum; where lazy horses stand head to tail, where chickens clack and cackle and sheep munch contently on grass. Here is a remnant of New Mexico as New Mexico onetime was, before art colonies and skiing, rural and peaceful and close to the spirits of the earth.

As here, at Rancho del Valle, where Shirley McClintock has recently come with her old friends J.Q. and Xanthippe Minging, and her foster daughter Allison. One more move in a long lifetime of moves. This one, they like to hope, the last.

1

THE WOMAN STAYING in the casita near the pond—the house they all called Frog House—came banging on the door in the middle of the night. It was the wrong door, the door to J.Q.'s quarters, which woke Dog, who barked disapprovingly in a husky, late-night voice. Though J.Q. had been oblivious to the door banging, the bark woke him, and minutes later he was in Shirley's room, shaking her by the shoulder and asking where the car keys were. They had not yet developed comfortable routines about such matters. Even now, months after the move from the ranch in Colorado, they all spent frustrated hours pearl diving for things they needed while awash in seas of stuff they didn't.

Shirley heaved her pajama-clad six-foot-three out of bed and stumbled across the half-lit room toward the dresser where the keys might have ended up when she went to bed last night. She'd stayed awake late, hooked on a PBS documentary, and her mind was full of screen-dream images, an angry collage, witches being burned, people being persecuted, accusing voices. She choked, put a hand to her throat where a protesting shout was threatening to come

4

out, inappropriate, surely at this hour of the night, morning, whatever.

She stopped, body sagging, trying to focus on the half-remembered horrors, and the whole thing wisped off illusively, leaving only the words she'd thought of since waking. Witches. Witch-hunt.

"Car keys?" J.Q. insisted.

"What did you say you need the car for?" she asked in a grumpy voice, as annoyed by this tantalizing vanishment as she had been by ominous images.

"The woman in Frog House is having a stroke or something," he muttered, sounding no happier than Shirley at being wakened. "She's in no condition to drive, and the fastest way to get her to a doctor is to drive her to the hospital in Santa Fe."

Alertness came suddenly, and with it a return of emotion, whatever she'd been feeling in the dream, as though someone had a fist in her chest, squeezing her heart. Ghastly foreboding, and what did one blame this on? Indigestion? The second (or was it third) glass of wine with dinner? Dissatisfaction with the world at large? Or just one more manifestation of that unwarranted grumpiness she seemed to be carrying around with her lately, the world on her shoulders and no convenient place to set it down.

She swallowed deeply. "Which hospital? I'll call ahead and say you're coming."

"Xanthippe heard all the ruckus and she's up. She can call ahead and say we're coming. I need you in the car in case this female passes out or has a convulsion. Get your robe."

She felt like shrieking, but didn't. No point nursing grievances, piling bad on worse. Things were moving, and she couldn't stop them. Discussion would only waste time, which she needed to put on a clean shirt and a pair of jeans instead of the robe J.Q. had suggested. Bathrobes conveyed neither respectability nor credibility, qualities that were often useful in a crisis. Her wallet was on the dresser where the keys had been, behind pill bottles that rolled and rattled under her hand as she groped. Credit was as needful as credibility, though she couldn't seem to find her pocket and would be damned lucky if she could even find her way! By the time she reached the drive, J.Q. had the woman in the backseat, the car door open, and the wheels making nervously skittish noises on the damp gravel. The air smelled of wet earth. It had been raining.

"What's her name?" Shirley mouthed to a slightly disheveled Xanthippe Minging, who was hovering beneath the lantern on the patio wall, mothlike in a light gray caftan.

"Tremble," answered her friend in a muffled voice, peering into Shirley's face as though into a crystal ball. "Are you all right?"

Shirley snorted. "Something I watched on PBS before I went to sleep, a documentary. I must have dreamed about it. Makes me feel as though I'd eaten spoiled fish. Her name, again?"

"Tremble, I think." She patted her white hair into its more usual configuration with a great flutter of fabric. "Alicia Tremble. Ms." Having said which, she flew off through the gate toward a phone while Shirley climbed in the backseat to take charge of the passenger.

The woman was excruciatingly thin, turkey-bone wrists and bird-claw fingers clutching her wispy night-black hair as though to keep her head from exploding. "Oh, God," she cried in an agonized whisper. "Oh, Oh, God."

Shirley perched beside her to be thrown abruptly forward as J.Q. backed up, then backward as the Cherokee raced off down the drive. Shirley eased back into the corner of the seat and braced herself.

"Where?" the woman shrieked. "Where are we going?" She was wearing a dark, high-necked, long-sleeved dress. Her legs were encased in heavy stockings. Not suitable for the time of year. Suitable only, Shirley thought inappropriately, for wearing to a funeral.

"We're getting you to a hospital," Shirley replied. "As fast as we can."

The woman leaned back, talons still clutching her forehead as she stared blindly upward. "I don't know what's happened. I've never had a headache like this." On her forehead and upper lip, tiny beads of sweat glistened in the lights of an oncoming car.

"Did you bump your head?" Shirley asked. "Have you had any trouble seeing?"

"No. No. No bumps, no vision problems . . . We took a drive this morning, into town. Monday I went back over to Jemez Springs—ah, God." She clenched her head again, sobbing for a moment until the pang passed. "We had dinner in Tesuque. Surely this couldn't result from something I've eaten. Could it?"

Shirley shook her head, at a loss. She wasn't aware that food poisoning gave people headaches, but then she wasn't aware it didn't either. Maybe it was an allergy. Maybe not. Malfunction of the human body was not exactly her field.

"You said we," she murmured, trying to focus through all this late-night mental clutter. "Is there someone with you?" And if so, why wasn't that person doing the midnight ride!

"I was meeting a client."

"A client?"

The pain seemed to abate, at least momentarily, for the woman took her hands away from her head, fished in a pocket for a handkerchief, and wiped her face. "No, no. I'm not thinking what I'm saying. It doesn't matter. Really, it doesn't matter. Oh, God. This is terrible!" She bent forward once more, shuddering.

Shirley braced herself in the corner, scrabbling with one hand for the seat belt. She started to buckle it, then realized Mrs. Tremble wasn't belted in. Before she could do anything about it, however, the woman went into another spasm. At the same moment they swerved outward and passed a lumbering semi at a speed that made the tires squeal.

Shirley took a deep breath. "Take it easy, J.Q."

7

"I'm only a little over the speed limit," he snarled. "I wish a cop would stop us. Maybe we could get an escort."

There seemed to be no cops abroad in the night. The highway was virtually deserted. The lights of Cuyamunge fled past, then darkness, then the road marker for Tesuque.

"Where are we?" the woman murmured. "Where?"

"Just coming up on the opera road," Shirley replied. "We'll be in Santa Fe in just a few minutes." J.Q. had had some tests done at St. Vincent, so he was probably headed there. Come to think of it, St. Vincent was probably the only place he could go. All the other local health centers were dedicated, if one believed their advertising, to drying out, coming down, or cooling off. What if St. Vincent's wouldn't let Alicia Tremble in? Lovely thought. To reach any other general hospital in the direction they were headed, they'd have to go all the way to Albuquerque.

"It came in the house," the woman said. "Amiss maculy, oh. Ahmiss maculy . . ."

She made a grating, hideous sound, grabbing for her head, then collapsed against the car door, her arms dropping limply into her lap. Shirley got the seat belt around her and moved her so her neck was straight against the seatback. The limp figure was now ominously still, breath barely moving the thin chest.

They crested the hill and started down the long slope into town, past the military cemetery, down St. Francis Drive to St. Michaels—with J.Q. running the red lights whenever there was no cross traffic—left on St. Michaels, forever on St. Michaels, past vacant malls and Santa Fe College and more malls, until they ran out of city and the hospital came up on the left, a storied pile of fake pink adobe, quiet as a mortuary—not a pleasant thought—even at the emergency entrance.

Shirley slid out onto the asphalt. J.Q. opened the door on Mrs. Tremble's side. She didn't move.

"She's out," said J.Q., leaning into the car, feeling the woman's neck. "We need help."

"I'll get someone," Shirley called, setting out at a stiff

8

trot for the emergency-room door. She was not up to running the mile, that was sure. After a long hot shower and some warm-up exercises, her new steel knee would function at a fast walk, but this was ridiculous. She clomped to a sliding stop at the nursing station. "We've got an unconscious woman in the car," she said, loud enough for the person at the desk to hear her over the phone conversation she was having.

The green-clad woman continued talking, but she gestured at the same time, an imperious summons to someone or something. In a moment another woman appeared, pushing a gurney. "Outside? Let's go, then."

As she turned, Shirley got a good look at her name tag. Patricia Micaela Garcia, followed by a long string of letters that Shirley decoded to mean she was an emergency nurse, or a nurse who did emergencies. Something of the sort.

The automatic doors hissed open as they approached and hissed again behind them. J.Q. was still half in and half out of the car, his wiry form twisted into an awkward tangle. He withdrew at the same moment the emergency doors opened again to disgorge two additional hospital workers. "We'll get her," said the nurse. "Just stand aside, please."

Shirley obediently stood aside. J.Q. stood aside with her, scratching his neck and yawning. "Don't suppose we could just go on home," he muttered. "Suppose we'll have to stick around."

"Oh, J.Q., I should think so. They don't know who she is or anything. Let's go in and get it over with."

They followed the gurney, stopping at the desk while the patient was taken away.

"Sit there," said the woman on the phone. "I'll get to you in just a moment."

The nurse, Pat Garcia, returned. "Tell me about her," she said, leaning down. "Was she conscious? What did she say?"

"She woke us, saying her head hurt," Shirley replied. "She was crying with the pain of it. She said she'd never had a pain like that before. I asked her if she'd hurt herself, she said no. She said she'd been on a drive Monday, and out to dinner tonight. Last night, I guess."

"She's your . . . what? Sister?"

"No relation," said J.Q. "We have a little guest ranch north of town. She's staying there, alone at the moment. She came banging on our door. . . ."

"What's her name?" asked the other woman, who had now finished with the phone and come up with a sheaf of forms on a clipboard.

"Alicia Tremble," said Shirley. "Don't ask me how to spell it, I don't know."

"Home address?"

"No idea. It'll be in our files back at the ranch. We didn't stop to pick up paperwork."

"She's from California," J.Q. offered. "The car she arrived in has a California plate. She left the ranch this afternoon in a car with a New Mexico plate. She may have a friend or acquaintance here."

Shirley added. "She said she came to meet a client. Then said she hadn't. Whatever."

J.Q. snorted. "The car I saw had a vanity plate. It said REBORN."

Shirley made a moue, shaking her head. What did that mean? A born-again? A mystic? Or one of those indefinable across-all-boundaries Santa Fe types who was sort of into-the-cosmos? Crystal gazers. Tarot readers. Channelers for prehistoric guides, returned through time. Wannabee Indians. Whoops, wrong term. Native Americans.

Pat Garcia tapped her bottom teeth with a thumbnail, ordering her thoughts. "The greatest help you could give us would be to find out where she's from, give us some clue as to where we might get a medical history. She's unconscious right now, so she can't tell us anything."

"Do what we can," Shirley murmured, suddenly overcome by both sleepiness and a strange sadness. Poor woman. Here all alone, with no one to help. "Do you think it's serious?"

"That much pain isn't reassuring. We'll have the results

of some blood tests in a few minutes, and that may help us treat her."

"I'll call you with what we have," Shirley promised. "Patricia Micaela, right?"

"An Irish family joke," the nurse replied, giving Shirley a once-over. "My mother was Irish. You're probably old enough to remember Pat-and-Mike jokes."

"Both saints, as I recall," said Shirley blandly.

"Oh, yes. In any language." Drawled. Laconic. She'd heard it before.

Patricia Micaela went away, leaving the other woman to write down names and addresses and phone numbers. "Please let us know if you find anything that might help," she said, not as a request, as an order. "The name of her doctor would be very useful."

Shirley nodded, turned, started for the entrance, J.Q. ambling along at her side.

"What time is it?" she asked.

"Almost half-past three."

"Wonder what's wrong with her."

"Haven't the foggiest." He yawned. "You want to drive back?"

"Might as well," she replied. "I'm wider awake than you are."

They made the trip in virtual silence. Shirley glanced at her watch when they arrived, muttering that Wednesday was half-over already. It was four o'clock. Dog was waiting outside the gate to do her usual welcoming shuffle bark: woof, sotto voce; mincing steps sidewise, mincing steps back, ears down, entire rear end in motion. She followed them as they went through the kitchen into the small adjacent area that served as combination breakfast room and office. One corner was devoted to business, with a recently installed desk that held the computer, the cash box, the journals, the envelopes and stationery and stamps. Shirley took out the file marked IN RESIDENCE and looked through it for Alicia. It was Alicia Tremple, not Tremble. In the space provided for home address there was only the address of a hotel in Phoenix.

"I remember making that reservation," J.Q. remarked. "She said she was calling from California and that's the phone number in California, but she was leaving the same day, so she asked us to send the confirmation to the hotel she'd be using in Phoenix."

"Not awfully helpful, is it."

"Well, we've also got her credit-card number. Someone can probably get an address from that."

Shirley picked up the phone and dialed the number on the reservation sheet. It rang repeatedly, then clicked, sighed, and said in a mechanical voice, "The number you have reached is out of service at this time. Please check the number."

Shirley sat, staring at the phone. It began rasping in her ear, one of those tones that was more an assault than a signal. She hung up and sat for a moment, rubbing at the lines between her eyes. Then she looked up the hospital phone number, dialed the area code on Tremple's number, then the information number.

"Police," she said.

"Is this an emergency?"

"I want to make a report."

Clicking, ringing. "She dialed it for me," said Shirley. "All I wanted was the . . ."

Babble. "I'm calling from near Santa Fe, New Mexico," Shirley said. "I run a guest ranch here. One of our guests has just been taken to St. Vincent's Hospital in Santa Fe. Her name is Alicia Tremple. We have reason to believe she is from your area, and it is imperative that the hospital locate someone who can give them a medical history."

Click switch, click switch. Shirley repeated the message twice more, virtually word for word. The last person on the line asked for her name and phone number and the phone number at the hospital.

"Why wouldn't her phone be working?" J.Q. asked.

Shirley nodded. "Your guess is as good as mine. Maybe

12

she didn't pay her bill. Maybe she moved just before she left and has a new phone. Maybe she had it temporarily disconnected because she was going to be out of town. Who knows?"

"An innkeeper's lot is not a happy one," J.Q. sang in a raspy baritone. "When there's Good Samaritaning to be done, to be done."

She groaned. "I don't mind, J.Q. It's just frustrating not to know where she came from, and it's our fault. We should have insisted on getting a home address when she called."

"How do you like innkeeping in general?"

"It's not all that bad."

"Wow. Your enthusiasm is overwhelming."

"Well, I'm not . . . invested in the place yet. Haven't put my mark on it. Pretty soon now. Maybe we'll start by redoing the gardens. Xanthippe thinks they're badly planned."

"You? You know pasture pretty well, but where gardens are concerned, you can't tell a petunia from a . . . pig's ear."

"I shall learn."

"Learn what?" asked a drowsy voice.

They turned to see Allison's adolescent form slumped against the dining-room doorway, noticeably nubile in her light pajamas.

"That lady? Is she dead?" Allison asked.

"No! Of course she's not dead. We got her to the hospital, and now we're trying to find out who . . . where she belongs, I guess."

"If they couldn't find out from her, that must mean she's pretty bad off, right?"

"Allison, I don't know." Shirley shrugged helplessly. "She's unconscious. That could mean something or nothing, I'm no medical specialist. Did we wake you when we left?"

"No. I heard Xanthy moving around. She told me the lady in Frog was sick. She was fine when the man picked her up this afternoon."

"You saw her?"

"She was waiting out in front of Frog House. I talked to

13

her. Alicia Tremple, she introduced herself, then she was all full of questions, you know, the same questions they all ask. Who owns the place. Who lives here. Are we open year-round. Do we have a weekly rate."

"We charged her the weekly rate on her credit card," said Shirley. "She should remember that."

"Of course you answered all her questions," said J.Q., in a wry voice. "Saving us the trouble."

"Yeah. Well. I try to be helpful." She started to say something else, then stopped. "Never mind. You guys look beat."

"The word is descriptive," Shirley admitted. "I think bed is the proper place for all of us."

Allison nodded, turned on her heel, and went, leaving Shirley staring after her. She was growing so fast. Shirley thought, not for the first time, that adolescence was like bindweed—before you knew you had it, you were swallowed up by it. Allison had been only eleven when Shirley had seen her first, a serious, troubled child, trying to look after Gloria Maxwell, her alcoholic mother, and Charles Maxwell, a father no better than he should be. When both mother and father had ended up dead, one right after the other, Shirley had managed to get custody of Allison. By chicanery, J.Q. always said, amused. By out-and-out chicanery. Shirley didn't care. She'd do it all over again. Allison at fourteen was still a gem of a child.

J.Q. mumbled something and went off down the corridor after Allison. Shirley yawned, fetched herself a glass of water, opened the kitchen door to let the night air in, sat back down at the table, suddenly too sleepy to move. Across the screen door a single tiny light made a dotted line, emerald flashes, once and again and again, a coded firefly message from the night. Within the last day or two, some creature, two-legged or four, had gone down along the river into the bosque and had returned with a firefly passenger on fur or hair or clothing. Now here it was, all alone, far from home, in the wee hours of the morning.

As was Shirley. Despite her brave talk, she didn't yet feel

at home. She felt like a visitor, too diffident to be settled, sorting through her mental baggage, searching for the one right thing. Many recent mornings had been haunted by unpleasant dreams. She kept feeling there was some chasm gaping in her way, something ugly dodging away from the light, something with teeth hiding in the dark.

It wasn't innkeeping that gave her the horrors. Innkeeping was easy compared with most of the things she'd done in her life, though responding to the oddities of the guests did eat up the hours. They locked themselves out or ran out of toilet paper at midnight. They found garter snakes in the swimming pool and had a panic about it. They saw something they thought was a mouse and immediately assumed they were going to die of hantavirus. One man from Brooklyn had heard Dog moving around outside his door and thought he was a bear. What continually astonished Shirley about these small crises was that they happened to city people accustomed to the daily risk of death as they moved among gangs and pickpockets and car jackers, presumably without histrionics.

To each his own dangers. To each his own loves and memories and nostalgia.

"What happened?"

This time it was Xanthippe standing in the doorway, her hair neatly combed. "How's Mrs. Tremble?"

"Her name seems to be Tremple, Xanthy, and I'm not sure how she is. She was unconscious by the time we got her there. There's no home address on the reservation sheet. The computer says her phone number is no longer in use. We've got the credit-card number we charged her week's rental to, but it may take the police or a physician to get information from the card service people."

Xanthy gave her a sympathetic but searching look. "You should be getting some rest."

"Indeed I should. So should you."

"I was worried about her. She seemed in such dreadful pain."

Shirley nodded, suddenly awash once more in that apprehension that was becoming all too familiar. "I know," she said, hushed. "Oh, Xanthy, I know." There was no doubt about the pain. The woman had been suffering. Migraine? Concussion? Shirley's fretting over it would do no good; the doctors would have to find out. She rose, turned Xanthippe firmly about, and walked beside her into the nether regions of the house. Here were quiet, thick walls and thick roofs, a whoosh of fan blades blowing out the hot daytime air to replace it by nighttime cool.

As they reached the end of the corridor Shirley staggered slightly.

"What?" asked Xanthy.

"Damn knee," muttered Shirley.

"Does it still hurt?"

She considered telling the absolute truth—that it hurt a good deal, most of the time—and discarded the idea. Other people's pain was always boring. "It does all right in the daytime, Xanthy. It's just at night it keeps me from sleeping. At least I suppose it's the leg. Not to worry, I won't die of it."

They reached the end of the corridor. Xanthippe turned to the right, toward her apartment at the end of the cross hall, and Shirley went left to her bedroom on the opposite corner. Allison and J.Q. had the two south-facing bedrooms along the hall. Of them there was no sign, and the only sound was the rush of air on its way from a multitude of open windows to the big exhaust fan above the corridor.

" 'Night," murmured Xanthippe from her doorway. "Don't fret over it, Shirley. Morning will be time enough."

" 'Night," replied Shirley. Her bed waited as she'd left it, the light cover thrown back, the sheets and pillows cooled in her absence. Through the western window she saw the bloated moon sinking toward the silhouetted mountains, a silver bubble on the darkest possible blue. She stripped off her jeans and shirt, pulled on her pajamas once more, stood at the dresser staring at the pill bottle, decided against it, fell into bed, and drifted into an uneasy sleep before she had time to think about why she might not.

16

* * *

Morning brought an annoying clarity. As soon as she was up and dressed, Shirley took her keys and went out the back door, around the house, over the acequia, and let herself into Frog House. Why hadn't she come over here last night? Of all the stupidity! She shook her head, angry at both herself and J.Q. Here they'd both talked and talked about identifying the woman, and neither of them had thought of coming here!

The living room was neat, almost as neat as when Alberta prepared it for a new guest. No papers on the table. Three paperback books on one chair. She opened one with a protruding bookmark, finding it pristine. New. Unread. She went through into the kitchen. Also neat, one clean pan on the drain board, the dishwasher containing only a couple of plates, three mugs, some silverware. No personal belongings, no ring in a saucer, no engraved watch beside the sink. Refrigerator holding only some cans of fruit juice, some coffee cream. Her puzzlement increasing, Shirley went into the front bedroom. The bed was disarranged as one would expect; a pair of shoes stood in the corner, a few articles of clothing hung in the closet. There was nothing at all in the dresser. The open suitcase on the chair held only underwear, stockings, folded slacks, a few casual shirts.

The windows were open, but it was hot in the house. Unbearably hot! She went into the hall and looked at the thermostat. It was set over ninety. Shirley tried to turn it down and found that the little lever was missing. Stuck on hot. How had the woman stood it? Why hadn't she complained?

In the bathroom the tub and shower curtain showed evidence of use and there was used soap on the basin beside a damp washcloth. Two of the neatly hung towels were still damp. As Shirley turned to leave, something caught her eye and she turned back. Dirt on the toilet seat. Muddy water that had dried. As though someone had put a slightly muddy shoe onto the seat, to tie it perhaps. As she again turned to leave, her eye was caught by reflected light. The sunlight was virtually blocked by the huge spiky bush outside the window, but one ray found its way through and was reflected from the radiator cover, just under the window. She peered at it from an angle, trying to catch the light. Something had dried there, soapy water maybe, leaving a shiny imprint of whatever it had drained off of. Less than an inch wide and perhaps two and a half inches long, with curved ends. Something from the medicine cabinet, perhaps. She looked in the medicine cabinet. A toothbrush, a tube of toothpaste, a round bottle of vitamins. Nothing that matched the elliptical shape on the radiator cover.

The other bedroom was unused, still immaculate. Nowhere in the living room, kitchen, bath, or bedrooms was there a single piece of paper, a wallet, a diary, an address book. It was as though the woman had no name, had no place.

And the all-too-familiar feeling swept over her again, the nastiness, the threat in the dark. She growled with impotent anger as she left the house, locking the door behind her. The morning was already warm with a gusty breeze from the southwest. The lilies beside the pond dipped and fluttered, like butterflies. Thirty feet away the black cat prowled along the pasture fence, the long fur of his tail tip whipping like a guidon. The sun performed an immediate exorcism. Whatever the nastiness was, it wasn't out here. Out here was free of it, cleaned by the wind and the light.

She called the hospital from the kitchen phone. No change in Ms. Tremple's condition at this time. This time was eight o'clock Wednesday morning. There was no change in the Tremple phone number when Shirley phoned it again. Still not in service at this time.

"You going to give them the credit-card number?" J.Q. asked from the doorway. He came in and poured himself a cup of coffee.

"I tried to give it to the nurse I spoke with, but she said it should go to the police."

"Police?" asked Allison, arriving via the dining-room corridor.

"She's an unidentified woman. Police identify people."

"Call the cashier's office," J.Q. suggested. "They'll take the credit-card number."

The person in the bookkeeping office was very interested in Alicia Tremple's credit-card number, and phone number, and the name of the hotel in Phoenix.

"I never would have thought of that," said Allison around a mouthful of cereal.

"You've never been hospitalized," J.Q. said. "Shirley was, remember? And, as I recall, the financial office had a legitimate interest in how the bill was going to be paid." He moved from refrigerator to stove. "Does anyone but me want eggs?"

Shirley rejected eggs. Allison, who was deep in a large bowl of cereal with milk and bananas, also rejected eggs. While J.Q. scrambled, Shirley worked the crossword puzzle in the morning paper. When J.Q. joined her at the table, she had another cup of coffee and a slice of toast with orange marmalade, just to keep him company.

"What's on the agenda for today?" she asked.

"Fences," muttered J.Q. "I've never seen such rubbish."

Shirley shrugged. It was true, the fences were rubbish. New Mexico fences were as idiosyncratic as everything else about the place. So-called coyote fences made of un-peeled saplings leaned in all directions at once. Some pastures were enclosed by ad hoc concoctions of rusted barbed wire strung to any convenient tree. Often fences only hinted at enclosure. Cows short on forage set their hooves pur-posefully at the bottom of unanchored stretches and pushed the fence flat, then walked across it into neighboring or-chards or gardens, retreating prudently to the riverside bos-que or up the arroyos when confronted by angry persons with dogs or guns. Property owners either fenced the cows out, reconciled themselves to providing free forage, or, as indicated by the not infrequent heaps of bones and hides along the river, took advantage of the incursion to fill the home freezer.

As though reading her mind, J.Q. announced, "There were thirty cows down in the riverbed this morning. Thirty of them. Just wandering around. Neighbor across the fence said they belonged to the pueblo down the road. Come summer, they just turn 'em loose."

"Probably just as well we don't have cows anymore," she commented, just to see what he'd say.

"We will have, if I don't fix the fences," he muttered, still focused on his eggs and toast.

Allison cleared her throat.

Shirley looked up from the paper, startled. It had been a formal, annunciatory sound. "What?"

"If you're all through talking about cows, I wanted to tell you what happened yesterday. Tuesday. Just after supper. You guys were outside, and I got a phone call. From Aunt Esther."

"From Mrs. Lawrence Brentwood?" asked Shirley unbelievingly. "When was the last time we heard from her, them?"

"Every year since we flummoxed 'em and I got to live with you, they've sent me a Christmas card with their names printed on it, Esther and Lawrence Brentwood, Melanie and Cheryl. That first year, when I was eleven, they sent me a Christmas present. It was one of Cheryl's old shirts, I recognized it. Last year they took Melanie's name off their Christmas card, so I suppose she got married or something. And Cheryl called me once last spring, right after we moved down here from Colorado. She said she just wanted to know how I was. That's the whole list."

"Why didn't you tell us at supper last night?" Shirley said plaintively.

"I didn't know how I felt," Allison confessed. "I sort of wanted to think about it first. I was going to tell you last night when you got back, but you looked really tired."

"Did they have anything special in mind?" asked J.Q.

"Aunt Esther wants me to come for a visit."

Shirley took hold of the edge of the table and held on, waiting for the vertigo to pass. It was a sensation she associated with childhood dreams of falling or rides on roller coasters, that dreadful moment when the bottom fell out, leaving only panic and a bubbling pressure in her throat, a scream trapped in silence. She had felt like this when her own children had been lost, when her second husband died. She had felt like this when Allison had been kidnapped, when they hadn't known where she was or if they would ever get her back. Now here it was, a black hole in her midsection, all too familiar.

She forced her voice to remain calm. "She wants you to come to Albany?"

"Um. She said it's time we got to know one another better."

"And . . . ?"

"She said Mother would have wanted us to stay family."

Shirley swallowed deeply. She had not known Gloria Maxwell intimately, but she knew without doubt that getting closer to Esther and Lawrence Brentwood would not have been high on her list of priorities: Allison knew this as well, or better, than Shirley did.

"And?" she asked.

"And nothing," said Allison. "I told her I'd think about it. Her calling like that. It felt . . . peculiar."

Shirley agreed it was peculiar. She took a sip of tepid coffee, made a face, and went to dump the residue and refill the cup with something fit to drink, meantime reminding herself sternly that Allison was not her daughter. Allison was her foster child. The possessive fury of a tigress with one cub would not be an appropriate response. Allison stayed with Shirley and J.Q. by virtue of an agreement with Esther and Lawrence Brentwood, Allison's aunt and uncle. Neither of whom, three years ago, could have shown any less concern for the recently orphaned Allison if she had been a totally unrelated person living in Somalia.

"Do you have any interest in making the visit?" J.Q. asked in a carefully neutral tone.

"Not really." Allison shrugged elaborately, shaking her hands as though to shake off some clinging stickiness. "Except maybe to find out what she's up to." She cleared her throat again, this time apprehensively. "I don't like it when she calls. I don't like it when I even think she's thinking about me. Even those Christmas cards made me feel all . . . like when you have a nightmare and wake up scared with your heart pounding and you don't even know why."

"I know the feeling," said Shirley.

Allison made an abortive gesture. "Am I being crazy?"

Shirley shook her head. "Let's just take it carefully. Your aunt may be having fits of conscience, but it could be something else. I just can't think what else."

"Money," said J.Q. "You can depend on it. Making it or squeezing it. One or the other."

Allison and Shirley looked helplessly at one another. Money was Lawrence's overriding interest; status was Esther's; but so far as anyone of them knew, Allison had neither. "You can tell them you have other commitments," said Shirley.

"What are they?"

"Helping me get through the busy season. Here it is, only July, and we're up to our ears in people. I need your help. Answering the phone. Trotting around with extra laundry soap and toilet paper when people think they've run out because they haven't looked in their cupboards. Making reservations. Making up the bank deposits. All that stuff."

"While you and Mingy play in the dirt? Making gardens? That's not fair."

"Well, considering that Xanthippe Minging spent a great deal of her time after we moved keeping you abreast of your studies, I think she's entitled to garden if she likes." Allison hadn't wanted to start a new school in February, and Shirley hadn't blamed her.

Allison asked, "Did you know beforehand that she was going to leave Crepmier School and move with us, just like that?"

"I had no such idea, though I'm very grateful that she did. Her assistant was quite ready to take over the school, one might even say impatient, and Xanthy knew that. One has to move along, make room for the young. . . ."

22

"The one who took over, she's at least sixty!" said Allison.

"Which is young," Shirley growled. "I myself am almost sixty. Anyhow, if you want to use me as an excuse to your aunt, feel free. If you want to use Xanthippe, I'm sure she wouldn't mind. Just don't make any commitments to the Brentwoods until we've talked about it."

"Deal." Allison rose, dropped a butterfly kiss onto Shirley's hair, put her dishes into the dishwasher, and departed.

"That's worrying," said J.Q. between his teeth. "What are they up to?"

"Conscience. Could be," Shirley commented.

"In a pig's putt." He took a deep breath, as though readying himself for a lengthy peroration on the subject of pigs' putts, but the ringing phone deflated him.

"Rancho del Valle," he muttered. "Yes. No. Ms. McClintock. She's here, yes." He handed the phone to Shirley.

"Ms. McClintock? This is Pat Garcia, at the hospital. Someone just called me from California, says she's a housekeeper for Mrs. Tremple. At least that's what I think she said."

"Good," Shirley said, with a sense of relief. "Then you've got the information you need."

"No. That's just it, I didn't. The woman wanted to know how Mrs. Tremple was, and I told her, but when I asked the name of Mrs. Tremple's doctor, she seemed to lose what little English she had. I tried Spanish, but I'm not sure she even understood what I was asking. Can we find anyone who knows her? We're in desperate need of information here."

Shirley lowered the mouthpiece and asked, "J.Q., did you see anyone with the Tremple woman? Anytime during her visit? I was over there this morning, and there's nothing to identify her."

"Far's I know she was by herself," he muttered. "Except for that car that picked her up, the 'reborn' car."

"Our housekeeper who may have seen her with some-

23

one," Shirley said into the phone. "Or one of the other guests. I'll make inquiries. I don't suppose the person who called you used a name?"

"Your guess is as good as mine. She might have been speaking Thai or something. I don't know."

"How is Mrs. Tremple? Do you know what's the matter with her?"

"No better and not yet. She's got the symptoms of a bad head cold—inflamed throat, runny nose. The doctors keep coming and going; they don't know what's wrong with her. All the tests have been inconclusive, so far."

"I suppose you're checking for hantavirus?" Shirley asked with a feeling of dread. That's all they needed. A guest dying of hantavirus. The so-called mystery illness had received nationwide publicity after several people from the Four Corners country had died of it and before it had been identified as a widespread virus carried by deer mice. Shirley had considered buying a terrier until J.Q. had mentioned the chickens. Terriers were death on chickens and rabbits as well as mice and rats. She'd decided upon additional cats instead. Perhaps a mama cat. From what Shirley had observed about cat territories, it would take at least seven or eight reliable cats to mouse the residential and barn areas of the property thoroughly, and she only had five on the job, three that had come with the property and the two barn cats she had brought with her.

Pat Garcia said, "We're testing for hantavirus, but the symptoms don't seem to indicate that. We desperately need to know where she's been, what she's been doing, what her history is."

"I'll ask around," Shirley promised again. "If I find anything out, I'll call you."

"Hantavirus?" asked J.Q. "Alberta cleans like a tornado. No way she'd have left any mouse dirt in Frog House, even supposing there'd been some there."

"They don't think she's got hantavirus. They don't know what she has."

"Anyhow, better put a cat out there," J.Q. went on.

24

"We don't have enough cats to put one everywhere. Besides which, you know very well one does not *put* cats. Anyhow, there was a cat out there. The big black one was hunting along the fence this morning, early."

J.Q. seemed puzzled at this. "The cats usually hunt at night, after we've got the dogs inside. That coyote dog your guests brought you, he doesn't have good sense yet, and he chases cats just for the fun of it."

"I should have taken him to the shelter, the way I planned." She shook her head. The pup had been presented to them by a guest one Saturday afternoon. The guest said she found it abandoned in the graveyard at Truchas, offering as proof a Polaroid snapshot of a wounded little ball of fur cowering behind a bouquet of plastic flowers in a metal enclosure constructed to look like two motorcycles—cause of death of the interred. Though the puppy finder flew home to Brooklyn on the morrow, she offered to pay whatever vet or shelter fees were necessary if Shirley would only take charge. That had been Memorial Day weekend, and the shelter wasn't open. By the time the shelter was open once more, the pup had already adopted them and acquired a name: Coyote, local lingo for anything of uncertain or mixed parentage, including children, dogs, and fences.

"He's a nice-looking little dog," said Shirley. "He has sensible manners."

J.Q. grunted. "He will when he quits chewing things maybe. For a mutt."

"Dog is a mutt."

"Dog is one of a kind. So you saw Nero out by the fence."

"Is that his name, Nero?"

"So Alberta tells me. The black one's name is Nero, because he likes to look at the fire. The white one is Desdemona Ladyfingers and the orange one is—"

"Baron Valter von Shenanigan, I know. I guess I never thought about the others having names." Shirley's iron-jawed father had not been one for naming animals, and he would certainly never have stooped to whimsy.

"Alberta told me their names, dating from the previous owner's time. Alberta herself has named the ones in the barn. I called one of them 'cat' the other day, and she said no—they're Mamacita and Consuelo."

"Both of them are males, J.Q."

"Alberta says not anymore." He laughed. "Anyhow, you must have been up awfully early to catch Nero still hunting."

"It wasn't that early. It was full daylight. First thing I thought of when I woke up was Mrs. Tremple didn't have anything with her when we took her to the hospital. Obviously she must have a wallet, a purse, papers, something in Frog House. I felt really stupid, not thinking of it last night. So I went to look."

"And you didn't find anything."

"Right. Nothing. No purse. No wallet. J.Q., there's nothing in that house to identify her. A couple of cotton dresses, some slacks, some shirts, underwear, stockings. A pair of shoes. A few paperback books. Nothing else. One bed slept in. No sign of anyone else being with her. She told me she came to meet a client, then she took it back. Funny. Maybe she's a lawyer, and it's something secret. Meantime I'm going to ask the other guests. Who've we got?"

"We've got the crazy lady in the Ditch House. The one with the Mercedes four-wheel drive and the twitchy guy."

"Who's in the Garden House?"

"A thirty-fiveish–fortyish couple and their teenage niece. Stevens, their name is. They've been back and forth a lot. Her mother lives here, and Mrs. Stevens has been visiting Mom. The Big House has the six guys who spent last week camping out in Chaco Canyon, and the Little House has Mr. and Mrs. Fley, the potter's parents."

"The potter's—"

"The woman who lives down the road, who makes the big pots."

"Oh. Toni. Right. I didn't know her name was Fley?"

"It isn't. It's Kirkpatrick, but her parents are Fley."

"I suppose now's as good a time as any." She heaved

herself up from the table and put her empty cup in the sink. "Be back."

"Who you going to start with?"

"The crazy lady."

The crazy lady had arrived in an immaculate, brand-new, fifty- or sixty-thousand-dollar all-terrain vehicle. The crazy lady had said she couldn't stay long, the place was too expensive. Shirley had agreed, gravely, that it was indeed expensive, about half what similar space would cost in Santa Fe. The crazy lady had said they would stay a week, she and her friend, who was a recovering alcoholic. Perhaps not really recovering, yet, but she intended he should recover. She would remove the toxins from his blood by feeding him organic food, she said as she lit a cigarette. She intended to cure his depression by holistic means, she said, inhaling deeply. She intended to give him something to look forward to, she said, shedding glowing ashes hither and yon.

"Something to look forward to, like lung cancer," Shirley had opined, quoting this conversation to J.Q. "They both smoke like they're curing hams. She caught me down by the animal pens yesterday and told me the story of her life, sort of. She said she bought that heavy vehicle because her friend felt insecure in her little two-seater. Seeing how she drives, I can understand why. She herself has recently returned from India, where she spent several years in a quest for the meaning of life. She told me she'd been working south of Albuquerque getting minimum wage for packing organic vegetables, but when she found her friend, she decided they needed to make a pilgrimage so he could find himself."

"Where did she find him?"

"In the hovel—her word for it—where she was living. She encountered him in the hallway when he fell, not *for* her, but *on* her. He was drunk. She got him to quit drinking, at least momentarily. She says he doesn't drink as much if they're traveling."

"It doesn't hold water, Shirley. Too many contradictions.

27

There's that Mercedes. Four-wheel-drive Mercedes' do not come in cereal boxes."

"Well, actually, it makes a kind of eccentric sense, J.Q. She believes in holistic medicine and organic food, and she smokes like a smelter. She believes in living in accord with nature, and she has an off-road vehicle. She claims to have lived in India, and I'd guess she really has traveled there, though tickets to India don't come in cereal boxes either, even if she did live on lentils and rice once she was there. Many, many contradictions, all of which disappear when she mentions she has a trust fund."

"A trust fund?"

"So she says. Grandpa's money. Normally she doesn't spend it because she doesn't believe in unearned income. I think she's into CVP."

"Which is?"

"Conspicuous Voluntary Poverty. It's what the hippies were into. If you're into CVP it is okay not to eat anything that requires fixing, okay not to keep your clothing neat, okay not to wear decent shoes, okay not to wash too often. It's also okay to go to India, because that's in search of truth. And it's okay to buy a Land Rover to save a friend's peace of mind. If she's got a nice trust fund to fall back on, I suppose she can go through life doing CVP."

"Why? Why would anybody . . .?"

"I think the attraction is sloth, J.Q. You have to do very little when you're in CVP. See, if you don't care how you live, you can exist on very little and feel good about yourself. Then, if you've got a trust fund to fall back on, you can justify both your lifestyle and your occasional break with it." She threw up her hands in admiration of the idea. "You can get away with any nutty thing that comes into your head."

When Shirley arrived at Ditch House she found that the latest nutty idea to come into the crazy lady's head was the building of a sizable fire on the carefully tended patch of lawn in front of the house. Beside the glowing flames, the crazy lady sat cross-legged, chanting breathily as she incinerated memorabilia.

"You're burning a hole in the grass," said Shirley in a quietly astonished voice.

"Am I?" asked the crazy lady, tearing what appeared to be a snapshot in two and adding the pieces to the flames. Her eyes were hidden behind enormous tinted lenses and her forehead was covered by a carefully pleated turban. What of her face was visible was pale, even to the lips. "Do you think it will grow back?"

"Probably not."

The crazy lady shrugged. Grass, the shrug said, was transitory. "I have emotions to be purged. Eradicated. They're destructive to my karma." She dipped into the pile next to her and added a plastic-backed looseleaf notebook to the conflagration. It smoked greasily and began to melt, the pages charring at their edges.

"There are three or four barbecues scattered around," Shirley suggested. "The little round ones, with legs."

"The implication of a barbecue would be all wrong. Charred meat, you know." She reached up with her left hand and ran her fingers around her ear, down to the lobe, then down her jaw to the tip of her chin, one finger resting on her lips. The finger remained there as she said, "One has to achieve a certain consistency of feeling, one has to concentrate upon release."

Shirley wondered briefly if strangulation might assist in the process of release, but decided it wasn't worth the effort. "I need your help," she said.

The crazy lady looked up, alarmed. "I try to avoid involvement!"

"No involvement. Merely an exchange of information. The woman who was staying in that house, there." Shirley pointed across the ditch to the house half-hidden beyond the pond foliage. "Did you happen to see her?"

"Is she gone?"

"She's ill. In the hospital. The doctor needs information to help make a diagnosis. Did you see her?"

"She dyes her hair," said the crazy lady. "I saw her doing that. At night. In the bathroom. She was wearing goggles, like you do when you go scuba diving. I guess it was to keep the dye out of her eyes. Maybe she's allergic to the dye. I would be."

"The bathroom's around the other side," Shirley remarked pointedly.

The crazy lady shrugged, unabashed. "I was walking. Meditating. My friend went out. He drinks, though he's getting better because now at least he's *aware* when he does it. He knows he's *choosing* to do it. I told him if he chose to drink, he'd have to do it on his own. I refuse to enable his self-destruction. So I went out for a walk to bring myself back into harmony." She made the ear-circling gesture again, as though to make sure it was still attached. Almost a ritual gesture. Like making the sign of the cross.

Shirley sighed. "Did you see her with anyone?"

"I saw her with a man, yesterday. Midafternoon, I think. He picked her up in his car. I wasn't here when he brought her back. Assuming he brought her back."

"And what did the man look like?"

"I really only noticed he had a tie on, then I stopped looking. That tightness around his neck told me he was snared in illusion."

Shirley turned on her heel, gulped twice, then managed a polite thank-you before fleeing to the safety of her own patio, where she muttered and choked to herself for several minutes, caught between anger and laughter.

"Big House," she told herself firmly. "Catch the campers before they depart."

Of the six young men occupying the Big House, four had already departed. The two remaining listened politely though languidly to Shirley's request for information, becoming only slightly more animated as she explained the situation.

"We saw her, Rob," said the short tanned blond with the haggard face to the muscular baldy with the improbably white teeth. "The really skinny woman. When we left yesterday. She was down by the mailbox."

"Mailing something?" Shirley asked.

The muscular baldy agreed. "Harry's right. She might have been mailing something, but we didn't see her long enough to know. We just drove past, waved, went on our way. She was sort of standing there, looking up and down the road."

"Could she have been waiting for someone?"

The haggard blond, Harry, answered. "It did rather look like that. If she were only there to mail something, she wouldn't have been *hovering* the way she was."

"What time did you leave?"

"The more energetic of us left around eight, but Rob and I didn't leave until around ten. We went into Santa Fe to walk up Canyon Road and meet the others for lunch."

"You didn't see her when you got back yesterday."

Rob shook his head ruefully. "Harry wasn't seeing at all well when we got back, and since I'd been keeping him company, I was about as blind as he was. As a matter of fact, given the condition we were in, we are extremely fortunate that Caliban drove us home. Caliban is boringly conscientious, but useful. And then, Alphonso or Arthur or Michael may have seen something. Shall we ask them when they get back?"

"If you'd be so kind. Do you know what time you got back?"

Rob looked at Harry. Harry shrugged. "It was after midnight and before dawn," he said. "The others can no doubt be more specific. We'll ask them and let you know."

Shirley thanked them kindly and left them to their recovery. Her next stop was the Garden House, locked up tight, curtains drawn, guests no doubt gone out, somewhere. The adjacent Little House was tenanted, however. Mr. and Mrs. Fley were sitting in the portal, he smoking a pipe and she crocheting something large and complicated.

"Bedspread," Mrs. Fley said to Shirley's questioning

look. "Takes forever. That's why I do it. The devil finds work for idle hands."

She said it as though she meant it. Mr. Fley quirked a lip, as though he'd heard it all before, many times.

"Nice place," he said. "Antonia said we'd like it."

"That was nice of her," Shirley said, trying to figure out who Antonia was.

"Pity our own daughter doesn't have room for us in her house," said Mrs. Fley in a crisp voice. "Though it's true she's going through a rough spot just now."

Daughter! Oh. Toni. The potter. "Perhaps she thought you'd be more comfortable here," Shirley offered. "And I'm very glad you are here, because just now I have a problem perhaps you can help with."

"Heard a lot of goin' on in the middle of the night," said Mrs. Fley disapprovingly.

"Illness," Shirley said. "Sometimes it strikes in the middle of the night, and all we can do is go along."

The woman's head came up, and she fixed Shirley with an interested gaze. "Illness, you say. Who?"

"The woman staying in the house over there." Again Shirley pointed. From this vantage point, Frog House looked as though it floated on the pond from which a bullfrog thrummed. "Our problem is, we can't seem to locate anyone who knows her. The hospital needs a medical history, they need to know where she's been, who she's been with. We don't know. I thought maybe you'd seen someone, something?"

"Well, surely she's got papers and things with her. Driver's license? Things like that?"

"We can't find anything. We've looked."

"Have you looked in her car?" asked Mr. Fley.

"The car's locked. I haven't found the keys. I haven't found a purse or a billfold."

Mr. Fley gave Shirley a look of complicity. "Want me to get into the car for you? I'm real good at it."

Mrs. Fley cast a troubled look at her husband and put

down her crocheting. "Maybe that's not a good idea. It might be better if you left such matters to—"

"Left to who? All the lady wants is her address." He laughed, thrusting his elbow at his wife, who dodged it as though she'd been dodging it for a lifetime.

"He can," she said, as though giving in to the inevitable. "Most unlawful man in the world, this one. On the side of righteousness o' course, but unlawful nonetheless."

"She's just talking. Happened I was a locksmith in my youth. Not much I can't get into if I try."

"Mr. Fley, I'd be very pleased if you'd open Mrs. Tremple's car and if you and your wife would be witnesses to whatever we do or don't find in it."

"Hah!" he exclaimed, rising to his feet to bustle into the house. "Give me a minute."

"You shouldn't encourage him," said his wife, with an odd little smile. "You'll set him off. Takes me weeks to settle him, then some little thing comes along and sets him off."

"Well, it could be life and death," Shirley remarked. "That's not necessarily a little thing."

Mrs. Fley cocked her head. "She's really sick, is she? Not just a bellyache or some such?" The words conveyed no real concern, merely a polite interest.

"Not some little thing, no. Not drunk, not overeating, not silliness, she's really sick. And the hospital can't find out what's wrong with her."

"Shame on me for not being sympathetic. Here I thought it was just foolishness. Most of those women, they get up to foolishness."

"Those women?"

"Women who try to look young. Gray hair, but they dye it. Putting on a little grandmotherly padding, and they diet themselves into skeletons. Chest dropped down where God intended it should be on a respectable old woman, and they go heaving it up again. Now you know what I mean. You and me, we're sensible women, and we know."

Shirley was not often speechless, but this oration left her

33

gasping as Mr. Fley surged out of the door, bearing implements in both hands.

"Get right to her." He chuckled. "You time me."

As it happened, after they arrived at the car, Shirley barely had time to look at her watch before Mr. Fley crowed, twisted something, jerked something else, and the car door came open.

"Ten seconds," she said in disbelief.

"Not my record time, but it'll do. Now you look and we'll witness you looking."

Shirley looked, though with an increasing sense of disbelief. The keys to the car were in the car, and they were all that was there. There was nothing in the glove compartment. There was nothing between or under the seats. There was nothing behind the visors. The car was as clean as a demonstration model. Only the few thousand miles on the odometer testified to the fact it had ever been driven at all.

She backed away from the vehicle and stood staring at it, lips compressed in annoyance. "Somebody," she snarled, "somebody is out to make things difficult."

"What's her name?" asked Mr. Fley, making a roosterlike circuit of the vehicle, beakily peering. "What did you say her name was?"

"Alicia Tremple. She's supposed to be from your part of the woods. Somewhere near Los Angeles. Of course, the car has a license plate—"

"No, it doesn't," said Mr. Fley. "That's kind of funny, too, isn't it?"

Shirley looked for herself. Quite true. The car did not have a license plate. "It did have," she said. "J.Q. saw it! A California license plate."

"I think you're right," the old man agreed, nodding his head, his cheeks quite pink with excitement. "I think somebody's trying to make things difficult."

Shirley's apprehension jerked one notch tighter and stayed there, like a drawn wire, thrumming.

"Looks like she didn't want to be identified, doesn't it?"

said Mrs. Fley, not without a certain grim relish. "Maybe she set out to do away with herself, and something went wrong."

"Insufficient poison," said Mr. Fley, with a crooked smile. "That's how they do it. I saw it in a movie."

"That was Maurice Chevalier said that, and we both saw it," said his wife. "In that movie *Gigi,* where they were raising up the little girl to be a hooker."

"To be a mistress, Mama. There's a difference."

"I imagine God puts them both in the same bed. Whichever. The movie had Hermione Gingold. She was in *The Music Man,* too. Now there's a sensible woman."

Shirley swallowed the laughter that was pressing upward from her lungs. She and Mrs. Fley and Hermione Gingold. What a trio.

"Thank you for your help," she said, offering her hand to each in turn. "I'll let the hospital know that we haven't found anything, and I'll pass on your idea that she planned it that way." Which wasn't a totally silly idea. Ms. Tremple had certainly left them with nothing but dead ends, except for the vanity license plate that J.Q. had seen. There couldn't be more than one license plate that said REBORN.

The Fleys wandered back toward their house, talking animatedly, while Shirley returned to the kitchen. There were at least six things she had planned to do this morning. Several roofs needed either mending or replacing, and she wasn't satisfied with the work she'd had done thus far. Ditch House had a smoky fireplace. Its chimney needed cleaning or it needed a rain cap or something. Some of the floor tiles in the Frog House bathroom were loose; she'd crunched on them this morning. That should be seen to. And the curtains in Ditch House were hideous! When she'd been talking to the crazy lady, she'd noticed they looked like old bedspreads. Something would have to be done about that. The list of things was infinitely expandable, and she was getting none of it attended to because of Ms. Alicia Tremple.

She poured herself another cup of coffee and sat down at

the kitchen table with the Yellow Pages and the phone. Ditch House and the Big House had recently been reroofed, but there were leaks other places. She would speak to roofers first, which she did, severally, and at some length, describing the problem and listening to various diagnoses. The cumulative information gave her a general idea of what she was looking for. The chimney question was easier. One chimney sweep and one mason agreed to come have a look. They said they'd be by as soon as possible. That should give her a choice among alternatives.

J.Q. wandered in, flushed faced and sweaty. "Hot down there," he muttered, leaning on the sink as he filled a tall water glass.

"I heard you pounding fence posts."

"We're gong to have to hire somebody to pound the rest of them. I've done something to my shoulder."

"Oh, hell, J.Q. What? Sprain?"

"Something. I've got the H-corners built and the guide wire strung on the north side, but the second post I pounded got to me. Damn, I knew I was going to do it. Darn thing kept twinging at me." He set down the glass and moved his arm experimentally, wincing as he did so.

"Get Vincente to help you."

"I don't know about Vincente. He's not real crazy about physical effort. He told me yesterday he thought it was time he and Alberta retired."

She nodded thoughtfully. Both the Luceros were being very careful to discuss what should be done and how. After years of more or less following their own desires about the place, they were now struggling with new ways of doing things. Or, maybe, trying to decide whether they wished to do them.

Shirley said heavily, "Thinking about retiring, is he?"

"He wouldn't be hard to replace. He doesn't do that much. Rides the lawn mower 'round and 'round, very slowly. Cleans the pool, very slowly, with a nice rhythmic movement. That's about it. She, however, is going to be an extremely hard act to follow."

36

"What're you saying, J.Q.? That he wants to leave and she doesn't?"

"I'm saying she's a worker and he isn't. All those years when the Fieldings were here, Vincente fell into the habit of doing less and less. I'm sure the owner thought he'd continue maintaining the place, but you heard Harry Fielding talk about all the maintenance he got saddled with. Now we're here, and Vincente catches me watching him, which he's obviously not real fond of. I took the lawn tractor apart the other day. He hung around, peering over my shoulder, listening while I talked to myself about the rust and grease and miscellaneous cross wiring and parts missing. He didn't offer to help when I cleaned it, or when I went after new parts, or when I put them in. He's not really into anything that requires either thinking or sweat."

"How old is he?"

"Fortyish. Maybe forty-five. That beer belly makes him look older."

"So the ideal situation would be keep her, replace him?"

"She wouldn't do that. She's a traditional woman. Her place is with him."

"What about we keep her, lay him off but let him live here?"

"That'd make trouble. It would interfere with his self-respect. You know that."

"I know that. Damn. I had hoped things could sort of trundle along status quo until I got the place in shape."

"Never happen," he said. "Allison said anything more about the Brentwoods?"

"I haven't seen her, J.Q. I've been talking to the guests. Mr. Fley broke into Tremple's car for me."

He raised his eyebrows at her, keeping them up while she described the Fleys and their opinions.

"She's a little too country to be true," Shirley opined.

"What do you mean?"

"I mean everything she says is slightly wry, as though she's slightly amused at herself. I think it's a part she plays, just for vacations."

37

"And she thought it might be suicide? Like maybe the Tremple woman took poison, and it didn't quite work? You believe that?"

Shirley shrugged. "Not in light of what she said to me on the way to the hospital, no. But maybe she didn't take it."

"You've got murder on the brain."

She sighed. "Actually, I've got roof leaks on the brain, and a couple fireplaces, and now you mention it, Vincente and Alberta. Tell you what. Let's pretend, just for the nonce, that everything is kosher with Vincente. Smile on him. Tell him the pool and the lawns look great. Let's get through the summer, then we'll decide what we're going to do when we don't have twenty or thirty guests around."

"You're the padrona," he said, turning back to the sink.

His back was a little stiff, she thought. A little annoyed. He'd like to tell Vincente what was what, but he knew it wasn't a good idea right now. He was feeling frustrated.

She started to go over to him, pat him on the shoulder, when the phone rang.

"Ms. McClintock? It's Pat Garcia." Her voice sounded inexpressibly weary.

"Lord, lady, do they work you twenty-four hours a day over there?"

"I stayed on when my shift was over. Mrs. Tremple was so sick. . . . Ms. McClintock, have you found out anything about her?"

"Nothing. It's almost as though she cleaned up after herself to make sure we wouldn't."

Silence at the other end. "I'm sorry," the nurse said. "I had hoped . . . well, it's too late now anyhow. She died about twenty minutes ago."

Shirley murmured into the phone, a few nonsense words, sympathetic sounds that meant nothing, turning a stricken face toward J.Q., who held his coffee cup to his lips without drinking.

"What did she die of?" Shirley asked.

The voice on the phone went on briefly, short phrases, not many of them. Shirley hung up.

"Well?" J.Q. asked, setting down the cup with a bang.

Shirley shrugged, sadly, helplessly. "They don't know. They're going to do an autopsy, of course. According to that nice nurse, they haven't any idea what they're looking for. Oh, J.Q., I feel just awful. She was our guest. . . ." Even as she said the words she knew the feeling was something else. Not simple sympathy or sorrow. Something more complex.

He came to put his arms around her, patting her on the shoulder. "That's all right. You're not responsible for 'em, Shirley. Besides, where this woman is concerned, you can depend on it, being a tourist isn't all she was."

And that was it, she thought. That was the complication. A tourist was not all she had been. She'd been something else, and now someone had to find out what.

2

The chimney sweep arrived about noon on Thursday while Shirley was out front trimming a huge thorny bush that had stabbed her in the past and was intent upon doing it again. She stuffed the clippers in her pocket and sucked a punctured finger as the van came down the drive in a barrage of flung gravel. When it stopped, the long-haired young driver unhinged himself and emerged bit by bit. The sign on the van said CHARLES FOR CHIMNEYS.

"The one that smokes is over here," she said, pointing eastward.

He stared vaguely in the direction she indicated, nodded almost imperceptibly, reached into the van for a large flashlight, and strolled after her to Ditch House. She unlocked the door and led him in. The crazy lady had said it would be fine to show him the fireplace because it really did smoke. Though how anyone could tell it smoked was beyond Shirley's comprehension. She counted six dinner plates set here and there for use as ashtrays, every one of them overflowing with cigarette butts.

"Stinks," said the chimney sweep.

"Sure does," she agreed, considering, not for the first time, a no-smoking policy for the place.

"Don't smoke, myself," he said as he lay on his back, knees up, head on the hearth, then eased his head and hands into the fireplace as he shone the light upward.

"Are you Charles?" Shirley asked.

"Na," he replied. "Charles was the guy left me the business when he went to Hawaii."

How did someone leave someone else a business? More interesting, why? She pondered this until he edged himself off the hearth and sat up. "Got a constricted throat in there," he said. "What I'll need to do is jackhammer that out, open it up a little, and make the opening of the fireplace a bit smaller. Less air in, more air out. That should solve the problem." He rose to his feet and stretched, brushing the low ceiling with his hands.

"How much?" Shirley asked.

Mumbling to himself, he wandered out toward his van while Shirley locked the door behind him. He exchanged the light for a dog-eared pad and wrote busily for a minute or two. "I make it nine hundred and a quarter. That'll take care of everything—jackhammer, new bricks to lower the opening, cleanup, replastering, paint it to match, the whole works. Take about three, four days." He offered the scribbled sheet between two fingers, and Shirley took it, noting that no word was legible, though the figures were unmistakably clear. She was about to ask him to elucidate the total, item by item, when she saw another car nosing down the drive, the two uniformed men in the front seat peering to either side.

She pocketed the estimate. "I'll have to see when the house is free before I can schedule the work," she told him. "I'll call you."

"That there bid is only good for thirty days," he said with an air of vague distress. "I've gotta break right now is how come I can take care of it right away. And I'll need half down for materials."

"When I schedule the work," she said, indicating the approach of the other car. The man who wasn't Charles glanced at the approaching vehicle and got into his van with suspicious haste. He busied himself there, head down, while Shirley went across the drive to greet the members of the Santa Fe County Sheriff's Office.

"McClintock?" asked one, referring to a piece of paper. "Got a search warrant for wherever this Tremple woman was staying."

"You didn't need a warrant. I'll unlock it for you," said Shirley, turning toward Frog House, somewhat dismayed at how quickly they left the car and how closely they followed her. Must be habit, keeping suspects in full view. If she was suspected of something. Good Samaritaning, perhaps.

"Anybody else staying in this house?" asked the shorter one of the two.

"Not that we're aware," she said, being as laconic as possible.

The two of them crossed the bridge almost on her heels, then watched her hands while she unlocked the door. She stood aside to let them in. Just to be on the safe side, she stayed just outside while they clomped about. No doubt they would have questions when they found no identification inside. God knows Shirley had questions!

Bingo. Back they came, the shorter one leading. "Is that her car over there?"

"So far as we know it is. When she arrived, it had a California plate on it. Sometime between then and when we looked at it this morning, the plate disappeared. I have no idea whether she took it off or someone else did."

"Hospital says you don't have an address for her."

"That's right. We have a phone number in California, and it's not in service. We have a credit-card number that we charged her rental to. It's a valid number; we got an authorization number on it. J.Q. saw her get into a car with a New Mexico vanity plate yesterday; the plate said RE-BORN. I imagine you can trace that."

"Don't need to," said the taller deputy. "That's Roger Reborn, Reborn Realty. You know, you've seen him on TV.

Don't just be in the market for a house, be Reborn. Makes my wife so mad . . ."

"Your wife takes things too religious," said the other. "Trouble is, she doesn't think God has a sense of humor."

"Well, that's not respectful, Cisso."

"Way I see it, Bible says we're made in God's image, right? So if we got a sense of humor, so does God. You tell her that."

"Think I'm crazy? According to Suze, God's exactly like her mother."

"Amen," said Shirley. "About Mrs. Tremple . . ."

"You got the credit-card receipt?" asked the shorter deputy.

"Back where we were," said Shirley, leading the way back across the driveway, from which Not Charles for Chimneys had made an inconspicuous departure, and into the kitchen cum office. The merchant copy of the credit-card form was stapled to the reservation form, and she handed the assemblage to the shorter deputy. Cisso. Short for what? His name tag had only initials.

"What's this hotel in Phoenix?" he asked.

"When she called, she said she was leaving California the same day, would we send her confirmation to the hotel in Phoenix. We did. See there, we sent it two weeks ago."

"And she got here when?"

"This is Thursday, she got here a week ago. Last Thursday night or early Friday morning. She reserved for a week. She would have left today."

"She came alone?"

"So far as we know. We don't wait up for guests. We put the key in the door and they let themselves in. I asked all the other guests if they'd seen her with anyone. One saw the man in the 'reborn' car. No one saw her with anyone else."

"Okay, so whatta we got here? We got a credit-card number that doesn't belong to this woman, maybe stolen—"

"Stolen!" Shirley gasped.

43

"Right. Either that or unauthorized use. You musta got your charge through before it was reported. The card belongs to some attorney in Los Angeles who says he never heard of this Tremple woman. And we got a hotel in Phoenix where maybe they got a home address or a different card number or something. And we got a phone number that's out of service."

"She said she was here to meet a client," Shirley offered. "Maybe she was a lawyer. There are professional associations for lawyers. One of them might have her address."

"Yeah, a lawyer might have a client, but so might a real-estate agent, and she went somewhere with Reborn, so maybe she's into property. Let's go over that. What exactly did she say?"

Shirley settled into one of the kitchen chairs and gestured an invitation. The shorter deputy, Cisso, sat down opposite her. The taller deputy lounged against the wall. Shirley repeated the few words the woman had said.

". . . and she'd been to Jemez Springs."

"With somebody, did she say?"

"She didn't say. She did say she'd had dinner at the restaurant in Tesuque. She asked if I thought it might have been something she ate."

"And?" asked the tall deputy.

"And she said something I didn't catch. Amiss makuli, macully. Something. Then she passed out."

"Amis?" said the shorter deputy. "Somebody's name?"

"It was more ahmis," said Shirley.

"Amish? A mess? Oh miss?"

Shirley shook her head. "I'm sorry. Honest to God, it was just a mumble. Have they any idea what she died of yet?"

The taller deputy shook his head. "They've done an autopsy, but some of the tests take a while. It wasn't any kind of poison, they know that much. Not deadly mushrooms or anything else she ate."

"Mushrooms!" Shirley hadn't thought of that possibility.

"I always think of mushrooms. When I first got on at the

sheriff's office, first DOA I saw died from mushrooms. He was a city guy. I guess these city guys, they think anything grows here in New Mexico, it must be peyote."

"I figure with this woman it's some kind of disease," said the shorter deputy. "Even though the house is weird, you know? No billfold, no purse. Women always have a purse. Like she didn't want people to know who she was."

"Or somebody didn't," said Shirley, without thinking.

"Well, if *somebody* didn't, then I'd need to find out what kind of somebody could just waltz in there and rearrange stuff, see what I mean?"

Shirley rubbed the lines between her eyes. "Most anybody," she confessed. "In the first place, we don't know what condition the house was in when the woman came pounding on our door. It was two in the morning, and J.Q. and I left with her in the car within five minutes. We went directly to St. Vincent's. We stayed there long enough to answer what questions we could, we came directly back here, arriving at about four. So we were gone most of two hours. When we got here, we looked at the record you're holding, and we went to bed. For some reason, I didn't think to search her house right then. Maybe I was just too sleepy or I didn't realize how sick she was. I did go through it first thing in the morning. I didn't move anything or mess anything up. I just looked for something with her name and address on it."

"What time in the morning?"

"Oh, seven-thirty. Seven forty-five."

"So anybody could have walked in there anytime between two and seven-thirty, nobody would know."

"I'd say probably before it got light," Shirley commented. "We've got a couple of eagle-eye visitors. Once it was light, it would have been risky."

"Could somebody get in easy?"

Shirley shrugged. "The houses were built back in the days when people didn't even bother to lock their houses. Even when the house doors are locked, the windows are vulnerable. Anybody could bash in one of these little panes.

45

Or, considering the condition of some of these windows, and if they wanted to take their time, they could knock out the putty, take out a pane, put it back, stick a few chunks of the dried putty on to hold it, and nobody'd ever know the difference. I didn't see any sign that anyone forced a way in. But then, I didn't check before we left to see if it was locked, either. She could have left it unlocked. I don't know where the key is. It isn't in the house."

The two exchanged glances, handed Shirley the reservation sheet, and stood up with a purposeful jingle of hardware.

"Hang on to that," said the shorter man. "Someone may want to see it, but I'm betting Roger Reborn knows who she is. Just in case he doesn't, we'll send somebody out to take fingerprints. If it does turn out to be natural causes, all we really need is a next of kin." `

"That's what you think, natural causes?"

The shorter deputy nodded slightly. "Yeah. Even weird like it is, I'm betting it's some disease or other. Like this hantavirus thing. Like bubonic. We get one or two cases of bubonic every year. Some kid handles a dead animal and gets flea-bit. There's probably viruses floating around nobody's died of yet, just because nobody lived where they were, right? People keep moving out, moving out, they're gonna run into new stuff."

Shirley agreed it was possible as she walked them to their car. "You got a nice place here," said the taller man.

"Thank you. We're enjoying it."

"Always have thought this place was pretty."

"You've been here before?"

"Oh, sure. Vinny Lucero, he's my uncle. I used to come help him and 'Berta get everything in shape when the Kingsolvers were coming for a while. Sometimes he'd hire four or five of us kids to get the pool cleaned, the grass mowed. Then every spring he'd hire us to clean acequias. That's a job on this place because of all the landscaping. Most places the ditch just runs through pasture and you can pile the dirt any old where."

Quite true. Shirley hadn't really considered the implications of ditch cleaning until she'd hired a crew to do it in March. Three quarters the cost of cleaning the ditch had turned out to be the time spent hauling the dirt away. Another thing she hadn't considered was Vincente and Alberta having a lot of friends and relatives in the area. That could prove to be an added little complication.

She shook hands with the deputies, agreed to keep Frog House as it was until the fingerprinting had been done, and asked to be kept informed. She was just turning back toward the house when the third visitor of the morning trundled down the drive, slowly, deliberately, crawling down the last few feet to where Shirley was standing. This one was a truck with a ladder rack on top.

"I'm the mason, John Diptick," announced the wiry individual at the wheel. He had shaved so close that his face looked polished, sun glinting from his cheekbones and pointy nose as he stared first at her, then at the houses.

The Tin Man, Shirley thought. All he needed was an oilcan.

He asked crisply, "Where's the smoky shimney?"

Shirley pointed and started back toward Ditch House. Before she got there, he had driven to the nearest corner, parked, removed a ladder from the truck, heaved it against the wall, and gone up it like a squirrel. She heard him on the roof, muttering and crashing. After a few moments he swarmed down once more and restowed the ladder on the truck with one economical and effortless heave.

"D'you have that place reroofed lately?"

"It was done this spring, yes. March or early April."

"Somebody put a rock on toppa the shimney. They do that, see, so's the stuff they're spraying around don't go in the shimney. That's why she smoked. I took the rock off. That'll be fifty dollars for the trip."

Wordlessly Shirley led him inside and wrote a check. "How come you got here so quick?" she asked. "I just called this morning."

"Had another job just down the road. You shoulda checked the roof."

Why hadn't she checked the roof?

Because I'm an old lady with a stiff leg, she told herself. No excuse, she answered. No damned excuse.

"Thank you for being an honest man," she said.

"Hell, I got work up the whatnot," he said. "Don't need pretend work when there's real around to be did."

J.Q. came out to join her as she watched the truck crawl slowly out the driveway.

"Chimney have to be rebuilt?" he asked.

"When we had the roofers here this spring, they put a rock over the chimney," she said in a toneless voice. "That kindly gentleman who is now departing charged us fifty dollars to remove the rock, which took him all of thirty seconds. Of course, either one of us could have climbed up there and removed the rock. Vincente could have climbed up there and removed the rock."

"I looked up the chimney!" he exclaimed. "There was light showing!"

"The chimney sweep also looked up the chimney. He, like us, didn't climb on the roof, however. Which didn't stop him from estimating it would cost nine hundred some-odd dollars to fix whatever was wrong. I think, in future, we will start any chimney or roof reconstruction plans with a personal view from above."

"Nine hundred dollars?"

"To jackhammer out what he called a constricted throat, rebuild it, and replaster. Damn it, J.Q., we should have had better sense. It didn't smoke last February. There were people in it burning firewood all month, and it didn't smoke. March was colder than a witch's tit, and it didn't smoke then! We had it reroofed, and then it smoked. As a matter of fact, it's smoked up so badly, it stinks. Anybody but the crazy lady would have refused to live there. We're going to have to repaint, and that's for damn sure going to cost nine hundred dollars. I've been so up to here with adapting, I'm not thinking straight!"

"Wonder how Vincente is on paint?"

Shirley told him about Vincente's nephew being a deputy sheriff who had identified the license plate as belonging to Roger Reborn.

"Reborn's a realtor?"

"According to the sheriff's man. I can't imagine anybody really being named that. Maybe it was originally something like Redburne or Raeborne. Lots of families lost parts of their names when they immigrated to this country. At any rate, we know who he is."

"And you want to go see him."

"I would feel a lot less nudgy if I knew for certain the Tremple woman died of something totally unrelated to this place. I can't imagine worse publicity. They said she didn't have the symptoms of hantavirus, but they don't know what she did have. And all this business about the phone number and the address and one thing and another. It's worrying."

"I'm a lot more worried about the Brentwoods. Their calling Allison that way . . ."

"Well, yes. So am I. But we haven't a clue what they're up to, and we do have one about Tremple."

"So you want to go see the realtor?"

"Would you mind, J.Q.? With that lame shoulder, you're not going to pound in any more fence posts. And we don't have any guests arriving or departing today. And Xanthippe would probably be perfectly happy to catch the phone for us."

"You want to go looking for him, or you want to make an appointment?"

"I thought we might catch him off guard."

"You'll be lucky to catch him at all. Still, I'm willing if you are."

"After lunch," she said, glancing at her watch. "And I'll call to see if he's going to be in his office, but I won't say what it's about."

Shirley fixed two plates of cold sliced chicken, bread and butter, and fresh tomatoes for herself and Allison; J.Q. had a bowl of beans spooned out of the big pot he'd had at the back of the stove for two days.

"How come you don't eat my beans?" he asked.

"I think of beans as more cold-weather food," she replied. "Like split-pea soup or clam chowder. Or, considering we are now residents of the great southwest, like posole. Like menudo."

"Why cold weather?"

"When I was a kid, the rest of the house had central heating, but the kitchen didn't. We had a wood cookstove, and Mama kept it going to heat the kitchen in cold weather. Since the stove was hot anyhow, she made soup. She'd have something bubbling away back there all the time. Beans, like you do them, with ham hocks. Vegetable soup. Beef and barley. She was a wonderful cook. And if the stove was hot, so was the oven, so she'd bake bread or rolls or biscuits, and that was supper in the wintertime. But in summertime, it was too hot to work in the kitchen except early in the morning, so we'd have salads and sliced ham and cold roast chicken, stuff like that."

"Winters sound like they were hard work," he said. "All that woodchopping."

"Well, you know, everyone was busy all the time, but I don't remember its being all that hard." She stared at the plate in front of her, suddenly not hungry. "We were close, though. We were a family."

"Something bothering you?"

"I'm nudgy," she confessed. "I've been having this nightmare."

"Before or after our late-night excursion?"

"Yes. No. Well, both, actually. Wednesday morning when you woke me, I had this head full of witches burning. That's really all I can remember, just witches burning. But then I think I had the same dream again this morning."

"Witches!"

She nodded, making a face. "I'm pretty sure it was because of this dreadful thing on PBS. Some small town, a couple and their employees were accused of abusing children at the day-care center they ran. The accusation was malicious, anybody could see that just looking at the woman who started it, like a cat caught in the cream jug. She was angry at the woman who owned the center, so she said her child had been molested there. She spread the idea. The couple and their employees were arrested and tried.

"It ended up, the man was sentenced to life and one of the women to twenty years and three or four people still to be tried, even though now the first set of jurors are admitting it was wrong, that they got confused, that they didn't believe the people were guilty. Some of them said they only voted guilty after they'd been at it a few weeks, just so's they could get out of the jury room. It was a full-fledged witch-hunt. I wanted to vomit. Someone was willing to send a man to jail for life because they couldn't stay in a jury room another week!"

"You're so upset you're shaking," he observed.

"It really did upset me," she grated.

"Now, why is that?"

"I never watched much television until I wrecked this knee, J.Q. Since then, evening comes, I sort of collapse, and I've . . . fallen into the habit. A lot of what I've been seeing and hearing scares me spitless. Every other show seems to be about the supernatural. People kidnapped by UFOs. People calling nine-hundred numbers to talk to a psychic network, for God's sake. Ghost stories. All done with great special effects so they're totally believable. I'm afraid we've got a generation of citizens who are illiterate in science but summa cum laude in superstition. They'll believe anything they're told."

"Are you mad at the world, or something in particular?"

"I guess it was the PBS thing particularly, the way the women went along, like sheep. Of course, girls are still taught that it's nice to be accommodating, to go along with people. It's what I call the 'Sure, if you say so,' attitude. All the mothers sent their kids to a quack psychologist, who told them their children had indeed been abused. Since she had a financial interest in 'healing' kids who'd been abused, what else was she going to tell them? So here were all these mamas saying, 'Sure, if you say so. I'm willing to send innocent people to jail on the word of an unscientific quack.'"

He extended a hand, patting hers. "I don't know why it got to you, Shirley, but I'm sorry it upset you."

She felt tears welling and hastily wiped her eyes. "I don't know why it got to me either. It's just part of the stuff I hate, I guess."

"You have rather seemed to be banging your head against the wall a lot lately." J.Q. finished his beans. "I'll just rinse off this bowl and be ready to go in a minute."

"Yeah," she mumbled around a mouthful of chicken. "Okay. I'll change my shirt and meet you out front." She stared at the three quarters of her lunch that was untouched, shook her head, went to the back door, and summoned Dog.

"You're not in a mood," she murmured, digging her fingers into the thick fur just above the wagging tail as she offered the chicken with the other hand. "Are you, Dog? Your appetite is not dependent upon how you feel about the world."

How did she feel about the world? She felt as she had for months now. That there was something bad around the nearest corner. Something smelly, barely detectable. Something out to get her. Not a normal feeling. Not normal at all!

She rinsed off her plate and was putting it into the dishwasher when Allison arrived at the kitchen door, out of breath. "What's for lunch?"

"Plate of sliced chicken and tomatoes in the fridge, glass of milk, and there's fruit in the bowl."

"What's the matter?"

"I'm grouchy. I'm emotional. I'm going off in all directions."

"Over my aunt and uncle?"

"Probably, though I've managed to convince myself it's over things in general."

"That lady dying, huh?"

"Also probably. And the fact we have to repaint Frog House. And the fact that injustice is being done near and far. And the fact that I almost got snookered out of nine hundred dollars because I'm getting old and creaky."

"I don't think you're creaky," said Allison, standing very straight, pink-cheeked and worried looking.

"Kind of you, child. Don't make a big crisis out of it. I'll figure out what's the matter with me, and we'll find out what your relatives are up to in due time, no doubt. Did you decide to call them?"

"No. I'm going to write Aunt Esther a note."

"Very good. Meantime J.Q. and I are going to beard Mr. Roger Reborn in his den." She took the plate and glass from the refrigerator and set them on the kitchen table.

"The real-estate man?" Allison asked, licking a white, milky mustache from her upper lip. "He's awful. You see him on TV along with the late movies. Sometimes he has his daughters do ads, and they look like cheerleaders. Buy Reborn and be at home in the world. Rah, rah, rah."

She took a mouthful of tomato and chicken. "Can I go with you?"

"Why would you want to?"

Allison started to answer, then stopped and thought a moment. "Because I want to be with you and J.Q., because I'm feeling insecure."

Shirley laughed shakily. "God knows that's going around. Sure. Let's all go meet Mr. Reborn."

Twenty minutes later they were headed south to Santa Fe, where, so the warm and confiding voice at his office had said, Mr. Reborn could be found on Tuesdays and Thursdays. The same confiding voice had remarked that Mr. Reborn spent the rest of each week at his office in Albuquerque.

"At least we know he was in Santa Fe Tuesday," Shirley remarked. "If he kept to his usual schedule, that is."

"He must be a busy little bee," remarked J.Q., weaving his way absentmindedly through the traffic at St. Francis and Cerillos Road. "Must be a hassle, personally running a business in both towns."

"If he's that big a deal, he probably has salesmen," said Shirley. "Which may prove interesting. Maybe the car was his, but the person driving was someone else."

J.Q. said, "Why don't we cross that bridge—"

Allison chirped, "Why do people say that?"

"Say what?"

"About crossing bridges. You can't cross it until you get to it, can you?"

It was not a question Shirley cared to deal with. For years she had made a career of crossing bridges before she got to them, sometimes crossing them in both directions simultaneously, or even blowing up the bridge before anybody else got to it. Her boss in Washington, Roger Fetting, had treasured the talent and paid her well for it. He had called her "his auspicier." A reader of signs and omens. Her talent for premature bridge crossing, though sometimes helpful, was often uncomfortable, Shirley thought, and maybe that's what had been wrong lately. Maybe she was trying to cross a nonexistent bridge before she got close enough to see the bridge wasn't there.

"Can you?" asked Allison stubbornly.

Shirley sighed. "It's a way of saying let's not speculate until we know the facts. Or worry does not change the outcome. Or talk is cheap. Or—"

"Least said, soonest mended," said J.Q. "Or a wise head keeps a still tongue. Or a closed mouth catches no flies."

"I don't think that's exactly the same thing," Allison objected, staring fixedly at what she could see of Shirley's face, her own smooth forehead creased in worried lines.

"Close enough," said J.Q., getting over into the right-hand lane behind a slow-moving car.

"Pull over," demanded Shirley. "Right here."

J.Q. obediently pulled over. "What?"

"It's the bone place. You guys wait a minute." She was out of the car and gone.

"What's she doing?" demanded Allison in a worried tone.

"There was a buffalo skull on the tree out front when we moved down," J.Q. said. "It was so old it fell apart, and Shirley wants a new one."

"Why does everyone down here like bones so much?" she asked plaintively. "There's a window downtown with nothing but painted skulls in it."

"Image of the Old West," opined J.Q. "Wagon wheels and cow skulls, cowboys and Indians, covered wagons and sunsets. Georgia O'Keeffe stuff. Looks like she's got one."

Shirley came toward them carrying a small skull with disproportionately long, curly horns.

"What is it?" Allison asked.

"Goat," Shirley replied. "We'll put it up where the old one was."

She stowed it in the back of the Cherokee, then got into the front seat, making a cavalry gesture. "Ho-oh."

They got back into the traffic, driving the remaining few blocks in silence until J.Q. said, "Does that large yellow sign say Reborn?"

"There's a driveway about three cars up." Shirley stuck her head out the window. "Is that he, Allison? The fat man standing outside the door?"

"That's him," said Allison. "He looks like the Tweedles in your mother's copy of *Alice* you gave me, Dee or Dum, either one. His mouth smiles and smiles, but his eyes don't. And his daughters are really pretty, but they have those same smiles."

"No doubt readying themselves for careers as game-show sex objects," Shirley remarked, unfolding herself out the car door. "We'll wait until he's disengaged." She propped one elbow on the car roof and stared fixedly at the neck of the woman talking with Reborn. In a moment the woman twitched, looked over her shoulder, resumed her conversation with frequent backward glances and an apparent lack of concentration. Shirley went on staring.

"That's witchy," murmured Allison.

Shirley gave her a startled look, then resumed her stare. Shortly the woman shrugged, gestured in Shirley's direction, and walked off down the street.

"Mr. Reborn?" Shirley moved quickly onto the sidewalk, catching him before he had a chance to get inside. "May I have a moment, please?"

"I have a client waiting. . . ."

"It'll take only a moment. My name's McClintock. This is John Quentin, and our daughter, Allison. We're from Rancho del Valle, north of Santa Fe. Tuesday, yesterday, someone with a 'reborn' license plate picked up a guest of ours. Would that have been you?"

He looked uncertainly from Shirley to J.Q. to Allison and back again. "Is there some problem?"

"We're trying to locate the person who drove the car."

"I picked up Mrs. . . . ah . . . Tremple yesterday. About three in the afternoon. She wanted to see some residential property. I showed her two houses we have listed."

"Did you by any chance take her to dinner?"

"No. I did drop her off in Tesuque about suppertime. She said she was meeting a friend."

"Mr. Reborn, did Mrs. Tremple give you a home address?"

"Just Rancho del Valle," he replied, his eyes narrowing. "She said she'd be staying there for some time."

Shirley sighed, shaking her head. Damn it. Dead end.

J.Q. asked, "When did she make the appointment with you?"

"Monday. That is, she called the office on Monday saying she'd like to see a particular house we had advertised in the Sunday paper. I called her back that afternoon and made the appointment. What is all this?"

"She died this morning," Shirley said. "We don't have a home address. The number she gave us is not a working number. The credit card she gave us was bogus. I'm surprised the sheriff's office hasn't already been in touch with you. They need to identify the woman."

Reborn bugged his eyes, looking momentarily toadlike. "I presume you've called information?"

"Which information?" Shirley asked. "Where?"

"You don't have a city? The area code?"

"We have no reason to think the area code is any more accurate than the rest of the noninformation we have."

"Well, you could try that."

Shirley nodded. "I'll try that. You're saying you don't know any more than we do."

"She wasn't very talkative. She didn't seem to be feeling well, said she had a headache, so after we saw the first house, we stopped by the office here, to pick up some aspirin. While we were here I returned a couple of phone calls. Mrs. Tremple talked to my daughter Zinny. Maybe Zinny remembers something."

"Is she here?"

He shook his head, pulled a card from his pocket, scribbled on the back of it. "Here's my home number in Albuquerque. You can call there tonight, around suppertime. What did she die of?"

"Nobody knows," said Allison, in a sepulchral tone.

The man glanced at her, startled, then bugged his eyes once more, an expression that seemed to be associated with mental concentration. "All she said was she had a headache."

"Didn't bite on either of the houses, did she?" asked J.Q.

"Didn't seem to, even though one of them was exactly what she said she wanted. Quite frankly I wondered if she was in the income bracket to buy it—it's not expensive for Santa Fe, but I thought it might be for her. She didn't balk at the price, so maybe it was just the way she was feeling."

Shirley gave him her hand and thanked him. They went back to the car.

"She could have had a blood vessel break in her head," J.Q. remarked. "A slow bleeder. The headache got worse and worse. When she got to the hospital, it broke loose and killed her."

"You're perfectly right," Shirley murmured. "That's the simplest explanation. If it weren't for all this purposeful anonymity, I'd believe that in a minute. Would you mind stopping in Tesuque on our way back? We can ask if anyone saw her last night."

"Oh, goody," Allison said. "Detective stuff."

"She's dead, Allison," Shirley snapped, putting her hand to her mouth. "I'm sorry. I didn't mean to sound ... I don't know what's the matter with me."

"You're tired," J.Q. offered. "And you're probably stewing over the possibility the woman caught something while she was with us."

"I never thought of that," said Allison, wide-eyed. "That'd be awful!"

"Right," Shirley said. "It would be awful. Would you mind stopping in Tesuque?"

They stopped. The only person available at the restaurant had not been there the previous evening. When Shirley outlined the problem, however, he looked through the reservations for the previous night. No Tremple.

"Do you know who she was with?" he asked.

Shirley shook her head helplessly. "No. She said she was meeting a friend."

The man ran his finger down the sheet. "Ten reservations for two, and there were probably a dozen more who didn't reserve. People don't always, not on a weeknight. If you'll describe her for me, I'll ask when the waitpeople show up tonight."

Shirley described the unnaturally dark hair, the extreme thinness.

Allison said, "When she talked, she put her head way over on one side, like this," and she cocked her head, almost laying it on one shoulder. "Maybe she only did it when she talked to kids, but I noticed it."

There was something sickeningly coquettish in the tilted head, the slantwise glance. A contrived and ugly confidentiality. Shirley shivered. J.Q. took her arm and squeezed it.

58

"My name's Al," the man said. "I'll call you if I find anything out."

Allison gave him the number. "Rancho del Valle," she said.

"Sure," he said with a smile. "I know the place. My aunt Alberta works out there."

Wordlessly they returned to the car.

"Are the Luceros related to everyone in the county?" Shirley asked.

"Probably," J.Q. answered. "After all, this area was populated from a very small base. The original Pueblos along the Rio Grande had only a few thousand inhabitants when the Spanish came, and the Spanish killed a lot of them, by warfare or disease. The Spanish weren't numerous, only a few hundred of them along with a tiny handful of European women, a few dozen concupiscent friars. Follow that with a couple centuries of exploitation, slavery, and interbreeding, you end up with a lot of interrelated people, even though the mixed children usually weren't recognized by their fathers."

"Why not?" Allison asked.

"Oh, either because they weren't supposed to father children at all or because status was based on race."

Shirley gave him a look. "What've you been reading?"

"An excellent book by one Ramón Gutiérrez," he said. "It's called *When Jesus Came, the Corn Mothers Went Away*. My point is, among longtime residents, a lot of people are related to a lot of other people here, and the known relationships are probably the least part of it. All kinds of alliances and mésalliances have been going on for hundreds of years."

Allison leaned forward, putting her arms on the back of the front seat. "What's a mésalliance?"

Shirley said sternly, "Allison, sit back and put your seat belt on. It's when somebody who's proud hooks up with someone who's supposedly inferior. Like if Beauregard was still a stallion, and you bred him to a plow horse."

"I'd never do that!"

"Well, that's what the proud Spaniards thought they were, stallions, but highbred Spanish brood mares were in short supply."

"So they had sex with the women who were here?"

"They did. They enslaved local women and used them sexually. The resultant babies were called mestizos."

J.Q. said, "The resultant babies were called all kinds of names. Some of the 'Spaniards' were from Hispaniola. Their parents or grandparents were African. Some of them had Moorish roots. And, of course, the original Americans came via the land bridge from Asia, so they included Asian genetic strains. Lots of coyotes around here."

"What difference does it make?" asked Allison.

"It doesn't," said Shirley. "That's the point J.Q. is making. Ethnic background is unimportant. Ninety-nine percent of our genetic material is the same as chimpanzees, so ethnically we're more ape than anything else. That doesn't make any difference either, but it's interesting."

"Ninety-nine?" J.Q. swerved the car slightly. "Ninety-nine?"

"Right. Which means only one percent separates us from apes, and probably less than one hundredth of one percent separates us from each other, no matter what color, sex, or gender we are. Which means, when we get upset at other people for being different, we are ignoring the ninety-nine-point-nine-nine percent of ourselves that are similar."

"I don't care," said Allison stoutly. "I think sometimes that little bit is important. I know some people I don't want to be like at all!"

"That's telling her, Allison."

Shirley actually grinned. "Right on, girlchild. Don't you ever tell me, sure, if I say so."

"What . . .?" Allison started to ask.

"Don't ask," said J.Q. firmly. "Don't get her started. She's on a tear today, being mightily dissatisfied with humanity. Best thing to do is get her home, give her a small glass of scotch, and stay out of her way."

The small glass of scotch and the approach of evening brought relative calm. The fingerprinters had come and gone from Frog House, after taking Shirley's fingerprints and Alberta's, for comparison. Alberta had packed Mrs. Tremple's clothing and books in the suitcase and stored it in the garage. Tomorrow, she said, she would clean Frog House.

"With disinfectant," she said. "With Lysol. Maybe it was catching, what she died of."

"I think if it had been catching, the doctors would have recognized what it was, Alberta." Shirley, being reasonable.

"Those doctors, they don't know everything," Alberta replied. "I still use Lysol. So people can smell it, they'll know the place is clean." She left the kitchen, back straight, face purposefully set.

"They'll wonder what the smell is covering up," said J.Q.

"I don't care," Shirley replied. "Nobody's coming until next week. By then the smell will have gone. Xanthy, hand me that head of lettuce, will you? Somebody see if the spaghetti's done."

"It's still hard in the middle," Allison said judiciously when she'd captured a strand and bitten off a piece.

"Salad dressing," mumbled Shirley. "Let's use the ranch dressing. J.Q., will you get that damned phone?"

The ringing stopped. Mumbling took its place. J.Q. was digging in the drawer for a pen. Shirley wiped her hands, reached past him, and handed him one from the pencil jar right in front of his face. Men.

He hung up. "Shirl."

"In a minute."

"No, dear heart. Now. Listen. That was Pat Garcia, from the hospital. They found out what killed Mrs. Tremple."

Shirley dropped the salad bowl with a clatter, a few shreds of lettuce flying to land at Xanthy's feet. "What. What?"

"Sit down." He said, implacably silent, gesturing them

all to take places at the table. "Now. Listen. Mrs. Tremple died of an infection in her brain. The bug that caused it is a kind of microorganism called . . . let's see," He put on his glasses and peered at his scrawled notes. "Naegleria."

"Oh, God, J.Q. Something she caught here?"

"Here at the ranch? Not possibly, no. It's an organism that grows in hot springs. Natural hot springs. And the only way it can kill someone is if it gets up someone's nose."

Xanthippe looked at him disapprovingly. "This isn't a time to be funny, John Quentin."

He crossed his heart, held his hand high. "I'm quoting precisely what the nurse told me. If you swallow this amoeba, your saliva or stomach acid will kill it. If it gets in any other . . . ah, orifice, it dies from lack of oxygen. It needs an oxygen-rich environment. Like the nose, like the brain. If it gets into the nose, it eats through into the brain, consumes the brain cells, and kills you. There's no treatment, no cure."

"There are hot springs at Jemez," said Shirley, her eyes wide, unfocused. "She said she'd been to Jemez."

"Reborn didn't take her there," Allison objected.

"No. She went to Jemez earlier. And she was waiting out by the road Tuesday morning. The young men from Big House saw her there around ten o'clock. Hovering, one of them said."

Xanthy shook her head sadly. "So, someone picked her up. Her client, whatever. And that's probably who she had dinner with, too. The poor woman was no doubt infected at Jemez Springs."

"Or it could have been at some other place entirely," offered J.Q. "She came here via Arizona. Either of the highways coming east from Phoenix are in or near the Gila National Forest, which is full of hot springs, and both of them bring you to the Rio Grande at Las Cruces. From there, you drive up the river to Truth or Consequences, which was originally named Hot Springs. She could have stopped at any of a dozen different springs on her way here."

62

"The point being," Xanthy went on, "it has nothing to do with us, or with this place. Shirley. Shirley! You don't seem at all relieved!"

"I'm not," she replied. "I mean, I am, but . . . but we still don't know who she is."

Though at the moment she couldn't say why that should matter to them. She'd never really known the woman. J.Q. had made the reservation. Alberta had cleaned the house. Others had seen her, spoken to her. Shirley herself hadn't laid eyes on her until she was dying. Perhaps that was it. To die among strangers seemed a horrid fate. Not to have people around that one knew. Not to have one's last breath listened for, one's last words . . .

What had her last words been? Ahmiss maculy. A mumble. Barely articulate. The brain, even then, being taken over, destroyed. Identity fading. Though, in this case, identity was just plain missing.

"I still want to know who she was," Shirley said stubbornly.

"We all do," soothed Xanthy. "And we will no doubt find out. If the police fail to do so, no reason you shouldn't do so, Shirley. You have a talent for such things, but please, don't go crazy over it!"

"I'm driving everyone up the wall, right?"

"You've been very edgy lately."

"Sorry." She gave them all individual grimaces of apology. J.Q. ignored her. Allison flushed. Xanthy peered over her glasses, as though measuring her sincerity.

"Have you lost weight these last few weeks?" Xanthy asked in a concerned voice.

"Haven't the least idea. My trousers still fit."

"You look a bit gaunt."

"I'll have a checkup," she promised. She would have a checkup. She was edgy. It was probably a combination of new place, getting used to her damned steel knee, and having no very clear idea of what her role would be from this time forward. When she had worked for Roger Fetting at the Bureau, in Washington, she had known exactly what

63

she was doing. When J.Q. and she were ranching in Colorado, they had known exactly what they were doing—most of the time. Here, in this place, she wasn't yet sure. Things happened that were unexpected and surprising. She had sudden emotional storms that were equally unexpected and surprising. There was no circle of workmen or suppliers she could count on to be honest and reliable. The involvements and intentions of the people in the area were unknown.

Which could be all very exciting, she told herself grimly. What was that old Chinese curse? May you live in exciting times. Well, at least she should try to do it more gracefully.

"The spaghetti's done," said Allison.

"Then let's eat it," Shirley directed.

As though by mutual agreement, J.Q., Xanthy, and Allison carried on a totally impersonal but very animated conversation during supper. They shared such a wealth of information about butterflies and frogs and the habits of hummingbirds that Shirley suspected them of having agreed upon and researched the topics in advance. Both the light chatter and the Chianti Classico J.Q. had furnished were extremely relaxing.

"Who's that?" Allison asked as a car crunched by outside, slowly pulling into a parking space.

"The Stevenses," J.Q. replied, half rising to get a better look. "Him and her and his sister's girl."

"I talked to her the other day," Allison remarked. "She's only a year older than I am."

"They don't seem to be enjoying their vacation very much," remarked Shirley. "What a bunch of long faces."

"It's not exactly a vacation," said J.Q. "We were talking early the other morning while I was feeding the stock. Mrs. Stevens was raised near here, according to him. Her father died recently, and she's actually been staying in town, to help her mother sort out the house. He says it only makes sense to sell it, property values in Santa Fe being what they are. Besides, it's huge and Mama can't take care of it. Nonetheless, Mama doesn't want to sell."

"I'm with her," said Shirley, wiping her lips on her napkin. "Since they're the only ones I haven't asked about Mrs. Tremple, I'll catch them before they get involved in something." She rose and was half out the door before the others could think of reasons she shouldn't. She kept going, leaving them spluttering to themselves.

"She's exactly like a rat terrier," muttered J.Q. "Gets hold of something and won't let go till she's shaken it to death."

Xanthy sighed. "It's not just that, J.Q. She's seemed different lately. I really want her to see a doctor. Shirley's always been volatile, but not over little things. Not until recently."

"Didn't she want to move?" Allison asked in a small voice.

"Of course not," said J.Q. "She wanted to live and die in the place she thought of as home. This isn't home yet. It may get to be. It has all the right elements. Now we need some time, calm time, easy time."

"Forlorn hope," murmured Xanthy. "It has not been my experience that Shirley ever has calm time."

Shirley, meantime, had her knuckles poised before the door to the Garden House when it opened before her.

"Mr. Stevens," she said. "I'm Shirley McClintock. I wonder if I might ask—"

She was thrust backward as he shouldered her out of the way, came out, and pulled the door to behind him.

"What?" he snarled. "What!" He was as tall as she, and heavy, with a bulldog's saggy face.

She stepped back, frowning. "We're trying to identify the woman who was staying in the house by the pond, Mr. Stevens. I've asked everyone else, and—"

"We didn't know her."

"That wasn't the question," she said, her voice dropping an ominous octave. "The question was, have you seen her, at any time, while you've been here?"

"No," he said, turning toward the door.

"I'd like to ask your wife, and your niece, if they've seen her."

He turned back, condensing the full weight of his visage into one long, weary look. "Look, lady, I've had a rotten day. I mean, measured on a scale of one to ten, this one has been minus eight! My wife's father died six weeks ago. My wife came out here to help her mom, and her mom does nothing but give her grief, you understand, like it was Riana's fault he died. And Ree can't stop crying, and my sister's girl, Vancie, is pregnant at age fifteen, for Christ's sake, and she's whiny, and the rental-car girl charged me an arm and a leg. I've had it with women. All women, including investigators, questioners, people sticking their nose in. So if you don't mind, just take the questions away. Maybe tomorrow. Maybe the day after. Not now!"

He departed, crashing the door firmly behind him.

Shirley blinked. After a long moment she turned and thoughtfully made her way back to the kitchen, where she found Xanthy and Allison doing the dishes.

"Where's J.Q.?"

"He took some salad trimmings to the goats," said Xanthy.

Shirley went to find him. He was leaning on the rail fence beside the goat pen, feeding shreds of lettuce to Isabel and her two kids. Shirley leaned on the fence beside him.

"So?" he asked.

"He's sick of women and he won't talk to me."

"Ah."

"So, when you see him next, see what you can find out. I'll talk to her."

"Which her?"

"Both, I guess. The niece is fifteen?"

"Allison said she was." He broke off, trying to hold on to the pan. Isabel was trying to get her entire forequarters into it.

Shirley mused. "That's right. Allison said she'd spoken to her. He says she's pregnant."

"Really." He put the pan down where Isabel could see that it was empty.

"It's his sister's daughter. Why would he bring his pregnant niece to Santa Fe?"

He sighed. "Act one, scene one—divorced mother, attempting to raise children alone, finds out daughter is pregnant. Daughter wants to marry the probably adolescent boy who caused pregnancy. Or maybe he's an older man, a nymphophile. Scene two—the mother asks her childless brother, since he is going to be out of town for a while, to take her along, talk to her, try to get her to see sense."

"I suppose that might have happened."

"Meantime his wife is having problems of her own and is not sympathetic to the niece. Maybe she, wife, actively hates her, niece. Maybe she, wife, actively hates her husband's entire family. Who knows?"

"I don't think it was that. Evidently his wife, Riana, is catching the devil from her own mother."

"You want that act and scene as well?"

"Thank you, no, J.Q. I can figure that one out for myself. One grieving relative turning on another—you didn't love him enough, you weren't nice to him, and so on and so on."

"Right."

They leaned awhile longer. Sunset was yet an hour away, but it was already cooling down. A group of magpies chattered at one another in the tallest cottonwood along the river bottom. From inside the barn, a rooster crowed, then came strutting into the pen, glossy black feathers gleaming with emerald lights in the late sun. He flapped his way to the fence rail opposite where they were standing, stretched and crowed once more, then began to preen, first one wing then the other.

"Pretty," she murmured, for the moment seduced.

"Very," he agreed. "Let's go sit on the patio and have another glass of wine."

"Good idea."

They walked companionably up the hill, and while J.Q. dusted off the chairs Shirley went in to get the wine.

"Vincente brought the mail," said Allison. "We forgot to pick it up today."

"So we did," Shirley agreed as she leafed idly through the pile. The phone bills. Three catalogs. A card from her cousin Beth. An envelope addressed to her. Return, Calworth and Carpenter, Attorneys-at-Law. Albany. New York. Now what the hell? She ripped it open and glanced at the page and a half, and again, and even more slowly for a third time.

"What?" asked Allison.

"What?" asked J.Q., standing in the kitchen door. "Shirl! What is it?"

Wordlessly she handed him the letter. When he had read it half through, he was almost as pale as she.

"What?" demanded Allison again, her voice rising.

"Your aunt and uncle," he said, the words rough, as though from a dry throat. "They've filed a legal suit to get custody of you."

In Ditch House the crazy lady and her friend lay before the fire, sharing an ashtray on the coffee table, he from the couch, she from her position cross-legged on the rug.

"Fireplace's stopped smoking," he remarked.

"Must have fixed it," said she, stroking her left ear.

"Think I'll go down to the pueblo, play the poker machines," he said.

"Emil, you always lose at poker."

"Thought maybe you'd lend me some money."

"Not for poker, not for drink."

"Don't you ever have any fun? God, woman, you're such a drag."

"I told you I'd keep you on this trip. I didn't tell you I'd keep your habits."

"Well, I've got some money."

She regarded him calmly, with the hint of a smile. "You didn't have any money yesterday!"

"So?"

"So, in order to drink, in order to gamble, you steal. Just so you know what you really do."

"Women. Bitches. You're no different!" He rose to his full height and moved toward the door.

"Don't try to take the car."

"How'm I suppose to—"

"You're not supposed to."

He slammed out, leaving her behind on the floor, staring at the ceiling through wraiths of cigarette smoke. Maybe she wouldn't wait for him to get tired and come back. Maybe she'd wait until he'd walked halfway to the pueblo, it was only a couple of miles, and pick him up. He'd have cooled down by then. Maybe she'd pack up and leave while he was gone. That might be simplest. There were a number of things one might do, at this juncture. Maybe . . .

She stared into the fire, focused on the end of a glowing log, and began to hum, a high, nasal hum, one that always reminded her of lamaseries and ancient, mysterious places. Beside her in the ashtray, her cigarette smoked. As it grew shorter it set fire to some of the other butts in the dish. The smoke grew thicker, but the crazy lady had taken herself somewhere else and didn't notice.

In the Garden House, Riana Stevens rinsed out the dish-cloth and hung it up to dry. The dishes were washed, the pans were scrubbed, the table was wiped down, as were the kitchen counters. Outside, the sky had gone from pale yellow to apricot to salmon to soft lavender. After spending the last week in the fusty old house with Mama, it would be nice to watch the sunset from outside.

She went to the door. Craig was on the bed, reading the paper. He had the curtains pulled across the west window, all that glory out there, and he'd shut it out. Vancie was curled up on the sofa bed, eyes shut, withdrawn from the world. Poor little thing. So in love with that dropout she couldn't see straight. Wanted to marry him. Wanted to live with him.

"Where," Ree had asked, "where are you going to live?"

"With him!"

"And where does he live?"

A blank expression, that look of baffled idiocy that Ree remembered finding all too often in her own mirror. Hormones at work; brain unavailable at this time. Vancie's love object lived, if Craig's sister could be believed, in an old garage with three other young men of similar persuasion.

The girl opened one eye.

"Want to come watch the sunset with me?"

The eye shut again, pushing itself into defiant wrinkles. Don't bother me. Don't ask me anything. I won't listen.

Riana let herself out the door, closing it softly, then went around the corner of the house and through the garden to sit on a bench placed conveniently beneath a tree. From here she could look out over shadowy canyons, up past the long, horizontal edge of mesa, and beyond to the crumpled mountains, stark against the fiery sky. To her right the land sloped away abruptly, down into the woods along the river, where the fireflies were.

Her father had always loved the fireflies. One of the earliest things she remembered was his helping her catch them, to put them inside a paper lantern and make it glow. First they had to cut a T-shaped piece of paper and fold it into a six-sided box, then they had to tape it closed, leaving only a corner flap free. He'd showed her how to prick each side with a pin, to make a design, and how to tape a loop of paper to the top, for the handle. First make your cage, Daddy had said. Then catch your firefly. . . .

Suddenly she put her head upon her knees and began to sob. Daddy was gone. Finally, irrevocably gone. She could never tell him thank you for the fireflies. And Mother . . . Mother blamed her. For everything.

Mr. Fley knocked the dottle out of his pipe and set about refilling it.

"Going to die of mouth cancer," said his wife, heaving her crochet work into the lamplight. They were sitting in a mostly darkened room, watching the sunset through the open window.

"Probably," he agreed, tamping the tobacco with a stained thumb. "Probably only live to be ninety-five or six before I die of mouth cancer."

"Tongue cancer, probably," she continued. "You'll be speechless the last ten years of your life."

"That should be fine with you," he commented, without rancor. "Seein' as how you're so bored with my conversation."

"Not really." She grinned, a particularly foxish grin. "Just like to get it offtrack sometimes. Otherwise I always know where it's going."

"D'you see her"—he gestured with his pipe—"sitting out there?"

Mrs. Fley looked at the seated figure in the sunset glow with blank, utterly incurious eyes. "First time I've seen her at all."

"That so? She's been here off and on. So've a couple of those young fellas. Do a lot of night stalking, they do. Prowling around in the dark. And that drunk, the one that came staggering down the drive day before yesterday. He went off just a while ago, walking, carryin' a sack. He'll be in the dark, too."

"There's a moon," she said.

"Old Chinese saying," he murmured. "Men who walk in the night are mistaken for tigers."

"Old Chinese saying, my foot." She yawned, surprising herself. "I'm tired."

"Been a long day," he said. "And there was all that hoo-faraw last night."

"I imagine tonight'll be quieter." She folded her work meticulously, set it on the coffee table beside her workbasket, and headed toward the bathroom.

"Think I'll go out to finish my pipe," he said.

"Turn the fan on," she remarked as she closed the door. "Get the smell of you out."

He grinned, turned on the fan, then took himself and his

pipe out into the courtyard. Through the gate he could see Mrs. Stevens hunched on the bench, her shoulders shaking, the dark folding around her. He leaned in a corner, himself hidden in that dark.

The door to the neighboring house opened quietly.

"Aunty Ree?" called a childish voice. "Auntie Ree?" A slender figure emerged from the doorway and went out into the garden. Murmurs came, and the sound of weeping.

So, they were both grieving over something. Two somethings, perhaps. He sucked on the pipe, seeing the red glow beneath the ashes, thinking, not for the first time, that life was like that. Something hard and hurtful was always smoldering just under the ashes.

He grunted, a small, slightly troubled grunt, as though some wandering thought had proven uncomfortable. After a moment he went in to keep company with Mrs. Fley.

In the Big House the six tenants were gathered in the kitchen around the remnants of a Chinese takeout, a dozen paper cartons, a jackstraw heap of chopsticks, scattered foil packets smeared with mustard and soy sauce.

"Too much," said Rob. "Cally, you always get too much."

"Better too much than not enough," said the huge, ugly man addressed as Cally. "As in life."

"Who's going to do the dishes?" Harry asked. "Rob and I did them this morning, for our sins. And Cally picked up the food."

"I will clear. Arthur and Alph and Michael will do the dishes," said Rob, rolling up his sleeves. "And we need to plan what we're going to do tomorrow. We only have a few more days." He began to stack the plates, then stopped. "Which reminds me. When we came home Tuesday night ... Was it Tuesday? Harry?"

"Tuesday night? Well, actually, it was Wednesday morning."

"Right. Did any of you see the woman staying in the house by the pond?"

"At that hour?" jeered Alphonso. "It was after three!"

"As a matter of fact, I did," said Caliban. "The porch light was on, and she was going into the house as we drove by. I remember thinking we weren't the only debauchees in the woods."

"We? Debauchees? Cally, how unkind."

Rob made a mental note of the time and circumstances. He would call Ms. McClintock as soon as he got around to it.

3

FRIDAY MORNING: SHIRLEY and Allison came into the kitchen to find J.Q. and Xanthy with their heads together like a couple of conspirators. They looked up guiltily, immediately averting their eyes. J.Q. cleared his throat.

"Are you going to call a lawyer?" he asked.

So they'd been discussing the Allison business. Shirley nodded. "Numa should be getting into his office right now. I'll call him as soon as I've poured myself a cup of coffee."

"It's fresh," said J.Q.

He drew away from Xanthy with a look of innocence so studied as to appear suspect. Now what were they up to?

Allison demanded, "Are you going to talk to him about me?" She handed Shirley the sugar bowl and a spoon.

"Naturally," Shirley replied, casting a questioning glance toward the breakfast table. J.Q. had disappeared behind the western edition of *The Wall Street Journal* and Xanthy was pouring out orange juice.

Before Shirley could query either of them, Allison asked, "Do you mind if I listen?"

"Of course not." She sat down at the desk, sipped her

coffee, dialed the Colorado number, and began a detailed exposition the moment Numa was on the line.

Xanthy and Allison listened unabashedly, though J.Q. remained hidden behind his paper, pretending noninvolvement.

Silence on Shirley's part.

"Numa, I just got the damned thing yesterday!"

"_____"

"Of course I'll fax you a copy. By eleven or so."

"_____?"

"Because I don't have a fax. I have gone to some effort not to have a fax. My religion forbids faxes. Everyone who does have a fax is several miles from here."

"_____?"

"In an hour or two. I can read it to you if you need it before then."

"_____?"

"Allison has no more idea than I do. She got a phone call from her aunt a couple of days ago. Aunty made vaguely familial noises and invited her for a visit. Aunt and Uncle haven't approached me."

"_____"

"No, of course she doesn't want to go live with them. If she did, she could go anytime she wanted to. Our arrangement is mutual, not one-sided."

"_____"

"I'd appreciate that, Numa. Thank you very much."

She hung up, made an angry face, and turned her chair around to join the others at the table. "He's going to find me a lawyer here in Santa Fe. He says we'll have to answer this thing from wherever we are."

"Is that all we have to do? Answer it?" Allison asked in a small voice.

"I have no idea. That's where we start, at any rate. First we have to find out what grounds they have, if any."

"I bet I already know," she whispered.

"Allison, why? Did your aunt say something?"

"No, it was Cheryl. Remember, I said she phoned me

once after we moved down. In April, maybe. And I said I wasn't going to school, I didn't have to for a while, but I didn't tell her about Xanthy and private tutoring and all. I just let her think I wasn't going."

"Well, if that's all," said J.Q. "I hardly think that will stand up—"

"That might be grounds," said Xanthy in a crisp, no-nonsense tone. "But it's not a reason. I'm interested in the reason."

"If they thought I wasn't being educated . . ." Allison faltered.

"Would they care?" asked Shirley. "Now honestly, Allison. Would they?"

The girl shrugged, flushed. "I don't guess so. No."

"Xanthy's right. What reason would they have?"

"Extortion?" suggested J.Q.

Xanthy frowned. "Wouldn't that risk publicity that might put them in a bad light? From my experience with them, I'd say they—or at least, she—would go to any lengths to avoid social disapproval."

Shirley said, "Unless they were desperate, of course. Or if they thought they could make a great deal of money."

"I say again, extortion?" J.Q. leaned forward, his jaw set.

"Like, maybe I'd pay a million or two for Allison?" Shirley demanded. "I would, in a minute, if I had it. But I don't."

"You have this place."

"For all they know, it's mortgaged to the hilt. No, that's a long shot, J.Q. They didn't seem like the kind of people who'd bet on long shots."

Allison was fretting. "I won't have to go there, will I? Even with one cousin gone, one cousin is too many."

"Not if the saints prevail, no," said Xanthy. "And we will not cross any bridges . . ."

Allison laughed. Shirley joined her, somewhat ruefully. Then Allison had to explain to Xanthy why they were laughing.

"Someone's hovering outside," interrupted J.Q.

76

They hushed, hearing Dog's annunciatory bark, the discreetly muffled "pay attention" sound that Dog had selected to mark an intrusion by guests upon private ground. Shirley opened the kitchen door, letting in a flood of morning sunshine and the heat that went with it. The muscular baldy from Big House stood outside, hand raised, smiling charmingly.

"Rob, isn't it?" Shirley asked.

"Yes, ma'am. Rob Clapton. We'll be leaving by noon, and I came to settle up. Also, you asked whether we saw anyone go into the house by the pond? Cally Frieze, one of our group, saw the woman when he drove in. She was going into the house at about three in the morning, that would be Wednesday morning."

"Not possible," said J.Q.

"I'm sorry?"

"We were at the hospital with her by two-thirty. She never left there. She died there. We got back around four."

"Well, he said he saw someone going into the house," Rob said.

"That could be," Shirley interjected. "Someone probably did go in. Is he sure he saw a woman? Or just someone going into the house?"

"Why don't I bring him over? If this is important, you should get it from him, not secondhand. About half an hour, okay? He's just having his first cup of coffee."

"We'd be happy to give him his second," said J.Q.

Rob flashed his white-toothed smile and departed.

"He's gay, isn't he?" asked Allison. "Vancie—Mr. Stevens's niece—says they all are."

"They give that impression," Shirley replied absentmindedly. "It seems the group takes a trip every summer. I heard them talking about having visited Sweden and Australia. This year they started out in Durango and came down through Chaco Canyon and Bandelier." She shook her head, bringing the matter at hand into focus. "If someone went into that house at that hour . . ."

"Well, if she didn't do it herself, someone else had to," J.Q. remarked.

"Did what?" demanded Allison.

Shirley murmured, "Cleaned out everything that might have identified her. Driver's license. Credit cards. Correspondence. Anything."

Xanthy looked out the window and rose from the table. "Here they are, back already. I'll just take the paper into the dining room, give you a little space."

The two had reached the kitchen door when Shirley opened it.

"This is my friend Calvin Frieze. We call him Caliban, he's such a monster." Rob gave his friend an openly admiring look, then winked at Shirley.

The giant bowed over Shirley's hand, stooped to avoid bumping his head on the low lintel, and took possession of the kitchen, occupying about as much room, Shirley thought bemusedly, as the refrigerator freezer.

"Rob says there's a dilemma," he rumbled in a mellow basso. "He says I must have seen an interloper at the house over there."

"Anything you can be sure of would be helpful," Shirley said, beckoning him to come to the table. He was not quite so imposing sitting down, though the chair seemed barely adequate. J.Q. gave him a cup of coffee, and he sipped it appreciatively, thinking the matter over.

"It was two-thirty before we could get Harry and Rob rounded up and headed for home. Harry's had a personal tragedy recently, and Rob was joining him in his grief."

"Someone needed to stay with him," said Rob with some asperity. "So he didn't do something silly, too."

The big man went on as though there had been no interruption. "They were both far too influenced to drive. I recall their being very little traffic on the highway; the road into here was completely deserted. So when I saw the figure standing at the door, it startled me a bit. I only assumed it was the woman I'd seen earlier, the one who was staying there. Nothing in the stance or the stature made me think differently."

Shirley said, "She was about five-six, very thin. Black hair. Probably dyed."

"Hmmm." He sipped again. "I remember a light above that door. I don't remember seeing hair. Light reflects from hair, you know. . . ."

"Cally does lighting for theater, and movies," said Rob. "He's won awards."

The big man smiled, a particularly charming smile. "Very small awards. My father's an electrician and my mother's a frustrated actress, so my chosen field is a natural consequence. Being a lighting professional does teach you to notice effects, however. Now that I think about it, I believe the person wore a loose jacket and something on his or her head. And trousers. Which could mean either a him or her, of course. I don't remember the feet. I don't think I could see the feet from the driveway. Just this rather amorphous shape, not too large, with one hand on the latch."

"You didn't see the face," Shirley said.

"Regrettably, no." He thought, tapping his finger on the table. "Tell you what. I'll go back out there and have Rob stand by the door. That could give us an approximate height. What are you, Roberto, five-ten?"

"And a half."

"We'll take Michael or Harry over, too. They're shorter than you are."

Shirley didn't pursue the matter. An approximate height seemed to be all they were going to get, along with confirmation that someone had gone into Frog House while they were at the hospital. She drank her own coffee and listened while J.Q. figured up the bill and elicited details of the journey through Chaco Canyon.

"We've been using those small nylon tents," Rob said, signing traveler's checks. "Light, easy to put up and take down. Ordinarily, I'd rather sleep out, but with this hantavirus thing, we thought it better not to be breathing dust off the ground. We're all rather into personal survival."

"Sounds sensible to me," J.Q. offered. "I've been concerned about what we'll do with all the guest houses this fall. Mice always try to get into warm houses in the autumn, when the cold weather starts."

Suddenly, out of nothing, Shirley felt her heart pounding, her breath coming quickly. She made an involuntary, strangled sound. Why had he brought that up!

From behind her she felt a hand on her shoulder and heard Xanthy's voice saying quietly, "Shirley, I need to talk to you."

Xanthy's hand remained on her shoulder as she rose and excused herself, falling to the small of her back, where it urged her along with a series of little pats. They went through the huge living room, down the corridor to Shirley's bedroom, where she leaned against her door, breathing heavily.

"When I came into the kitchen you started breathing like that, red in the face, making gargling noises. What's the matter?"

Shirley breathed deeply once more. "It's been happening to me lately. Someone says something, and I get frantic. This time J.Q. said something about mice. I suddenly felt ... I don't know. Angry at him for having mentioned it. Panicky at the thought of having to deal with it." She collapsed onto the bed. "How silly. What's the matter with me!"

Xanthy went to the dresser and picked up one of Shirley's pill bottles, then came to sit beside her on the bed. "How long have you been taking this?"

Shirley took the bottle and peered at the label. "Since about the first of the year. I take it at night, with one of those pink ones."

"What are you taking it for?"

"So I can sleep! Whenever I lay down, my knee ached like a rotten tooth. It was driving me crazy. First the knee, then I'd get muscle cramps in my calf, in my foot, then a shooting pain down the back of my leg! I'd get up, walk around, take a hot shower, it would go away. I'd lie down, it was back again. I wasn't getting any rest and I felt like

80

a sick old dog. The doctor said the combination of the two pills would relax the muscles and let me sleep. And they do."

"This is Halcion."

"So?"

"So, I read about it in *Consumer Reports*. It's marketed as a sleeping pill, but it's a close chemical relative to some medications used to treat panic attacks, medications that are being, shall we say, reevaluated. This one—listen to me!—is said to make some people paranoid and hostile. Being paranoid and hostile does fire up the adrenaline, and perhaps that explains the frantic feelings you've been having."

Shirley bit down a flood of angry words. She took a deep breath. "You said I'd been edgy. . . ."

"In recent months you have been. Before that you were unusually crabby, because of the pain, I think, but you were very much yourself. Recently you've been strange. I couldn't explain it, even to myself, until this morning when J.Q. told me about the chimney."

"What about the chimney?"

"Another strange effect of this drug is that it makes some people forget what they've just done."

"I haven't—"

"Shirley, shortly after the roofers were here, you climbed up on the roof of Ditch House. I held the ladder for you."

"I didn't!"

"Yes, indeed you did. You went up, you looked over the edge, you cursed, very much in your usual manner, you came back down, telling me to leave the ladder there, you had to go back up and remove a rock from on top of the chimney, but you needed to change your shoes first."

"Change my shoes?"

"You didn't want to get tar on the shoes you were wearing. When I went by later, the ladder was gone. I assumed you'd gone back up and removed the rock."

"Why didn't you—"

"I didn't realize there was any connection with the smoking chimney until J.Q. told me the story early this morning.

81

Before you got up. J.Q. says you've been forgetful about other things as well. He put it down to mere distraction."

"My God." She didn't doubt it was true. Xanthy was truthful in all things, often uncomfortably so. "What else have I done that I don't remember? And how can a pill do that?"

"I've read that daytime memories may be stored during sleep, particularly during dreaming. That's why dreams are often so odd; storing memories is like opening a file cabinet and riffling through batches of associations to get to the right place. Perhaps this medication disrupts that process, like a computer malfunction, destroying files instead of putting them away. Or misfiling them, where you'll never find them."

Shirley stared at the bottle on Xanthy's palm with revulsion. Such an innocent-looking little cylinder. "Why did the doctor prescribe them?"

"You said it yourself, so you could sleep. But it seems to me the better part of valor, since you need all your wits about you just now, that you taper off."

"I'll just quit."

"I think tapering off should work better. Stopping abruptly seems to cause even more sleeplessness and anxiety than prompted the drug in the first place. I'll bring you the magazine, and you can read the article for yourself. And for the next week or so, while you're getting off this stuff, maybe it would be a good idea to stick close to one of us. Me. J.Q."

"Does he know about these pills?"

"I told him what I suspected when he told me about the smoking chimney. The whole episode seemed absurd, so unlike you, that I came in here a little while ago to check the labels on your pill bottles. If you weren't losing your mind, then you had to be taking something. It was the only explanation I could think of."

Shirley compressed her lips, not knowing whether to laugh or cry. "What if it isn't pills? What if I really am losing my mind?"

"We'll have to cross that bridge—" Xanthy stepped back, offended, as Shirley collapsed in half-hysterical laughter. "My dear, it is not funny."

Shirley sobered. "No. None of it. Least of all the thought I may have been blundering about, committing all kinds of foolishness without remembering it. Maybe I've done something so egregious that the Brentwoods have latched onto it."

"I think we'd have known."

"Maybe I called them. Maybe I wrote, saying something awful."

"You're fully capable of that, as we both know, but you wouldn't have done it out of the blue. You don't write to them ordinarily, do you? And Allison didn't mention hearing from them until Wednesday morning. You haven't had time since then."

"Maybe I'd better keep a notebook. Write down what I'm doing at any given instant."

"Just get off this medication. Put your fertile mind to the problem of why your leg hurts at night. Figure out some other way to sleep. I'll bring you the article a little later." She left. Shirley heard her footsteps going down the long corridor to her own apartment. She tossed the bottle in her hand. Where did she go from here? It had been so wonderful to sleep again! She'd managed to get through a few painfully impossible days on the strength of being sure she'd sleep at night. Could she sleep without them?

Whether she could or not was irrelevant. She couldn't go on taking them, risking some chemically induced Alzheimer's for a few comfortable hours! Tonight she'd take three quarters of a tablet. Then only half. She'd refilled the prescription two weeks ago. If she took only half for a while, then only a quarter, an eighth, what was here in the bottle would be enough. She wouldn't refill the prescription again.

Her resolution was somewhat diminished by a familiar flutter, a premonitory pressure in her head, a desire to change the subject. An anxiety attack. A panic reaction. A feeling that had grown altogether too familiar recently.

Prior to this year she had felt real panic only a few times, just often enough to make it recognizable. She'd seen it often enough in animals, of course: a shivering of the senses, a disabling flutter, an irrational and frantic desire to hide from the reality of what was happening. To flee, to hide, and if that was not possible, to attack! And here she was, acting more or less like a terrified rabbit!

She lay back on the bed, an arm across her forehead, trying, just for the moment, not to think of anything. She breathed deeply, in and out, concentrating on relaxing shoulders that had knotted, jaw muscles that had tightened. Footsteps in the corridor, the small creak as her door went from half-closed to open.

"Shirl?"

"Yes, J.Q."

"Did Xanthy talk to you?"

Poor J.Q. He actually sounded worried. "She did. Scared me spitless. I don't know what I may have done lately."

"I doubt you did anything irrational. You just may not remember some of the rational things you did."

"For a start, we'd better cross-check the reservations."

"I'd thought of that. I'll do it this morning."

"We don't use a computer. We can't blame mistakes on a computer error."

"I'll think of something. There may not be any mistakes."

"I'm actually kind of relieved," she said, taking her arm from over her eyes.

"Relieved?"

"That chimney business. It wasn't like me to let something like that get by. I'm usually right on top of things."

He snorted. "As you were in this case. Right on top of the house. Don't make a big thing out of it. We'll all keep an eye on you."

"Yeah. Thanks. Maybe you'd better put a leash on me."

"Now you're overdramatizing."

"What I need is something tiring to do today. Something really laborious that will wear me out."

"Weed the front garden. Xanthy says it looks like a jungle."

"I'd thought, maybe, cleaning the barn . . ."

"It was just cleaned last week. Do you want that thing faxed to Numa?"

"Of course!" She sat up straight. "I'd even forgotten that!"

"You were distracted from that. After I check the reservations, I'll take the letter into town and fax it while you weed the garden. It'll be a good way to get yourself calmed down."

"Xanthippe will have to get me started. I'm not sure I know what to pull and what to let alone."

"I'll ask her."

Half an hour later, wearing a borrowed straw hat and with a soft pad under her steel knee, Shirley was on hands and knees digging out tough strands of Japanese clover with a sharp trowel. Also on the extirpation plan, according to Xanthy, were wild lettuce, a thing called mallow, and grass in any form.

"Think of mushrooming," Xanthy had said. "Your father didn't teach you to recognize every mushroom. He taught you to recognize a few very tasty ones, to know them so well you couldn't make a mistake, and not to eat any others. Weeds are similar. You don't learn every weed. You learn the most prevalent and noxious ones, and while you're pulling them, you learn what the garden plants look like, and eventually you'll know enough to pull everything except what you want there. Work on this stuff with the little yellow blossoms, that's the Japanese clover, and on any kind of grass—doesn't matter what kind, it doesn't belong in a flower garden. Also pull this rather pretty round leafed one—it has a taproot like a parsnip—and these tall ones with the prickly leaves. Oh, and dandelions. You know dandelions."

It was a pleasant, almost mindless exercise, mildly interesting if one cared how many kinds of grass there were. Some of them grew in neat little clumps that pulled out cleanly. Others had such an underground network that pulling one bit did no good at all. The only way to get it out was to dig up a great trowelful and sort out all the roots. Though her leg felt slightly uncomfortable, it wasn't unpleasant work. She hadn't knelt down like this for the better part of a year.

"Ms. McClintock?"

Shirley swiveled her head, caught the brim of her hat on a stalk, and dragged it off, standing her hair on end. The crazy lady was at the end of the garden path, wringing her hands dramatically.

"What can I do for you?" Shirley smoothed her hair and tried to extricate her hat from a large, multistalked plant that held it in a death grip. "What is it?"

"I wonder if you could help me."

"I have no idea," said Shirley, starting to sit back on her heels, recoiling at the sudden agony that went down her leg all the way to the ankle. That far it wouldn't bend! Kneel, yes. Sit on her heels, no! Hastily she shifted position, rising laboriously to her feet. "Ouch. Damn." She shifted back and forth. "What's your problem?"

"You ought to try meditation," said the crazy lady in an interested voice. "It's wonderful for relief of pain."

"Your problem," repeated Shirley in a wooden voice that made her feel like the cuckoo in a clock. She did not want to discuss relieving her pain.

"Emil. He went off last night and he hasn't come back."

Shirley limped over to a garden chair and sat in it, working her knee back and forth. Maybe at first she shouldn't kneel too long. Maybe she should work up to it slowly. Maybe she should have worked up to innkeeping slowly. She could not feel any real interest in the crazy lady's problem.

She fished for something to say. "Was he committed to coming back?"

"I don't understand?"

"I mean, had he promised you he would come back. Had he made a commitment, to you, to return to you."

The crazy lady stared, looked away, then looked back again. A classic double take.

Shirley slogged on: "You told me the two of you aren't married, right? You're not engaged? You picked him up, he was drunk at the time, and you invited him along? What obligation does he have to meet your expectations of his behavior?" She relaxed against the chair back, watching the crazy lady's face.

"None, I guess," said the crazy lady, rather carelessly, as though it didn't really matter. "None at all." She stroked her left ear with an outstretched finger, ran it down her jaw to the chin, one finger on her lips.

"Well, then, I'd suggest you get on with your life—"

"But I . . . I . . ."

"—or your spiritual quest, whichever."

"They're the same thing," she cried expressively, with a gesture that was both graceful and well used. "Living is a spiritual quest."

"Right," Shirley agreed, surprised that she could agree.

The woman's voice rose, an impassioned howl. "I thought he was improving."

Shirley worked her knee again, trying to decide between truth and diplomacy. One told friends the truth. One was diplomatic with guests. What the hell. The crazy lady was due to leave today anyhow.

"All you were doing was making it inconvenient for him to get drunk. Alcoholics don't stop drinking because of inconvenience. They drink because that's what they do, like what you do is . . . ah, meditate. If someone made it inconvenient for you to meditate, you'd find a way to do it anyhow, wouldn't you? There's no way you can help an alcoholic from outside." She spoke sadly, surely. After Allison's mother had been killed, Shirley had done a lot of reading about alcoholics. "They have to want to help themselves."

A long silence that the crazy lady filled with tortured expressions. Shirley shifted uncomfortably. Why did she feel this was some kind of soap opera?

"Emil took her wallet," the crazy lady whispered. "That's where he got the money. I found it under his bed."

This was no soap! Shirley's ears pricked, her face flushed as her disinterest was replaced by an avid curiosity. "Whose wallet?"

"That woman who died. The one who dyed her hair."

"You mean he took it from her house?"

"All I know is, I found it under his bed. It has her driver's license in it, with a picture."

"Do you think he broke into her house?"

"I don't know. Do you want me to get the wallet?"

"I'll come with you," Shirley said, rising stiffly to her feet and following the younger woman to Ditch House. The house still stank of smoke, though less so than previously. The wallet was lying on the coffee table. Shirley sat down and opened it. Driver's license with an address in Los Angeles. No credit cards. No money. Alicia Lenore Tremple, age forty-six, black hair, brown eyes, height five-foot-six, weight 106. Shirley doubted that. Ninety-five, more likely.

"He took the credit cards and the money, I suppose." Shirley put the license back in the wallet and stared at it reflectively.

"I don't know."

"Had you given him any money?"

"No. I wouldn't give him any. And I slept with mine under my pillow."

Shirley considered the implications of that. A very strange relationship. Based on what?

She spoke slowly, thinking her way through it. "How does this sound? Alicia Tremple woke in the night feeling very sick. She got dressed and got into her car, to drive herself to the hospital, then realized she couldn't make it. So she left the car, maybe engine running, maybe lights on, almost certainly unlocked, and came knocking on our door. Emil may have been awake, or he may have been wakened by this racket. He waited for us to leave, then he went over to take a look at the car. He took the wallet—which may or may not have been inside a purse—locked the car, and brought the wallet back here. Yesterday he saw the sheriff's car here. Maybe he has reason to avoid lawmen. So he took the money and the credit cards and left."

The crazy lady shrugged, saying plaintively, "I suppose he might have."

"It's possible he took the license plate, too. I suppose one might get a few dollars for a current license plate." And in that case, there had been no effort to hide Alicia Tremple's identity. The mystery was the unintended result of a simple theft. "How tall is Emil?" she asked.

"Five-ten," murmured the crazy lady. "You don't think he's coming back?"

"What was the next step in your spiritual journey?" asked Shirley, resolutely serious.

This surprised the crazy lady, for her eyes opened wide, just for an instant. "Just to . . . be," she replied, eyelids lowering once more.

"Well then, why don't you just be somewhere nearby for the next few days while things are being sorted out. If he comes back, he comes back. If not, it means he's not ready. Right?"

"We'd . . . I'd already rented us a house. In Peñasco."

"Was he with you when you rented it?"

She jerked her head, a reluctant affirmative.

"Well then, he knows where you'll be, doesn't he?"

The crazy lady pursued her out of doors, as though unwilling to be left alone. Beneath the newly hung goat's skull, she stopped, looking at the horns, making a strange noise.

"What?" Shirley demanded.

"When did this get here?"

"This morning. I put it up before I started weeding."

"Do you . . . do you know what it is?"

"It's a goat's skull. A male goat's skull, as a matter of fact."

"A sign," breathed the crazy lady.

"A skull," Shirley reiterated impatiently. "A decorative

item. A Western motif, if you will. Let's not overdramatize what is dead and gone!"

Perhaps she only imagined the slight flush on the crazy lady's cheeks. If so, it was the only response. Shirley left her and headed for the kitchen phone. The sheriff's office should certainly be advised about the existence of the wallet, and about Emil. She couldn't find the paper she'd written the deputies' names on.

"Somebody there named Cisso?" she asked.

"Narcisso Pacheco? Sure. You want him?"

"Please."

There was a great deal of confused noise at the other end. Someone yelling. Someone else yelling. Shirley almost missed the voice in the general confusion.

"This is Cisso."

She launched into explanation.

"What's his last name, this Emil?"

"Don't know. You'll have to ask his friend, and she may not know. But we've got an address for Alicia Tremple." She read it off, apartment number, street address.

"We'll need the wallet."

"I know. I've got it for you."

"We ought to search this house where the woman's staying, in case he left anything else there."

"I don't think she'll care. If she does, I'll let you in."

"I guess that'd be all right. It's not his house, right? He didn't rent it?"

"It's not his house, he didn't rent it. As a matter of fact, this is her last day. I doubt she'll be here by the time you get here."

"We'll be out."

"I thought you were weeding," said J.Q., coming into the kitchen, carefully carrying his hat, which was full of eggs. "A coyote got a hen, right while I was watching, grabbed her up and carried her off into the bosque. There's a hole in the fence."

Shirley wasn't listening. "The crazy lady's friend stole Mrs. Tremple's wallet."

"Too heavily populated around here to use the rifle. Thought I'd try the new shotgun—what?"

"Emil somebody stole Mrs. Tremple's wallet."

"When?"

"I'm guessing, but probably while you and I were on the hospital trip. I'm betting she had the wallet, got into her car, then realized she couldn't drive herself and got out of her car, leaving the wallet. I'm betting Emil heard the ruckus and went over after we'd left to see what he could pick up."

"He was the guy Caliban saw at the door?"

"Don't know. We'll have to see what he thinks about the shape he saw at the door, how tall it was."

"There's a hole in this story, you know. Most women don't just carry a wallet. They carry a purse, with a wallet in it. Or if they take the wallet, they still have a purse, somewhere. You didn't find one."

"I know, J.Q. Maybe he took it. Perhaps it was a good purse, eelskin or ostrich or something, and he thought he could sell it. Maybe he took her key, went in her house, and took other things, thinking he could sell them."

"I suppose that's possible." He put down his hat and burrowed in a bottom drawer for an egg container. "Time to take eggs to the Salvation Army," he muttered. "I've got about nine dozen saved up."

"Don't the guests want any?"

"The crazy lady doesn't eat eggs. Mrs. Tremple no longer eats. The Fleys took half a dozen. The Stevenses drove off while I was feeding the rams this morning. Said they were going to Chimayo for the morning. And the gentlemen in the Big House are moving on today, down to Albuquerque, where they're spending a day before flying off home."

"I'm sure the Salvation Army will appreciate the eggs."

"Did the last time. You want me to go hunt for Emil?"

"Heavens, no! Let the sheriff's office do it. Cisso and his partner are coming out to get the wallet, and to search

91

Ditch House to see if there's anything else left over there. I think maybe Emil took the license plate, too."

"Why would he do that?"

"Sell it to a car thief, maybe. I don't know, J.Q. I guess it simplifies the tangle if I can believe one person did it all."

"One person went into the house and cleaned it out, and that same person took her wallet, locked her car keys in the car, and stole the license plate."

"Right."

"So there's no mystery."

"Also right."

He shook his head, closed the egg carton, and put it on the counter. "Have you called yet?"

"Called who?"

"Information. In Los Angeles. As Reborn suggested. You've got an address now."

"Didn't think of it again," she said, abruptly chastened. Why hadn't she thought of it? Because she'd forgotten. She went to the phone. "What's their area code?"

He handed her the phone book. She fished her reading glasses out of her shirt pocket and peered at the listing. "Two thirteen," she said, dialing.

While she waited for the information operator to answer, she watched J.Q. take everything out of the refrigerator to get at the back where the cartons of eggs were. He stacked them on the counter before reloading the refrigerator.

"What city?" asked the voice. Shirley told it, city and name.

"Your number is . . ." said a recording, and Shirley reached for a pen, writing it down once and then checking it as the digits were repeated. She punched in the numbers and waited while the phone rang and rang and rang. She was just about to hang up when a breathless voice answered.

"Tremple."

Shirley took a deep breath. "Who's speaking, please?"

"Who's calling, please?" snapped the other voice.

92

"Sorry. My name is Shirley McClintock. I own Rancho del Valle, north of Santa Fe. Ms. Alicia Tremple was staying here, and I need to speak with someone who knows her."

"Was staying? What do you mean, was?"

"Who's speaking, please."

"This is her sister! I'm here because the housekeeper called me. Has this got anything to do with the house being broken into? Did she find out about the house?"

Shirley gritted her teeth and fought down the sudden urge to hang up. She hadn't thought of running into a close family member who didn't know. Briefly she considered putting the question off, referring it to the sheriff's office, but the questioning voice at the other end was too involved and demanding for that.

"Is your name also Tremple?" she asked, delaying the inevitable.

"My name is Elaine Scott. What is this?"

"Ms. Scott, your sister woke us very early Wednesday morning. She was having a terrible headache. We took her to St. Vincent's Hospital in Santa Fe."

"Is she there now? What's the number there?"

"She's . . . I'm not sure. . . ." Oh, Lord. She simply had to say it, that's all. "She . . . she died on Wednesday."

"Died! My sister? That's impossible. She was never sick. Never. She had some little allergies, but she was healthy! You can't mean my sister. You must be mistaken. It must have been someone . . ."

Voices at the other end. More than one person. Female voice yelling, one loud male voice, one quieter male voice. Then the phone went dead. Shirley turned. J.Q. was standing beside a tower of eggs, his large hands resting atop the pile, watching her.

"Well?"

"Her sister. She hung up. Maybe by accident. I think someone was there with her, possibly the police. She said her sister's house had been broken into."

"You didn't give her this number."

"She didn't give me a chance. I'll call back, a little later."

She did try to call back around noon, but the phone rang endlessly and no one answered at all.

The family lunched al fresco, sandwiches on the patio, after which J.Q. went to the feed store in Espanola to pick up some supplies and Xanthy said she had letters to write. Allison, seeing the Stevens car returning, went to pay a call on Vancie. She returned a few moments later saying she'd been invited to join Vancie's family on an afternoon drive to the Puye Cliff Dwellings.

"I said I'd ask," Allison reported.

"Who invited you," Shirley asked, "Vancie or her uncle?"

"Vancie."

"Allison, I don't know. Mr. Stevens was relatively hostile the other evening when I asked him about Mrs. Tremple. He was quite resentful about his own family problems, and you might be in for an uncomfortable afternoon."

Allison stood on one leg, storklike, scratching her ankle. "I'll see," she said, strolling off.

A few moments later Mr. Stevens came personally to ask Shirley's permission.

"Allison told me you were afraid she might be in the way. I apologize for the other night. It had been a rotten day. Today's better. I'd really like Allison to come along. Frankly speaking, Vancie is a lot easier to get along with if she has company her own age. And having the two of them chattering away will keep Ree from brooding."

If not a different man, he was a man in a better mood. "Family problems are the worst, aren't they?" she remarked in her most sympathetic voice.

He sighed and ducked his head, rubbing the back of his neck with one hand, an accustomed gesture. "It's really a difficult situation. I've never had anything like it in the twelve years we've been married. We've always been really happy; we've really enjoyed our life together. Then about a

94

year ago she got this new boss at the lab, and ever since then life has been hell! You know what I mean?" The words bubbled out of him like water from a faucet, under pressure, needing release.

Shirley wasn't sure and said so.

"I'm no psychologist. Part of it might be the new boss is a woman and she resents other women? Or maybe just a boss who's determined to hold all the power in her own hands. I've seen that over and over again in places where my firm does the audits. Ree's a top-notch technician. Up until now she's always felt very secure in her work and she's had high performance ratings. Now Ree hears from other people that the woman is talking about firing her. Or she hears somebody else got a raise and she didn't. My wife is not a confrontive person. She simmers and boils and gets angrier and angrier. She started coming home and taking it out on me, night after night. I guess she took it out on her father, too. Then to top everything, her dad died, and Ree blames herself. I guess that happens, but what makes it impossible to deal with is her mother blames her.

"I wouldn't want to live through this past four or five weeks again, believe me. Tears every five minutes and blaming herself in between and screaming at me that I don't understand."

"Why does her mother blame her?"

He made a face, part resentment, part pity. "Who knows! Maybe it doesn't matter. She's been much better the last couple of days, as though she's come to terms with it. Having Allison along would give her someone new to talk to."

Shirley regarded him thoughtfully, seeing a man in distress, but a reasonable man for all that. "If Allison wants to go, it's all right with me."

Allison went. Shirley wandered through the house, finding no one in it but herself. Well, if she was alone, there were some unimportant little jobs she'd been putting off, sorting through boxes of things she'd moved but wasn't sure she wanted to keep. Old financial records, old correspondence. She was just getting settled to work when she heard Dog's muffled bark in the patio, announcing someone.

The giant from the Big House had dropped in to leave the key and to tell her that Rob was taller than the late-night visitor to Frog House. Michael, who was five-foot-five, was about the right size, give or take an inch.

"Thank you, Mr. Frieze."

"Call me Cally. Everyone does. And by the way, we're so glad Harry thought of this place. You can expect to see some of us again, I should think."

"Thank you. That's nice to hear. We've enjoyed having you with us. Do come again."

She had been pleasantly surprised at the genuine enjoyment she had in dealing with most of the guests, who, if not always charming, were at least civil. Though Shirley had never considered herself a hermit, she had whenever possible avoided people in groups, committees, mobs, clusters, communities, or any other aggregation. Here at Rancho del Valle she'd promised herself that she wouldn't ask people to come back unless she really meant it, and she wouldn't let people come back if they were a pain in the ass. A very few had already gone on what she called privately her ad calendas McClintochas list. There'd been the viciously misanthropic lawyer from California who threatened lawsuits against her and against guests staying in other houses for all and every reason. (You allow *children* here—I heard them outside at *seven o'clock this morning*. . . . Your dog *touched* me with its nose.) There'd been the giddy girl from Denver who had intended a delirious weekend for herself and Prince Charming and, unable to admit the Prince was a toad, had blamed it on the place. (The wrong ambience, I thought it would be romantic!) And there'd been a really nasty woman from Dallas, with long false fingernails, who found fault with the housekeeping (Filth! Filth everywhere!) in an effort to get a reduction on the rates. Even the crazy lady was a gem when compared with memorable bastards like these, creatures who left trails of aggravation behind them like snails leave slime.

Cally and his friends had been enjoyable and she was grateful for their help, even though Cally's judgment about the height of the interloper threw a wrench into her easy dismissal of the mystery. If it hadn't been Emil who had entered the house late at night, then who had it been? And why!

Shirley was at the door, ready to return to her self-imposed duties, when Deputy Cisso and colleague arrived. She took the two of them to Ditch House and sat on the portal while they searched the house. It was empty except for a few scraps and bits. The crazy lady had departed.

"Was he a friend of hers? Lover? What?" Cisso asked Shirley.

Shirley shook her head. She wasn't at all sure what the relationship was, not anymore. "I thought he was just a guy she picked up in Albuquerque, the way some people pick up stray cats and dogs. She doesn't seem all that upset about him, does she? Did you find anything?"

"No purse, if that's what you mean. And nothing belonging to a guy. When he took off, he took everything with him. One thing might interest you, though. We got a call at the office, just before we left. The victim's sister from Los Angeles. She says you talked to her? She's flying out this afternoon. So I guess the mystery's really solved. The woman soaked in a hot spring, caught a bug, and died of it. Then this guy Emil stole her ID."

"That could be one mystery solved," Shirley agreed, "but there's a much bigger mystery so far as I'm concerned. Why are people allowed to soak in these hot springs when there's a deadly bug in them? Do the public health people allow it?"

Cisso took off his hat and wiped his forehead. "How would you stop people? There's springs everywhere. All through the Jemez Mountains, and down in Gila National Forest, and at Truth or Consequences—"

"At Ojo Caliente, too," offered the other.

"And not just in New Mexico. In Arizona and California, too. How would you stop people skinny-dipping?"

"If enough people had died of this bug, the springs would be fenced off. So what's the real story?"

"Well, people have died of it," Cisso replied. "But not that many. One here, one there."

"How many?"

It was the other deputy who answered. "Sixty, seventy people, all over the country, over thirty or forty years. Not that many. See, the only ones who get it are the ones who dive in, or get the water up their nose. If they just sit there nekkid, soaking up the rays, they don't get hurt. A little sunburn, maybe."

Cisso nodded agreement. "The pathologist said that's only how many they knew of for certain. There were probably some others, but the disease is so rare, doctors probably diagnosed it as something else when the people died."

"Something about it still bothers me," Shirley said stubbornly. Something did. She couldn't put her finger on it, but something definitely did.

"Hey, some deaths just happen," Cisso said, trying to be comforting. "Sometimes people just up and die."

She waved as they drove out, his words still resonating. People did just up and die. It reminded her of her father's comment on sheep. A sheep is an animal just looking for a place to lie down and die. And, don't let one sheep see another one die or it'll get the idea. It's true, people—and sheep—sometimes did just die, but she couldn't accept this in the Tremple woman's case. Some beast of suspicion was swimming around at the bottom of her mind, making ominous currents and eddies, not surfacing, something more than mere suspicion or simple paranoia caused, supposedly, by her medication.

Of course, some concern was legitimate for any business owner. She herself had sent guests to one place or another for the baths; she herself had mentioned the springs in and near the town of Jemez Springs. If she recommended a place, and someone died from it, did that make her liable?

In these litigious days? All too likely. But there was something more than that, something to do with the woman herself or the way she had died. Shirley circled the subject, teasing at it. How had the woman looked? What had she said? She came up with nothing useful. No matter how she went 'round and 'round, she couldn't come up with the piece that didn't fit.

If she did what she usually did when troubled, she'd saddle Zeke and ride out into the country while her subconscious worked away at the problem. Given Xanthy's warnings, however, riding off alone wasn't a smart idea. Maybe if she went for a walk, it would come to her. At one time in her life, when she'd worked in Washington, going for walks had been a good release of tension. Many an evening she'd strolled along the Mall, or in the National Zoo, where she'd leaned on railings and watched animals engaged in their intensely present lives.

She had her own equivalent of a zoo right here. Sheep and goats and assorted poultry, awaiting inspection down in the pastures. She strolled down the hill, went through the gate, and shut it behind her. An alert goat put its head out of the barn, saw her, and came trotting over to see if Shirley had anything good to offer. Like a bit of corn? Or a bite of bread? Shirley offered her hand and the goat nosed it to be sure it was empty, then put its head back to scratch one shoulder with the tip of a horn. The does were horned as well as the bucks, but their skull ornaments were simple back-curved ones, suitable for chastising other mothers' kids or fighting out matters of precedence or, occasionally, explaining to a dog or coyote why he did not belong in the pasture. Unlike the sheep, who were relatively helpless at protecting their lambs, the goats seldom lost their kids to predators. Female horns were actually more serviceable than the long, spiraling skull ornaments of the males, ones that grew longer and more impressively burdensome with every passing year. The skull she had hung on the willow tree, out by the garden, must have been growing horns for at least ten years.

The goat left her, and the other females, who were watching from the barn, went back to what they'd been doing. Since there was no food in the offing, Shirley did not merit their attention. Something about that idea teased at her, like a fish seen through murky water, now there, now gone. What had she read, seen lately? Animals and food. Animals living in the present, interested in what was going on, sharing so many attributes with humanity. They remembered things, they reasoned, they rejoiced, they grieved: there'd been a chimpanzee in the Washington zoo, a mother who had lost an infant, sitting against the rock wall, head back, eyes staring into nothing, grieving, refusing to eat.

Refusing to eat. The thought swam closer. Food avoidance. Bingeing, vomiting. Bulimia. Anorexia. Alicia Tremple, in the car, her bony shoulder beneath Shirley's hands. That extreme thinness.

But surely she had been too old for an anorexic. Weren't most anorexics girls in their teens, in their twenties? Still, there was something there, some facet of the idea she couldn't pin down.

No good. She set the search aside as she strolled along the bottom fence, kicking at twigs. Leave the matter of the Tremple woman for now. Think, instead, about the Brentwoods. Why, after three years, during which they'd shown no interest in Allison at all, were they now seeking custody of her? Had the idea originated with one of them, or both? Shirley could understand it if Allison had won a lottery or come into a fortune. But Allison's mother and father had been penniless. And Allison's aunt had made it clear there was no help on that side of the family.

So what about the other side of the family? Allison had never mentioned any kinfolk, but Charles Maxwell had to have come from somewhere. He'd been a petty crook and a wastrel. Shirley hadn't questioned where he came from because she hadn't cared. Shirley had assumed that if there were any kinfolk, they were more of the same. Charles, however, could have been a bad apple in an otherwise unexceptionable barrel. Or even in an exceptional one!

How would one find out?

She turned and trudged back the way she had come. This time the goats didn't even glance her way.

She went directly to the large closet off her bedroom where cartons of papers had been stored during the move: all the stuff from her desk and files, checks and bills and miscellany, more of the odds and ends she'd been sorting through that morning. Somewhere among the cartons were a couple of sealed boxes containing everything left in the Maxwell house after Allison's mother had been killed, after the furniture had been repossessed, after the clothing had been given away. Allison had been eleven then.

Eleven. Still a child, with a child's directness, growing slowly as a tree grows, reaching toward the sun. And now, here she was a teenager, suddenly burgeoning like bindweed! Her emotions and needs spreading out in all directions, entangling the world!

Be that as it may, the cartons had sat among the family belongings for three long years, but Shirley had never looked inside them. Now she found one of the dusty cartons at the front of the pile, excavated it, and carried it into her bedroom, where she slit the tape and dumped the contents on her desktop. It seemed to be mostly what she'd assumed—trash. Newspaper clippings dated over three years ago. Some credit-card receipts. Cash-register receipts. Paper clips. A plastic hair clip. A small, rattly box: seashells. An almost empty lipstick tube. A birthday card, sans envelope. *Happy Twenty-fifth Birthday, Charlie,* signed Sally Preston. No return address. Prescription bottles, half a dozen of them, in a small tin box that might once have held cookies or fruitcake. Two of the prescriptions were from doctors in Colorado, one in Columbine, one in Pueblo. One prescription each from El Paso, Texas, and Roswell, New Mexico. The earliest date was 1983, one filled in Albuquerque. *Charles Maxwell, take one tablet as needed for pain.* Dated July 12, 1983. There were four tablets left.

Charlie seemed to have moved back and forth a lot. He'd gone from New Mexico down to Texas and up to Colorado.

How long did pharmacies keep their records? Maybe they were on a computer. Even if they were on a computer, they wouldn't give out an address over the phone. Besides, there might be an easier way to get it. City directories would be available in the Albuquerque library. That would be a good place to start.

"What are you up to?" asked Xanthy, from her door.

"Something occurred to me," Shirley answered. "I never knew who Charles Maxwell's people were. There might be family on that side, kin of Allison's."

Xanthy considered the matter. "You're thinking of an inheritance?"

"It would explain the Brentwoods' sudden interest."

"The explanation would be more persuasive if it were the other side of the family, wouldn't you say? Esther Brentwood would be more likely to learn about money coming through her family rather than through Maxwell's."

"Not necessarily. Allison's parents were living in Columbine when they were killed. If someone went looking for Charles Maxwell at his last known address, the paper trail would lead to his wife, and through her to her next of kin, either Allison or Esther Brentwood. Esther paid for the funerals."

"There's something to that. What are you going to do?"

"How about we wait until J.Q. gets back so he can answer the phone, then you and I'll take a run to Albuquerque. The library there will have old city directories."

"Albuquerque?"

Shirley handed her the pill bottle. "He lived there. At least he consulted a doctor there. Allison would have been just a toddler at the time."

"Allison doesn't remember any family on her father's side?"

"She's never mentioned anyone. Of course, I never asked."

Xanthy picked up the birthday card. "Sally Preston might be kin."

"Not using the last name that way. Wouldn't a sister or cousin or aunt just say Sally?"

"Unless there were more than one Sally. This whole line of investigation seems rather farfetched."

"Xanthy, you want a reason for this sudden interest of the Brentwoods. You're the one who mentioned it, in fact. Allison's coming into some kind of inheritance is the only reason I can think of. Nothing else makes any sense at all. You met Esther and Lawrence. Surely you don't think they're being moved by a newfound sense of familial piety."

"Well, if you're going, I'll go with you. You shouldn't go alone."

Shirley flushed, simmered, then gulped, waiting for the sudden spate of annoyance to subside. She herself had said she shouldn't go alone, so why did Xanthy's saying it make her angry? "I'm sure that's wisest, Xanthy."

"Should we be away today? Are any guests expected?"

"The Big House. Tomorrow. Two couples and one child, from New York."

"When J.Q. gets back, then."

J.Q. returned about two, heard their plan without comment, and offered to have dinner ready when they returned.

"We'll bring something," Shirley said. "Pizza or something. And we'll be back by seven."

"That only gives you an hour in Albuquerque."

"How long does it take to look through old city directories?"

Longer, as it turned out. At five-thirty, Shirley shut the last one of the dusty volumes and growled something Xanthy did not quite hear.

"No luck?"

"No sense! The alphabetical listing is fragmentary. I tried back-checking ten people at random. Out of ten people listed by street address, the alphabetical listing only had five of them."

"Who publishes the directory?"

"It's a commercial effort. I suppose the less they spend

checking entries, the more money they make. So long as the street listings are fairly correct, who cross-checks? Charles Maxwell could have been living with someone else, or he could have been called something else. We're going to be late getting home. Tell you what, Xanthy. Let's call a pizza place in Santa Fe. We'll start back right away, but on the way out of town we'll stop at the drugstore where Charles filled his prescription."

"Call the pizza place and the ranch," Xanthy said in an admonitory tone. "J.Q. worries about you."

"Yeah, well, I worry about him, too."

They found the drugstore without trouble, plate glass and concrete block, current but not new, a barn of a place in a mall that looked to be several decades old. Xanthy made the calls from a booth out front while Shirley went back to talk to a pharmacist. The two younger ones disclaimed any knowledge of what had gone on eleven years before. Both of them indicated a white-haired man, glasses at the tip of his nose, busy at the computer keyboard.

"This is the story," she told him, when he'd finished tapping numbers, had pushed his glasses back up, peered at her through them, and acknowledged her presence. "My foster daughter was orphaned about three years ago. We have traced her mother's family. We've been unable to trace her father's. Among his belongings I found some prescription bottles, and I've been trying to find an old address for him. This one was filled here."

She passed it over. The pharmacist let his glasses slide down his nose until they rested on the bulbous tip as he focused on the label.

"You say he's dead?"

"Three years ago, yes."

"This thing's eleven years old!"

"I know. I thought it was worth a try."

"Maxwell. Maxwell. Now, why does that ring a bell?"

"No idea."

"Oh, sure. This is Stupe Maxwell's son. Was, I guess, heh?"

104

"Stupe Maxwell?"

"Sure. Didn't you ever see them, the Two Stupes. Ronny and Donny. Kenny and Benny. Was that it? Something like that. The Stupes' real names were Sheldon and Hardin. They grew up here. I went to school with them, and that's where they got the nickname. They were all the time pulling something stupid, see."

"Ronny and Donny?"

"Whatever they called themselves in their act, I forget. They were twins. One of them died some time ago, there was a piece in the *Herald* about him. But Stupe—Sheldon—he's still alive, far's I know. They weren't identical twins, you know, but they looked a lot alike. They did short films, before TV, then they did some early TV stuff. Like the Three Stooges, only funnier."

"Let me get this straight. The man's name was Sheldon Maxwell, nicknamed Stupe Maxwell—"

"They were both nicknamed Stupe Maxwell. They used to introduce themselves, 'I'm Stupe Maxwell, and this is my brother, Stupe Maxwell.' "

"Sheldon and his brother did a comedy act together under the name the Two Stupes?"

"That's it. On the show, Sheldon and Hardin Maxwell called themselves Ronny and Donny Stupe, or Benny and Henny Stupe, or Terry and Jerry Stupe, I don't remember." He shook his head, a smile moving across his lips like the shadow of a cloud, there and then gone. "Anyhow, this is Stupe Maxwell's son, Charley. And the prescription was for a painkiller, by a dentist. Wilson, see here. He's retired now, but he was the dentist."

"How did you know Charley was Stupe Maxwell's son?"

"He told me so."

"Stupe?"

"No. Charley. He asked me if I was the Chuck Flannery his dad knew in school, back in the thirties. He told me he was Stupe Maxwell's son."

Xanthy came up beside Shirley and paused, one foot

raised, as though for imminent flight. "We do need to get on our way," she said.

"Just a minute, Xanthy." She turned back to the pharmacist. "Isn't that kind of a strange thing for someone to tell you? I mean, do most people tell you who their parents are when they're filling a prescription?"

He felt his chin, fingertips searching for whiskers, up the cheeks, thinking about it. "Not really. People tell me all kinds of stuff. Besides, I knew his daddy pretty well. We played baseball on the same team."

Shirley sighed. "Was there an address?"

"No idea. What was this, eighty-three? We didn't go on the computer until eighty-four. All the old files are over in the warehouse. If it's a matter of life and death, we could look, we've got the date here. But otherwise . . ." He left it hanging.

"Stupe Maxwell," Shirley said. "Well, it's a place to start."

She left, trailing Xanthy, who commented as she climbed into the car, "You know, I used to see the Two Stupes on TV. I thought they were very funny. Rather in the tradition of the wise fools, you know. Giddy innocence falling on its face only to emerge triumphant. Chaplinesque."

"I never saw them," Shirley replied, buckling her seat belt. "I never hope to see them. One of them is dead. The other one is Allison's grandpa. Or so we are led to believe."

"Her grandfather? How very odd. And how very typical of you, Shirley. If it had been up to me, I'd never have come. I certainly would never have asked those questions. And yet you seem to bumble from fact to fact, rather like a bee, eventually getting to the honey."

"This honey may not be that sweet, Xanthippe! If I'd had a choice, I wouldn't have gone uncovering any other kinfolk for Allison. The kinfolk she's had up till now haven't done her much good."

They drove back in virtual silence, exchanging only a few comments on the view or the traffic. They stopped in

Santa Fe to pick up the pizza, then drove back to the ranch, arriving only an hour late.

"You're starved," Shirley said in a contrite tone when both Allison and J.Q. came out to meet them.

"I'm starved," admitted J.Q. "Allison had a late lunch in Taos, so she's not starved."

"I'm hungry, though," Allison asserted, taking one of the pizza cartons and leading the way to the kitchen. "We had a sort of strange lunch. The Stevenses do Chinese no matter where they eat."

"What do you mean, do Chinese?" Shirley got a fresh bottle of milk from the refrigerator and passed it to Xanthy, who poured and dispensed.

Allison said around a mouthful of pepperoni, "They each order something, then they pass it around, so everybody gets a taste. I was just going to have a chiliburger, but that doesn't pass very well, so I had turkey enchiladas with sour cream. They were pretty good. What I really liked was the chicken in red chili sauce. The lady there said she got the recipe out of Diana Kennedy's book. We've got that book."

J.Q. leaned back and fetched it from the shelf, leafing through it with one hand. "Pollo, pollo, pollo. Is this it? Chicken in red chili sesame-seed sauce?"

"Does the recipe call for an avocado leaf? The lady at the restaurant said she'd never managed to get an avocado leaf, but it was really good without."

Silence while J.Q. read the recipe aloud. More silence when he had finished. How did one respond to a recipe?

"Did you find anything out?" asked J.Q.

Shirley's glare came too late.

"About what?" asked Allison.

J.Q. grimaced. "Sorry."

"You didn't want to tell me!" Allison challenged. "It's about me, isn't it?"

"Only partly," Xanthy commented, blotting tomato sauce from her lips. "Shirley may have found an Albuquerque grandfather for you. Then again, she may not."

"A grandfather! My father's father?"

107

Shirley gave in to the inevitable. "Did your dad ever mention Sheldon Maxwell? Or the Two Stupes? Or—"

Allison's mouth dropped open. "When I was little," she cried. "We had tapes of them, the Two Stupes. Dad used to watch them sometimes, but Mother hated them, so he never did it when she was there. We never watched them in the last house, it was in the house before that. The one we had in Palace Pines."

J.Q. said, "Why don't you fetch the Albuquerque phone book, Allison."

She fetched. J.Q. traded the cookbook for the phone book and found the Maxwells. "There's a Sheldon listed. Want me to call?"

Allison said, "No. Not yet. Don't. I don't want . . ."

Shirley reached across to pat her. "We went looking because we're trying to figure out your aunt Esther and uncle Lawrence. We thought maybe there was a reason for their wanting you so suddenly. Maybe an inheritance. Something like that."

"I get that, it's just . . . I just want to think about it a little."

"Fine," said J.Q. "You think about it. As a matter of fact, we can probably find out some additional information without bringing you into it at all. Like, is he alive? Does he have an estate? Has he, by any chance, been trying to find you?"

"He doesn't even know about me. I mean, if he knew about me, wouldn't he have written to me, or something? Wouldn't he have come to Dad's funeral? Wouldn't . . . ?"

Allison put down the slice of pizza and stared at her plate.

Shirley took the child's lax hand in her own. "Allison, this is why I didn't want to talk about it just yet. We don't know anything. An elderly man who works in a drugstore remembered your father telling him that he, your father, was Stupe Maxwell's son. The pharmacist may not have remembered correctly. Or he may have remembered correctly, but your father might not have been telling the truth. Or maybe your father was telling the truth, but his father is no longer alive, which is why he didn't try to find you earlier. The name in the phone book could be a widow or a totally unrelated person."

"If it was a widow, she'd be my grandma, wouldn't she? She'd use her name, wouldn't she?" Allison argued.

"She might be a second wife. And she might continue to use her husband's name because of those nasty sorts who look for women's names so they can make dirty phone calls."

"I wish life would just settle down," Allison said angrily, her eyes full of tears. "All the time my life is just so . . . complicated."

"Allison—fourteen going on seventy-four," said J.Q. "I'm with you, kid. Life is just too darned complicated. Speaking of which, Shirley, you got a call from Numa. He's talked to a fellow attorney here in Santa Fe, and you have an appointment for tomorrow morning, nine-thirty. Fellow's name is Yesney. Pascal Yesney. Numa said to tell you he's already filled him in on most of the details."

"Well, I'm glad he has because I certainly can't." Shirley took a final wedge of pizza, ate the tip, pulled off the crust, and dunked it in her milk glass. Dunked crust was her favorite part. "Allison, eat your supper and forget it."

"Let me just get used to the idea overnight, okay," Allison begged. "Before you let anybody know maybe I'm related to them."

"Deal," said Shirley, all too willing to comply. Unless it were necessary, she might not let anyone know even after tomorrow. Allison was right. Three years had been long enough for anyone who was really interested.

They straightened up the kitchen in troubled silence. Allison went thoughtfully off to her room, and the others to theirs, leaving Shirley sitting on the patio, staring up through the branches of the pine at a wedge of moon. Frog House, the Big House, and the Ditch House were all dark. Crunching feet on the gravel told Shirley the Fleys were taking their customary evening walk.

"Good evening," she called, not loudly.

"Ms. McClintock?"

She rose and went to the gate. "Pleasant evening," she remarked.

"We've been down to see the fireflies," Mrs. Fley said. "I haven't seen fireflies since I was a child. I was talking to that Stevens woman about them. She said she used to make lanterns, little paper lanterns, and put the bugs inside. Isn't that something. I never would have thought of that."

"I think the Japanese do that, too," Shirley said. "Firefly lanterns and cricket cages."

"Crowded like they are, I guess the smaller the pet the better," growled Mr. Fley. "Rather have a dog, myself."

"Place is kind of empty tonight," his wife said.

"Filling up again tomorrow," said Shirley. "New York people coming to the Big House. Ditch House is people from Germany."

"And over there, where she was staying?"

"Nobody this weekend. People coming Monday, I think."

"Well, you have a pleasant evening. Think we'll get back before it gets too dark to see." He took his wife by the arm and they ambled off, around the corner of the Big House and back to their own.

It was too dark to see. Shirley went into the house and back to her own bedroom, changed into her pajamas, brushed her hair and teeth, pushed the purring Baron to the far side of the bed, and slid beneath the light cover. Beside her on the table the pill bottles gleamed. One of the pink ones. Three quarters of a blue one.

Three quarters was evidently sufficient. She slept like an innocent child.

4

Mrs. Fley was leaning on the fence Saturday morning when Shirley went down to feed the wethers.

"I'll be sorry to leave," she said. "Got to go back next week, and I'm not eager."

"Back where?" Shirley asked, tipping a sack of mixed grain into the trough, careful not to give them too much. She wanted them fat and sassy, not sick. Sheep stomachs were evolved to eat grass and other forms of roughage. They reacted badly to too much grain.

"Near Los Angeles. Not for much longer, I hope. Wallace and I've been thinking of moving. Place is getting unlivable. Too many people. Like Sodom and Gomorrah, just waiting for the destruction."

"You mean earthquakes?"

"Wouldn't surprise me if God just sank the whole business."

Shirley stood erect, lips quirking in a smile. "You think you ought to get out first?"

Mrs. Fley smiled in return. "You mean, do I think I'm

exempt from God's judgment? Well, I guess. Wallace and me, we've always been on the side of the angels."

"Which side is that?" Shirley asked. "Vis-à-vis earthquakes, for example."

"Oh, let's see. The angels' side is probably pro-earthquake. Pro-viruses, too. With a celibate pope still preaching unreason, machismo breeding in the benighted lands, and the threat of nuclear war receding, how else is the Good Lord going to get us weeded down to a reasonable number."

"You think there are too many people?"

"Well sure, don't you?"

Shirley had to admit she did.

Mrs. Fley nodded, considering the question. "But not for long. First this AIDS thing, then this hantavirus thing, now this new one that killed the woman across the way—"

"That wasn't a virus," Shirley objected.

"Well, I know that. Call it a Naegleria fowlerii or call it divine retribution, you just watch. It'll spread, or something else will." She grinned, teeth showing, the skull beneath the flesh clearly limned, dark-ringed eyes and all. "Cholera, maybe. There's a new strain of that. And TB, of course."

Shirley frowned, obscurely troubled. "I don't think I can enjoy the idea as much as you do."

"Oh, honey, this isn't enjoyment." She grimaced again, this time letting the anguish show. "My grandson, Antonia's child, he died because of AIDS. Needlessly. He didn't have to die. That wasn't his fault, that was someone else's. Whatever you call it, what I feel, don't call it enjoyment."

She turned away from the fence and went up the hill, stumbling a little, leaving Shirley openmouthed behind her, wondering what all that had been about.

At breakfast, Allison said she'd thought about having a grandfather and decided they should go ahead and find out. "It scares me a little," she said. "But it would be better to know, wouldn't it?"

112

Accordingly, while Shirley scrambled eggs J.Q. dialed the number in Albuquerque. After a lengthy pause someone answered, and J.Q. entered upon a muttered conversation. Finally he said, "I see. Thank you very much," and hung up the phone. He turned to them with a troubled look. "He's in a nursing home. Alzheimer's."

Shirley pulled the frying pan off the burner and stared at him. "How bad, did they say?"

"The person who answered is a housekeeper hired by the realty company. She keeps the place neatened up because the house is being shown for sale. So far as she knows, Mr. Maxwell has no family."

"Somebody had to have listed the house."

He shrugged. "A conservator, maybe?"

Allison, who had been following this exchange, swiveling her head like a tennis fan, asked, "What's a conservator?"

"When people are incapacitated, the court can appoint someone to look after their property," J.Q. answered. "The woman told me the name of the realty company, Braunsmier, and they'll know."

He returned to the phone and Shirley to the eggs, a furrow between her eyes. "Ask them how much the house is listed for," she said. "Ask them if it's got a mortgage on it."

"Why do you care?" whispered Allison.

"Because your aunt and uncle would care. If the man died without a will, or if he willed it to his son, you could inherit it."

"I don't want it," she said shrilly. "What would I do with a house?"

Xanthy said, "Allison, don't worry about it. Nobody's making you inherit anything, nobody's going to burden you. Shirley and J.Q. are just trying to find out what's going on."

"Also pursuant to what's going on," said J.Q. "Shirley is due at the lawyer's office in one hour."

"Why is he in his office on Saturday?" Shirley asked.

"Probably because Numa asked him to be," said J.Q. "Numa no doubt feels this is an emergency."

Shirley distributed eggs to go with the melon, toast, and sausages already on the table. J.Q. forked a sausage onto his plate, cut it, placed a small bit in his mouth, and chewed reflectively.

"Not up to the Sausage Company's standard," he said sadly.

"How many local markets have you tried so far?" Xanthy asked chidingly. "Why don't you give up and just order them from the Sausage Company?"

"One should patronize the local folk. One is, after all, a member of the local economy," he said loftily, taking another bite.

"I don't think the local folk are into gourmet sausage," Shirley commented, seating herself and pouring a cup of coffee. "So far as local sausage goes, I think everything goes in that wasn't used up otherwise. Hide, hooves, ears, and tail."

"This is probably a bit of hoof," said J.Q., putting a hard bit of something at the edge of his plate.

"Yuck," said Allison.

"Since Sheldon Maxwell's in a nursing home, we need to proceed carefully," Shirley remarked, after a moment's silence. "If Allison has a grandfather, or if there's an estate, we don't want to compromise anything. . . ."

Xanthy looked up, surprised. "Well, that's a first. Usually you're into everything with both feet, and the devil take the hindmost."

Shirley looked Xanthy full in the face, saying significantly, "I just said I want to be careful. I don't want to go blundering in and forget anything important."

"Oh," Xanthy said. "I see your point."

"What point?" Allison demanded.

"The point is, everything must be done by the book," J.Q. said firmly. "So that no criticism will attach to anyone."

"You mean so Uncle Lawrence and Aunt Esther can't say she did something wrong."

"To minimize that likelihood."

"Got to go," Shirley said, taking the last gulp of coffee. "I should be back by noon at the latest."

"I'm driving you," said J.Q.

"You are? I don't ..." She caught Xanthy's eye. "Oh, how thoughtful of you. Maybe you can pick up some lightbulbs and paper towels while I'm seeing the lawyer. We're almost out."

She went to the hall mirror to check her appearance. No egg on her face. Not visibly, at any rate, though Xanthy and J.Q. seemed to think she had it all over her. When she reached the driveway, carrying her folder of papers, J.Q. was already in the driver's seat.

"Did you find any mistakes in the reservations?" she asked in a stiff little voice as they went down the driveway.

"One little one, but you didn't make it. I did."

"So I haven't been wandering around, making errors right and left," she said.

"Not that we know of."

"My making booboos is a rare thing, in other words. I am not a raving maniac."

"No, dear heart, you're not, but yes, I'm still going to drive you. I don't know what provokes these amnesias. I went over to the pharmacy yesterday and picked up a package enclosure. Bunch of gobbley-gook. Not what I'd call useful. Maybe you only forget things if you're stressed. Back when we had the roofers here, things were pretty stressful. We'd just moved down. We couldn't find anything. We didn't know our way around. So maybe that explains the chimney bit. Thinking of losing Allison is about as stressful as we could get, so you might do it again. Consider me a reference work and relax. I'm not going to spoil your fun."

She relaxed to the limit of her ability, watching the land flow by on either side: the shiver of cottonwoods, the spotty clumps of piñon, the swell and sink of the hills, up to stony rims and down to tree-feathered valleys, veins of green in the reach of desert. The city, when it suddenly appeared around them, seemed almost a natural consequence, a crystallization of the pink soil and stony prominences. Seen from a distance, it could have grown there.

The illusion was lost up close. Narrow streets. Too much traffic. Too many people in shorts and sandals with cameras around their necks. The law office was in a Victorian building just off Marcy, a converted house, one of the few in Santa Fe not built or rebuilt according to Santa Fe style.

"What's his name again?" Shirley asked.

"Pascal Yesney. Yesney and Peake."

"Pascal Yesney? I'll bet he had a lovely childhood. Though as names go, it's really no stranger than Numa Erlich."

J.Q. said firmly, "I'm going to drop you off here. I'm going to get the lightbulbs and a carton of paper towels. I'll come back and park if I can. I'll be waiting for you in the waiting room or out here. Don't go off without me." He checked his watch. "You've got five minutes before your appointment."

She got out, clutching the folder of documents and patting her pocket to be sure her checkbook and wallet were inside. The place looked vacant, weekendish. The driveway to the rear parking lot had a chain across it, but the front door was open and so was the door to the ground-floor office. She went in. No one in reception, but at the end of a short hall was another open door through which she could see a gray tonsured head bent over the desktop. "Pascal Yesney?"

He looked up, taking a moment to switch gears. "Ms. McClintock? I'm Pasc Yesney. Come in and take a chair. You've brought the agreement Erlich worked out for you? Good. He faxed me a copy, I just wanted to check the signatures." He took the envelope. "Numa tells me you don't have a fax. Says you don't believe in them."

Shirley sat down, crossed her legs, and considered the matter. "Well, I'll tell you. When I was a girl, some fiftyish years ago, we had an automatic clothes washer and a mangle—something you don't often see in houses these days—and I can remember my mother saying how much harder she had to work than before she had either of them. Since she had the new washer, instead of the old one with the wringer on it, people expected clean clothes every day instead of maybe twice a week. Since she had the mangle, she had to iron the sheets all the time, not just for company. She said conveniences weren't all that helpful when they raised expectations so much.

"Now, of course, we've got gadgets up the gizmo, and I consider we've reached the point of diminishing returns. We spend more time and effort getting and keeping up conveniences than the so-called conveniences free up. If I had a fax, for instance, I'd be running back and forth taking messages to and from all the guest houses. Either that or I'd have to put one in each guest house, and then I'd have the maintenance and the supplies to worry about. And the guests wouldn't get a real vacation, they'd be pursued by paper. I figure I save time and money and the guests' peace of mind not having one."

He grinned at her.

Thus encouraged, she went on, "The McClintock Brief Law on conveniences—they often are anything but."

"What do you want to do about this?" He waved the letter she had received from the Brentwoods' attorney.

Shirley stared at her hands, busy knotting themselves together in her lap. "Allison isn't fond of her aunt and uncle. Before you ask, I'm not responsible for the animosity. She had reasons for disliking them before I'd ever met her or them. I want you to find out why they're doing this, then Allison and I want you to fight them."

"What do you mean, find out why?"

Shirley described the Brentwoods from her brief encounters with them. "Money or status," she said. "Those are the only things that might have moved them to do this. We need to know what money or what status."

She fished the pill bottle out of her pocket, set it on his

117

desk, and went through the previous day's investigation, point by point, concluding, "Sheldon Maxwell is in a nursing home. He's said to have Alzheimer's. If the pharmacist was right, his brother died some time ago."

"Numa told me about Allison's parents," Yesney remarked, swiveling his chair so he could look out at the passing people and traffic. "I take it you're fond of the girl."

Shirley started to speak and found herself unable to do so. Tears spilled from her eyes. She gasped.

Surprised, he fished a box of tissues out of a drawer and handed them over. "Sorry. I didn't realize."

She gritted her teeth, spoke between them. "Numa may have mentioned that I lost both my own children years ago. One might suppose, therefore, that Allison serves mostly as surrogate. One would be wrong. She's a member of the family in her own right. She's very dear to us all."

"You and this man Quentin."

"And Xanthippe Minging, who lives with us now."

"The girl, excuse me, Allison. She's healthy?"

"Very."

"She doesn't go around sporting bruises or anything?"

"Only if she falls off her horse, which she very seldom does. Why?"

"I'm thinking of possible grounds. Abuse would be one. Neglect. I take it she isn't neglected."

"She attended a private school in Colorado, one with an excellent reputation. She's had what amounts to a private tutor the last four months, since we moved here. She didn't want to go into a strange classroom late in the school year, and I didn't blame her. The move was hard on all of us, even though in one sense we were looking forward to it. Changes are hard sometimes, even when they're for the better, and we've weathered the worst of it. As for Allison, she's well clothed, well fed, and her emotional needs are tended to. What else can I tell you?"

"Religion?"

"What about it?"

"Is her . . . ah . . . spiritual development also tended to?"

"What do those words mean?"

He frowned. "I'm not sure. I guess what I mean is, does she go to church?"

"Sometimes she goes with friends. J.Q. and Xanthy and I are not churchgoers. We talk about religion, however, and read about it. Belief, to me, is an essentially private matter. We also talk about morals and ethics, which I consider more important among persons."

He shook his head. "I don't think it makes much difference, myself, but you never know what this kind of suit will involve. Do the Brentwoods attend church?"

"I have no idea. You think we should attend church?"

"Ms. McClintock, I think you should do what you feel best. It's still a free country, though there are always those who try desperately to make it otherwise." He hummed to himself tunelessly, twiddling his pen, swiveling his chair like a child on a swing, twist, twist. "What's your gut feeling about this?"

"What I said before. Money. I think Esther and Lawrence Brentwood have found out that Allison is worth money to them. I don't know how. I don't know when or who. But I'd bet my own money on it."

"Have you excluded any possibility as the source of this hypothetical money? Allison's mother's kinfolk, for example?"

"According to Esther, she was Gloria Maxwell's only kin. She practically reared her younger sister. If there'd been anyone at all, surely they should have come forward and offered some assistance when Esther and her sister were young."

"You never know about this kind of thing. Families split up and have no contact with one another for years. Branches go off to some other state, some other country. Decades later they come back, alone, looking for their roots. You just never know."

She nodded her agreement, asking, "May I leave this matter in your hands? You'll answer the complaint."

"You may. At this stage of the game, everything is pro forma. They challenge, we respond. We don't know what they're after, they don't know if we know. But if you're right and this isn't delayed familial feeling, we need to know what they're up to."

"Can you find out?"

"Not any better than you can. You've already done what an investigator would have done. I can hire one, of course, but it'll be expensive and you'll no doubt second-guess him every step of the way. You're like my aunt Til, an incurable mixer-in. I know the signs." He grinned at her. "Besides, Numa told me about you."

She found herself flushing. "I seem to get involved in things."

"Well, it keeps one young, so I'm told. Why don't you just go on finding out what you can. If you reach an impasse, we'll consider hiring someone. There's no real need for haste. These matters move slowly."

She offered to write a check for a retainer, which he accepted. They exchanged small talk. She waited out front for a quarter of an hour before J.Q. showed up.

"Where to?" he asked, when she'd climbed in and settled.

"Marketplace, for groceries," she grunted. "I've got a short list. I want blue potatoes. I want some of that good rice and some fresh vegetables."

"And then?"

"And then . . . let's call home and tell Xanthy we won't be back for a while. I'd like to go to Albuquerque again. Alzheimer's or not, I want to meet Stupe Maxwell."

The Braumsmier office had only one bored young realtor manning the phones. He knew nothing at all about Sheldon Maxwell, but he had the phone number of the realtor who had the listing, one Socorro Tapia. Shirley borrowed his phone and called her, afterward reporting to J.Q.

"Mr. Maxwell knew he had Alzheimer's, but he was still signing his own papers when Tapia got the listing agreement. That was some time ago, however, and she's heard that he's gone downhill some since then. She took him an offer recently, and he didn't focus on it very well, but the people at Cedar Rest say he's still okay part of the time. That's the Cedar Rest Home."

Shirley looked up the address, thanked the young realtor for the use of his phone, and went with J.Q. back to the Cherokee, where he burrowed a map out of the glove compartment and found the route they would take.

"Every time I come down here, I'm surprised," Shirley commented, when they had driven about halfway. "I expect Albuquerque to be more Santa Fe, and it's more like Wichita or Tulsa."

"It started as a commercial town, not an art colony," muttered J.Q., his eyes fastened on the rearview mirror, which showed him the usual New Mexico rearview, a pickup truck riding their bumper at over fifty miles an hour. He switched on the hazard lights. When this did no good, he slowed down to twenty miles under the speed limit. The pickup blared its horn and went by in a cloud of dust and loud radio music.

"Go kill someone else," J.Q. said firmly to the dwindling truck. "Which you will."

"We're becoming old farts," said Shirley. "Aren't we?"

"Where driving is concerned, I always was an old fart. I don't understand the internal combustion mystique. Cars, fast boats, snowmobiles, all-terrain vehicles ... Anything that makes noise and goes fast and is inherently dangerous."

"Young men like to flirt with death," Shirley commented. "Most male animals do it. It's built in. The less brain, the more movement."

"No brain required to make loud noise and go fast. Proof of manhood, I suppose. Is that the road coming up?"

Shirley referred to the map. "One more," she said. "Next big cross street."

They turned left at the light. Now they were in a residential area, large old houses set back on green lawns under trees that had been there awhile. The Cedar Rest Home was one of them, converted from its residential purpose without losing its residential character. Surprisingly there actually were cedars, a high, dark hedge of them between the building and the street.

Shirley shivered. "Those black cedars make me think of the graveyard south of Columbine. That funereal color . . ."

"They're not exactly cheerful. Maybe that's why they're here. To get people in the right mood."

They parked in a small, empty area of blacktop near the side door marked OFFICE and went through to an anteroom, where a bored-looking woman was filing a stack of forms.

"Help you?" she asked brightly, hands poised to lay down their burden at the least excuse.

"We'd like to see Sheldon Maxwell," Shirley announced.

"Shelly. Of course. They should just be finishing with lunch. Down that hall, ask Ellen, the woman in the green smock."

She went disconsolately back to her filing. They walked down the wide corridor, past a number of closed doors, toward the unmistakable clatter of crockery. The woman in the green smock was just inside the dining-room door, keeping an alert eye on the diners. Shirley introduced herself and mentioned Maxwell's name.

"Shelly? He's right over there, see, the red sweater. They've got to their coffee and dessert, so he'll be finished in just a bit. Why don't you sit out there and wait. It won't be long."

"Out there," was a wide, furnished space between the large front doors and the dining room. It wasn't long before the diners came straggling out, some in wheelchairs, others hitching along step-by-step to the thump of walkers. Sheldon Maxwell was one of the last, stepping along easily, headed for somewhere, obviously needing no help.

"Mr. Maxwell?"

"Yes?" He stopped, turned toward them, his eyes clouding. "Do I know—"

"No," Shirley said hastily. "You don't know me, Mr.

Maxwell. My name is McClintock. This is John Quentin. Would you mind if we talked with you a few minutes?"

"Not about the TV show, is it? Told them I couldn't do that. Don't remember lines that well . . ."

"Not about a TV show—no, sir."

"We can sit here." He gestured vaguely toward a settee and several chairs grouped to one side. "I sit here sometimes."

They sat. Shirley hitched herself forward, catching the old man's eyes with her own. "We've come to ask about Charles Maxwell."

Sheldon Maxwell shook his head. "He's a devil, he is. I told Hardin so. Told him it grieved me to say that about family, but Charley's just no good."

"You haven't seen him for a while?"

"Hardin? No. Hardin died."

"Charles. You haven't seen Charles."

"Charley? I told him to go. I said, you can't get along with your father, that happens sometimes, but you're old enough to get by on your own. I told him that."

Shirley sat back. "When was that?"

"Long time." He sat back. "I kind of lose track."

"Did you . . . ah, disinherit him, Mr. Maxwell?"

"Disinherit? Charley? What's to inherit from me? I turned everything over to these people—the house, whatever they get for it, whatever they can sell it for. They'll keep me. Church runs the place. Never thought . . ."

His eyes went first, their involvement fading, their focus lost. Then his face collapsed, becoming for an instant anonymous, anyman's face. The green-smocked woman appeared beside them.

"Is he having a little trouble?" She shook him by the shoulder lightly, almost playfully. "Shelly. Come on, Shelly. It's time to have a nap. Let's get you back to your room."

She lifted the old man, seemingly without effort, one strong arm around his waist as he went along beside her, legs moving, right, left, right, left, in rhythm with hers. They disappeared down the hall.

123

"She'll be back," said Shirley. "Let's just wait."

She was back, within minutes. "I'm Ellen Fleshman. Is there something I can do for you?"

"Just a question or two. We're trying to trace a relative of Mr. Maxwell's. Just now he said that he'd turned over everything he owned to Cedar Rest. Is that the usual procedure?"

"It's a church-run place," the woman answered. "We have a volunteer board of managers. Lawyers, accountants, real-estate people. When someone wants to come here, they turn over their property, and the board sells it or leases it or whatever they can to make the most of it, and whatever money there is goes into the endowment. In return, we take care of the person as long as he lives."

"Even if they need hospital care?"

"We've got a hospital. On the other side, facing the back. It's more a hospice, actually. Mostly when people come here, they aren't going to get any better." She made a sorrowful face. "With Alzheimer's, there's only one direction, and that's down."

J.Q. asked, "In tracing this person, we've run into a dead end. Do you suppose your board would allow us to look through Mr. Maxwell's house? See if there's any old correspondence or anything."

"You'd have to ask Reverend James, and he's not here today. Probably it would be best to write him a letter. The board meets every week, so you wouldn't have to wait long for an answer."

Shirley thanked her, and they rose to leave.

"Such a nice old man," said Ellen Fleshman. "And a lot of the time, he's okay. He used to be on TV, did you know that?"

Shirley said they'd known, yes, thank you again, and good-bye.

They drove home in virtual silence. Just before the turnoff, J.Q. asked, "What's next?"

Shirley shook her head. "I'll tell Pasc Yesney about the church home, Cedar Rest. He can check the details of the agreement. I have a hunch it's exactly as represented and Sheldon Maxwell probably owns little more than the clothes on his back. I'll ask to look through his house. That may give us something."

"What's all this?" muttered J.Q., looking ahead of them. Beside the Rancho del Valle mailbox Xanthy stood, nervously shifting from foot to foot and peering in their direction. As they approached she stepped into the road and waved.

"Xanthy! What is it?" Shirley spoke through the open window.

Xanthy climbed into the backseat. "Drive," she told J.Q. "Just down the road a bit."

Obediently he drove.

"Pull in here," demanded Xanthy, when they reached a wide spot with a shady space along the side of the pavement. "I had to catch you before you went in. You know the people who were coming to the Big House today? The people from New York?"

"Sure," said J.Q. "I made the reservation a month or so ago. Two couples, and one grown-up child. Evans, I think the name is."

"Evans may be the name of one couple," Xanthy exploded. "But the other couple are Esther and Lawrence Brentwood and, I believe, their daughter, Cheryl."

J.Q. drove them around behind the house where they could disembark out of sight. Shirley went in through the back door while Xanthy went to intercept Allison, who had taken Beauregard out for an amble along the bosque. Meantime, Xanthy suggested, Shirley might wish to deal with Alberta, who was waiting for her inside.

When Shirley got to the kitchen she found Alberta seated primly at the kitchen table, steam rising visibly from her brow.

"What's the trouble, Alberta?"

"That woman, the one in the Big House, she is not nice. She says the house is not clean. The house is clean. The

125

floors shine. The kitchen is polished. All the towels are neat, and the beds."

"You always clean beautifully, Alberta."

"Him her *esposo*, he says there is ex-cre-ment on the portal, and I tell him it is the peacocks who ex-cre-ment there, and each day we clean it away."

"Quite right."

"And they ask for candles, for when the electric goes. I tell them the electric does not go. Still, she says she needs candles. I say no candles."

Shirley waited it out.

"And her, the young one, with her nails so and her teeth so and her hair so, she says the bathroom will not do. For her it must have more mirrors."

"Why don't we let them go somewhere else, Alberta?"

"This is what I say! Go to the big hotel. Go to the Holiday Inn. Go to La Fonda. Go to the Hilton."

"This is what you say—said to them?"

"This is what I say."

"And what did they say?"

"They say it is Spanish Market in Santa Fe, and they are forced to stay here. All other places are full."

"When they made their reservations, Santa Fe wasn't full, Alberta. They made their reservations some time ago, according to J.Q. No, they meant to stay here. I don't know who the Evans couple is, but the others are Allison's aunt and uncle and cousin."

"*Familia?*"

"No. Aunt and Uncle, but not *familia*."

Alberta's brow furrowed, then cleared as she understood the distinction. "Not nice people," she said firmly.

"No," Shirley agreed. "Not nice people."

"Have they been giving Alberta fits?" asked J.Q. as he came in from the corridor.

Alberta repeated her story for J.Q.'s benefit, this time with less anger and more eloquence. By evening, it would be a full-fledged production, with a chorus line.

"Allison got back just as I was coming in," J.Q. said during the first lull. "She'll be up as soon as the unsaddles Beau."

He turned back to Alberta. "Pay no attention to them, Alberta. We'll offer them their money back to go elsewhere, or stay if they decide to. Meantime, you and Vincente pay them no attention."

"Vincente says we should retire," said Alberta, angry all over again. "We should not have to put up with these Anglos."

Shirley chose not to be offended, though she realized what Anglos Vincente was no doubt talking about. She shrugged, hands up. "Oh, I agree, Alberta. No one should have to put up with the Brentwoods. If you wish to retire, then you must retire."

"Vincente says we can stay here in the house, pay you rent."

"Well, no. No, I would need the house for the people who are doing the work. But if you decide to retire, you would be welcome to stay for two weeks while you find someplace else."

Her brow furrowed once more, Alberta departed.

"Thought you wanted status quo," J.Q. remarked.

"I thought the ground rules should be made clear," Shirley said. "Before Vincente builds too many *palacios* in the air. I wonder, by the way, why he plans to pay us rent. That sounds to me like a ploy. If he pays me rent, in effect he has a lease, so even if they retire, I can't necessarily get them off the place. Maybe they're fond of the place, it wouldn't surprise me. Did he think of that, or did someone else? Or am I being paranoid?"

"No telling." He turned his head, listening to approaching steps. "Here's Allison and Xanthy."

They came in, Xanthippe tight-lipped, Allison obviously distressed.

"Why are they here?" Allison demanded. "I don't want to see them."

"There's no reason you have to," Shirley said. "While Alberta was going on about them I got to wondering why

127

you and Xanthy don't go up to ... oh, say Chama for a couple of days. Maybe you could look around Abiquu. Or ride the narrow gauge."

"How long are they reserved for?" asked Xanthy.

"Just the weekend. Tonight, tomorrow night. They're leaving Monday, so it wouldn't be a long exile."

Allison fretted. "If we went, would it be running away? I don't want to leave you alone if I can help."

Shirley snorted. "I don't see it as running away. More like beating a strategic retreat. I'm not comfortable with them around when I don't know what they're up to. I don't like their sailing under false colors either. If they'd tried to make a reservation under their own names, we wouldn't have taken it. This place is too small to provide a comfortable distance between animosities. No, if you're gone, Allison, I don't have to worry about you. That's a help, right there."

"Did you find my grandfather? Is that why you were gone so long?"

"We found a man who is probably your grandfather. That is, when we asked about Charles, he said he'd severed relations with him, he had not disinherited him, but there was nothing to inherit. Sheldon Maxwell turned over his property to the home he's staying in. We'll have someone check that, of course, but so far we've got nothing to help us with the Brentwoods."

"Does he ... does he want to meet me?"

"Allison, we didn't tell him about you. He's not altogether capable, you know. I'm not sure he'd understand who you are."

"I might ... I might like to meet him, anyhow."

"Then we'll go meet him. Whatever you like."

"But not right now."

Shirley bit her tongue until she could reply patiently. "It's entirely up to you ..."

"I think visiting her grandfather would be a very good idea," said Xanthy firmly. "I think Allison and I ought to go down to Albuquerque for the weekend. We can ride the

128

tram up to the top of the Sandias. We can go to the Old Town. And we can visit Mr. Maxwell if Allison decides she wants to."

Allison asked, "What do you think, Shirley?"

"The idea has some merit."

"If I'm visiting my grandfather, that's not running away, is it?"

J.Q. said through gritted teeth, "Don't worry about the running away. Shirley's right. Sometimes a strategic retreat is called for. We don't know what they're up to, and until we do, we're at a disadvantage."

Allison shifted from one foot to the other, thinking the matter over. "Can I ask Vancie to go with us? She'd like to get away from her relatives for a while. Her aunt is really sad and crying all the time."

Xanthy nodded. Shirley said, "Mr. Stevens would probably welcome the break."

Though they worried the subject a bit longer, the matter was decided. Xanthy went off to pack. Allison went around the back way to ask Vancie if she could come along. Shirley stayed in the kitchen, keeping an eye on the Big House, but none of the tenants showed a face. Half an hour later Xanthy's car went off down the drive with the two girls in the backseat, and Shirley took a deep breath.

"Now what?" asked J.Q.

"Now we go about our business as though they weren't here," she replied. "So far as I'm concerned, they're not."

During the early afternoon the Brentwoods continued in seclusion. Come five o'clock Shirley went down to feed the stock. When she returned, the car that had been in front of the Big House had gone. A crumpled paper bag lay where it had been. Shirley picked it up and smoothed it. From Luz de Nambe, a candle-and-gift shop along the road to Santa Fe. Typical of the Brentwoods to throw their litter just anywhere. Let someone else clean up. They weren't alone in that attitude. Shirley had been amazed in the past few months to observe the housekeeping standards of some guests, particularly some of those she had judged to be quite well-to-do. A few families who had arrived quite expensively accoutred had been unable to manage even the simple routines of putting dishes in the dishwasher and garbage down the disposal. Shirley, who had always assumed slovenliness and slum went together, had come to the reluctant conclusion that it was the well-to-do who didn't know any better. Without household help, they were just plain dirty. Alberta had summoned her on more than one occasion to look at the condition of a just-vacated house, and more guests had gone on Shirley's never-again list for slovenliness than for any other reasons.

No matter, the Brentwoods had gone out to dinner, and very nice of them. She thought briefly of exploring their house in their absence, seeing what clues to their motivation she could find, but discarded the notion. If discovered, it would cast her in a very bad light.

"Did you have time to write Reverend James?" J.Q. asked, when she entered the kitchen.

"I did. The letter's on the desk."

"How about calling Zinny Reborn? The guy's daughter. The one he said talked to Mrs. Tremple."

"I didn't do that. I'd forgotten about her."

"It's around suppertime now. Probably a good time to call."

"If I can find the card."

"You were wearing your blue shirt. You put it in the pocket. You want fajitas for supper?"

"Fajitas would be fine." She went back to the bedroom and found her blue shirt in the laundry basket. The card was in the pocket. She returned to the kitchen, where J.Q. was busily slicing onions and peppers, seated herself at the desk, and punched in the number. No one answered the phone at the Reborn house, but after eight rings a machine cut in. Shirley left a message.

"Be damned," said J.Q., hands idle as he stared through the front window.

"What?"

"There's Emil whatshisname. Staggering down the drive, headed for Ditch House. While you were down at the barn the people from Germany arrived. The son speaks English, but the old people have about twelve words of English between them."

"Go sidetrack him, J.Q."

"Too late," he said, rinsing the onion juice off his hands. "He's already there. I'll have to extricate him."

J.Q. went out. Shirley watched through the open door. A very drunk Emil was attempting to enter Ditch House against the wishes of a very German gentleman. J.Q. arrived and took him by the arm. Emil swung at him. Whoops. Better help J.Q.

Shirley arrived just as Emil collapsed into a heap.

"Get his other arm," urged J.Q.

"What is this?" demanded the younger guest, who had just arrived.

The old people drowned him in words.

Shirley heaved, and Emil came up, almost a deadweight.

"He is your family?" demanded the younger guest in an angry tone.

"No," said Shirley firmly. "He was a guest of the person who rented this house last week. He is too drunk to realize she has moved on."

"Ah."

"*Ach?*"

Voluble explanations. Shirley and J.Q. each took an arm and continued heaving. Emil's toes dragged on the driveway, twin furrows leading toward the patio gate.

"What the hell are we going to do with him?" asked J.Q.

"Whatever, so long as it's outside," she answered. "He smells to high heaven. And he'll probably throw up."

No sooner spoken. Shirley and J.Q. moved to a distance and waited until the spasm was over.

"I'll get the hose," said J.Q.

Emil rolled onto his back and swabbed at his face with one forearm. "Don' feel so good," he mumbled.

"I should imagine," Shirley commented.

"Where's Tanya?"

It took Shirley a moment to realize who he meant. Tanya Roth was the crazy lady. "She's gone to Peñasco. She rented a house there."

"Why'n hell she go to Panyasko? Hell'n gone." He rolled over and tried to sit up. "Wait for her inna house!"

"No you won't, buster," said J.Q., returning with the hose to rinse the mess off the driveway and, over Emil's objections, off Emil himself, while from Ditch House a plaintive voice demanded explanation of the process. The younger guest assured his mother they were not trying to drown the man. When Emil stank slightly less, Shirley and J.Q. dragged him into the patio and dropped his dripping form into a chair, behind shut gates, out of sight of the guests.

Shirley went in to call Cisso Pacheco. She returned with a cup of warm coffee, not that it would sober Emil up, but it might keep him occupied.

"I was just asking Emil what he did with Mrs. Tremple's purse," said J.Q. "He says there wasn't any purse. Just a wallet, in the front seat of the car."

"Did you lock the car with the key inside?" Shirley asked.

A furtive look fled across the man's face, finding no-where to roost. Emil was too drunk to be furtive. "Yeah," he mumbled. "I guess. Keys were inna car."

"And you went off the next day?"

"Yeah. Play a lil poker."

"How much money did you take, Emil?"

"She didn' have much!" he exclaimed indignantly. "Onny a couple hunnert. Dollars. Anna credit cards. Jimmy gimme somethin' for the credit cards." He hiccuped his way to silence.

"Did you take the license plate?"

It took several repetitions before he understood the question. "What I wan with a license plate? Don' hava car! Don' need no license plate." And with that, he dropped off, head sagging onto his chest.

"Thus endeth the tale of Emil," said J.Q. "Think I'll go call the sheriff."

"They're already on their way," Shirley told him in a resigned voice. "You know what this means. It means we've still got a mysterious stranger going into that house. Mrs. Tremple had a purse. All women have purses. She probably had other things with her name on them as well."

"Skinny as she was, I bet she was taking something," said J.Q.

"You mean she'd have had medicine. Probably labeled. Bottles." Shirley thought about it. "There was a shiny place on the radiator cover. Like somebody had set something down that was wet and soapy, and the soap ran down the sides and dried. It didn't look like a medicine bottle, though. Not the right shape."

"What shape?"

"Not round. Not square. Kind of oval, with straight sides. There was nothing in the medicine cabinet except her toothbrush. If she had medicine, it was gone, along with everything else that might identify her."

They sat, regarding the unconscious Emil with mutual disfavor. Whatever appetite they might have had for supper was in abeyance. J.Q. excused himself to put the food away. Twenty minutes later the sheriff's men arrived. Shirley gave them a statement as to what Emil had said, including the bit about Jimmy, who had ostensibly bought the credit cards. J.Q. verified her statement. They got Emil on his feet and took him away.

"Are you going to let her know? His companion, Ms. Roth?" J.Q. asked, when the sheriff's men had gone.

"I'm not going to make any great effort," Shirley replied. "She might have gone to Peñasco, and she might not. The place may have a phone and maybe not. He'll probably get hold of her, when he sobers up. He'll need bail money, if they charge him with theft."

"There's no proof. Nothing they can use in court."

"Maybe the wallet will be enough. And maybe they'll find Jimmy and he'll have the credit cards on him."

A car came sneaking down the drive. Dog gave her "guests arriving" bark. Car doors opened and closed. A firm knock at the front gate. J.Q. went to open it.

"Hello," said Esther Brentwood, with a bright, false smile. "R.J., isn't it? Mr. Jensen? We've come to see dear Allison."

In Garden House, Riana Stevens sat by the window, watching the shadows of clouds move across the canyon lands to the west. At one moment there would be only an obscurity, a darkness hiding all detail. Then the shadow would creep eastward, trailing light behind it, disclosing crenellated rimrock, tall towers, looming walls, all shining in the evening sun. Fascinating. So much there that one never saw unless the light was right. Someone might tell you that marvels and complexities lay there, but if the light wasn't right, you wouldn't believe him. It took the light to see what was real.

"What are you thinking about?" her husband asked, in a fond but slightly apprehensive tone.

"Just how hard it is to see what's true. How easy it is to believe something false if there's no light on the subject."

"Ree. Come on now. You're still going over and over it. It's time to—"

"If Mother had told me . . . about Dad. If she hadn't hidden it."

He took a deep breath, biting down angry words. "He didn't want people to know. Men . . . a man wouldn't want people to know. It has to do with self-respect."

"But she should have told *me*!"

He shook his head. "This isn't getting any better, Ree. I haven't wanted to intrude on your private stuff, but maybe it's time. Why don't you talk it out? Tell me exactly what you said to him."

She turned her head angrily, tears flying. "I don't want to talk about it."

"All right, damn it, don't talk about it. But you've got to stop this."

"I know. It's so stupid. I should have handled that job thing by myself. I do good work! I didn't need to stay there and work for her, for God's sake. I could have gone somewhere else. With my experience, I'd probably make more money somewhere else. And instead, what did I do? I killed my own father!"

"You didn't kill him."

"I as good as killed him, Craig."

"If you want to blame someone, blame the person who made the mistake! For your sake, let's straighten this out. Let's sue!"

She wept angrily against his shoulder. "That isn't what I want, Craig. I want Daddy back. I want justice. That's what I want. An eye for an eye."

In the house next door, Mrs. Fley looked up from her crochet work. "She's crying again."

"Have you put the whole story together by now?" he asked her. "Eavesdropping a bit here, a bit there."

She flushed, though only momentarily. "Don't need to eavesdrop; I know all about it. Seems the woman in there said something awful to her father, then the old man had a heart attack and died. Then the mother blamed her daughter, told the daughter she'd killed him, talking that way to him."

"Now how in the devil did you find that out?"

The old woman looked innocently out the window. "Ah, well, I guess the niece told me some of it. Girl was wandering around this morning, just wanting someone to talk to."

"So much unhappiness around."

She paled and was silent, pausing a long time before saying, "There is indeed. So many people looking for help."

"You think Kevin should have come to you?"

"Of course he should, yes. I could have helped him. And what help did he get? Falsity and lies. Depression. Despair."

"He didn't come to you, Mama. And Toni didn't either."

135

"I know it. Would to God they had."

"You're putting blame—"

She drew herself up, eyes snapping. "Papa, I'm putting blame right where it belongs. On profiteers. On people without ethics. On people who fatten on misery. Those so-called professionals."

He said nothing for a moment, startled by her manner, which he had used to see often, though not recently, not since she retired. Since then she had been someone else, an altogether easier person. He said doubtfully, "But he committed suicide."

"I know. And it's a tragedy Antonia may never live down. It's why she doesn't want us there, in her house. She didn't come to me, and now she can't face us."

"It wasn't her fault."

"Of course it wasn't." The old woman put down her crochet work and leaned against the back of the chair, eyes closed. "I know whose fault it was."

Shirley rose from her chair, forced her mouth into the semblance of a smile, and went to the gate, holding out her hand. "Why Hester, it is Hester, isn't it? No, no, don't tell me! Esther! That's right. I thought I recognized you. How very surprising to see you here! Is dear Terrence with you?"

Dear Lawrence was only a few steps behind, with dear Cheryl behind him. They straggled into the patio, and Shirley indicated chairs. "How very nice of you to drop in."

"Actually, *Lawrence* and I are staying here," said Esther. "With our friends, the Evanses."

"Are you! Why, how nice. And how sorry Allison will be to have missed you."

"Missed . . . ?"

"She and a girlfriend are spending the weekend sight-seeing. Where did they talk about going, J.Q.? Chama? To ride the narrow gauge?"

"There were words to that effect," he said. "I think Chaco Canyon was also mentioned. She'll be very surprised to hear you've been here."

An almost covert exchange of glances. "But, surely, she'll be back." Lawrence, asserting question as fact.

"Oh, next week sometime. When they run out of sightseeing to do."

"A girl that age? Allowed to go off by herself—"

"Oh, no, no, no," said Shirley, waving the words away. "Of course not, Esther. She's with a girlfriend, as I said, and a responsible adult. Well, do sit down, and tell us what you've seen and what you're going to do while you're here."

None of the Brentwoods seemed to have seen anything or intended to do anything.

"Did you fly in?"

"Yes."

"Well then, you came up through Albuquerque?"

"Yes," said Cheryl.

"No," said Esther, too hastily. "That is, yes. We stopped there just long enough to rent a car. That is, the Evanses did."

Cheryl seemed about to say something else, but she caught her mother's eye and was silent.

"I . . . ah, understand Allison hasn't been going to school," said Lawrence.

"Private tutor," said Shirley. "She didn't want to go into a new class just a few weeks before the end of the year. I don't think she's decided where to go this fall. There are a couple of good college-prep schools in Santa Fe."

"Will *she* be allowed to decide?" he asked disapprovingly.

"Within limits, of course." Shirley smiled. "What about you, Cheryl? You were just off to college when I last saw your parents. You should be graduating this year?"

Cheryl flushed and turned away.

"She dropped out for a year," said Esther. "To get some work experience."

Shirley, her eyes fixed upon Cheryl's lengthy and brilliantly painted false nails, allowed a little skepticism to shade her smile. "Modeling, no doubt."

137

"I work in an office," she said.

"Business."

"I'm a receptionist," she said, casting a rebellious glance at her mother. "In a law firm."

Possibly she worked for some of Daddy's colleagues. "Well, what brings you to Santa Fe?"

"Just . . . vacation," said Esther. "And we thought we'd visit Allison. . . ."

"Oh, inasmuch as you're suing for custody, I do think that's a good idea," Shirley said calmly, biting off each word, noting another quick exchange of glances and Lawrence's flaring nostrils. "She's fourteen now, you know. Quite old enough to tell the judge what kind of living arrangement she prefers. Still young enough, of course, to remember how kind you were to her and her mother and tell the judge about that also."

"She's family," said Esther, cheeks red, mouth tight. "We have to remember that."

Lawrence growled, "She's growing up now. Blood is thicker than water. She needs the care of a family. We do hope this matter can be resolved quietly."

"Vain hope," said Shirley. "I prefer the full blaze of publicity. Since you're so prominent in your community, I'm sure reporters will want to cover the matter fully. Like that child in Florida who recently divorced her biological parents. The media will eat it up."

Esther drew away, her face now completely red. Lawrence, on the other hand, remained unmoved. "We will need to see her while we're here," he said in a tone meant to be threatening.

J.Q. drawled, "Chama's a tiny place. Should be easy to find someone there. Same with Chaco Canyon. No more than a handful of tourists there at a time."

Another significant exchange of glances. Esther rose, smoothed down her skirt. "We'll plan on that, then. Tomorrow. Sunday. I'm sure we'll be able to find her."

They departed, as though to a rattle of muffled drums,

with a bitter wind in their wake. Shirley closed the gate and leaned against it.

J.Q. drawled, "Thought you weren't going to mention the custody thing?"

"Didn't intend to. Woman made me mad. Did she think we didn't know? That we hadn't received notice? That we didn't care?"

"I think so."

"Think what so?"

"Think it was a trial balloon, to find out if we cared. I also think they were up to something in Albuquerque. Mama was all too eager to indicate they hadn't stopped there."

Shirley sat down. "She was funny about it, wasn't she? And Cheryl seemed a bit uncomfortable about her job. Of course, there could be more than one reason for a student dropping out of school for a term."

"Like?"

"Like she's pregnant, like she's expelled, like Daddy's in financial trouble?"

"Possibly. Are you hungry?"

"Ravenous. Hating Brentwoods gives me an appetite."

"Let's go get the food out again. I have a hunch it's going to be a long tomorrow."

The phone rang at ten that evening. Though Shirley had an extension by her bed, she did not ordinarily answer it after eight o'clock. This time, since it could be Xanthy or Allison calling, she picked it up. The voice at the other end was familiar, but male.

"It's Cally, Ms. McClintock. Remember me? I was with the group that just left."

"Of course, Cally. What can I do for you?"

"Rob and Harry and I are wondering if you have anything available starting Monday? It turns out the job I was due to start is delayed awhile, and the three of us thought we'd extend our vacation."

"But not Alphonso, Michael, or Arthur?" she asked.

"They've all gone home. Back to California."

"Well, as a matter of fact, I've got the Big House available Monday night for a week. It's occupied right now, but the people are leaving no later than Monday." Having the house rented as of Monday night would assure that fact!

"Wonderful! You've got my credit-card number on the reservation we made last time. Use it for the deposit, and we'll see you day after tomorrow."

Shirley hung up the phone, then sat up in bed and stared thoughtfully at the large orange cat lying athwart her feet. "We are successful," she said. "Our guests like us well enough to return. One must, of course, ask oneself why."

There was one more phone call, this time Xanthy, reporting in, giving Shirley the name of the hotel in Albuquerque where they were staying.

"We're going to see Sheldon Maxwell tomorrow," she said softly. "Allison has decided she has to. She says if she waits, and he gets worse before she sees him, then she'll be sorry."

"Very sensible of her. Just don't let her expect too much, Xanthy. He's variable."

"Have the Brentwoods made themselves known?"

"Oh, indeed." Shirley took five minutes to expand on how the Brentwoods had made themselves known, to Alberta and to her.

"So you've sent them up to Chama?"

"We didn't actually lie, Xanthy. We merely said that location had been mentioned, which it was, by me. J.Q. dragged in Chaco Canyon as well."

"I'll call before we start back. You think Monday will be safe?"

"I've just reserved the Big House for Cally and his friends. They're extending their vacation. So even if dear Esther and dear Lawrence want to stay longer, we're full up."

When Shirley hung up the phone, she sat for a long moment, looking at the pill bottle. Tonight she would cut down to half a tablet. She shook the blue oval tablets into the

140

palm of her hand and sat looking at them, finally breaking one in half with her thumbnail, then staring at the halves.

No. This was taking too long. She couldn't afford to risk what they might be doing to her, to her memory, to her judgment. Sleepless or not, she would have to do without them.

By four in the morning her resolution was weakening. She had a favorite book propped on her chest, the cats were breathing easily on either side of her. Nero. Ladyfingers. The Baron. They had no trouble sleeping. She, on the other hand, felt no drowsiness at all.

No ones dies from a night's lost sleep, she told herself, turning the page. No one dies from several nights' lost sleep.

At five-fifteen she yawned, turned off the light, and fell into an uneasy doze. At seven-thirty, she awoke, cotton-mouthed and sticky-eyed, snarling. The foreseeable future was not going to be great!

The Brentwoods and the Evanses departed early on Sunday morning. J.Q. was on his way to the dairy when they drove out, and he followed them as far as the highway, where they turned north, he said. Toward Chama.

"And may they find the Bluebird of Perpetual Discord," growled Shirley. "A pox on both their houses."

"Who are these Evans characters?"

"I have no idea." Nor had she, then.

"Now you've got Hollywood types," said Mrs. Fley across the fence, when Shirley went down to feed the chickens.

"Who's that?" Shirley asked, straightening up and paying full attention.

"The man in the biggest house, the new one. Told my husband he's a screenwriter. Out here working on a project."

"Indeed." She tossed the rest of the corn into the pen and

went to lean on the fence beside the older woman, eager to find out more about Mr. Evans. "Did he happen to mention what he's working on?"

"Nope. Just said he's working on a biographical treatment. That's what they call them, you know. Treatments."

"Like medical treatments?"

"Sort of like that." Unaccountably she laughed. "Actually, a lot like that. Try this, then if that doesn't work, try that. Can't just tell a story. Have to do a treatment of it. Something the actors can manage. No good putting subtle emotion in the script if the actor only has two expressions, asleep and awake. No good prescribing a medicine the patient won't take."

"You sound like you have firsthand knowledge."

Her face clouded, then cleared. "Oh, yes. I was married to a screenwriter. For a while. Back in the forties and fifties."

"You were a kid in the forties and fifties!"

"My husband was twenty-five in fifty. Old enough to get blacklisted. They thought he was a commie."

"Was he?"

"I went to a meeting with him once, with a friend of ours who was maybe a commie. Nicest man you'd ever want to meet. Interested in justice, you know. Back then, anybody interested in justice pretty well had to be a commie." She laughed, a dark, aching laugh. "Like now. If you're interested in justice, you pretty well have to be black, a feminist, or gay."

"Or all three," said Shirley.

"Well, for sure you can't be a general or senator with your big balls and little brain invested in killing other people," the old woman said viciously.

A moment's silence while Shirley thought this over. "Would you care to elucidate?" she asked at last.

Mrs. Fley pursed her lips and half turned away, then back again, with sudden decision. "My grandson was in the army. He loved the army. Wanted to stay in the army. Was

142

afraid he might be put out because he was gay. He thought maybe somebody could help him with the problem. Didn't want to ask Grandma, who would have told him how to keep his private affairs private and how to keep himself healthy! I could have told him he wasn't any different from some hetero cross-dresser who's into garter belts and high heels, or some woman, only way she can come is on the kitchen counter with ketchup on her belly. They'd get kicked out, too, if they started talking about it on the firing range. Private stuff is private."

Shirley bit down the amusement that threatened to break loose. "He didn't ask for your advice?"

"Didn't come to me. Didn't go to any M.D. Went to a Ph.D. She told him he had to come out. Tell everyone. Confront the influences that made him that way. Be cured. Sweet, innocent little fag!"

"Your grandson."

"Mine. Yes. And I loved him."

"Loved."

"He's dead."

"But you said ... AIDS."

"That's right. He didn't have it, but he died of it. My daughter, Antonia, she could handle what he was, but she couldn't handle his blaming her, blaming her husband. Lord, they tried so hard with that boy. Did without things to provide for him, try to build him up, make him know they loved him, regardless, and he came to them with that filth in his mouth, blaming them. She finally said go. Be what you are, I accept what you are, but I don't accept the blame. So he did. Went away, was what he was, got kicked out of the army, got a false positive on his HIV, thought his life was over, didn't care enough to try to live, didn't live. Died. Him and his friend both. Dead."

"When was this?"

"Last year. About this time last year."

"You're very bitter."

"I'm an old woman and I'm very bitter, yes. He died

143

thinking he wasn't human. Career gone. Family rejected. All because of that damned fool he went to for help. Told him he wasn't normal. Told him he had to purge himself, admit his abnormality, face up to it, blame someone, and cure himself. Well, he couldn't. Was no one to blame. Was no cure. He never chose to be that way, and God knows my daughter never chose it for him."

She turned away angrily and started up the hill.

"I'm sorry," Shirley called after her. "I've . . . lost people I loved, too."

The old woman turned, her face crumpling. "Sometimes don't you wish you'd died? Before it happened?"

Behind her, Shirley did not answer. The question was too close to what she had felt . . . more than once.

"What was all that?" asked J.Q., coming from inside the barn. "I just heard part of it."

"What is she?" asked Shirley, wiping tears from beneath her eyes. "Really?"

"What do you mean?"

"Nice old lady, hmmm? Talks like a country woman. You'd figure her for natural intelligence, untrammeled by education. Then yesterday she comes out with Naegleria fowlerii. Is that what the people at the hospital said?"

"Just Naegleria."

"She stated some decided and rather cynical views on overpopulation. And just now I asked if her grandson came to her, and she said, no, 'He didn't go to any M.D.' Do you think?"

"You think she's a doctor?"

"Something like that. See if you can find out, J.Q."

"I'll talk to her husband, Wallace. He's out by the pool, and I can drop by to check up on the pool filters."

"Interesting," she said. "All very interesting."

5

Dog was barking her "stranger alert" when Shirley came back up the hill. The people, whoever they were, had not driven in as guests did, going to a particular house and stopping there. They had left their car in the middle of the parking area and were wandering around like loose chickens. Dog disapproved of this on principle.

"Can I help you?" Shirley asked.

A stout, dark-haired woman turned toward her and came hesitantly over the gravel in shoes inappropriate for anything but carpeted hallways. "Are you the owner?"

"I am."

"I'm Alicia Tremple's sister. I think you're the one who called."

"You're Elaine Scott?"

"Yes. This is my husband, Gerald. I couldn't take it in, you know, when you called. It was so unexpected."

"Come in." Shirley held the gate wide, ushering the woman and her companion onto the patio. "I was about to have a cup of coffee. Will you join me?"

They would, thank you. Shirley fetched a tray, and they

seated themselves around the patio table, Gerald and Elaine, side by side, holding hands in an accustomed manner, as though they often sat so.

"The people at the sheriff's office told us her things were here," the woman said. "We came ... we came to pick them up." She dabbed at the corners of her eyes with a soggy tissue. "It's all so unbelievable."

"Because of how sudden it was," Shirley suggested, offering sugar. Gerald took three spoonfuls. Elaine shook her head. No sugar.

"No. No, it wasn't that. People do die suddenly. I mean, our mother, she died suddenly. Sometimes it's better that way. Not to draw it out. But first to have her house broken into, and then this."

"Her house?"

"Sonia called us, that's Licia's housekeeper. Somebody broke in and just made a horrible mess of the house. We went over there to tell the police if anything was missing. All I could say was, I didn't think so. I mean, she doesn't keep anything valuable there. Her stereo, her TV, what else did she have? And her office wasn't even touched, even though the door in between was broken down."

"Her office is in her house?"

"I say it was some addict, looking for easy money," growled Gerald. "Just before she left, I told her that house needed grilles on the windows. She was going to see to it when she got back."

"But then, on top of that, dying like this ..." Elaine wept into her sodden hankie. "She's always been so careful of herself. So kind of ... well, fearful, I guess you'd say."

"You'd think, her profession, she'd get over that," he said. "A little less scaredy-cat, a little more caution, that's what she needed."

"Well, that's why she went into it, of course, to understand herself." She patted him on the knee and turned toward Shirley with a confidential little moue. "Our father was not a nice man. Our mother died. She wasn't there to protect us. He ... well, he mistreated us right up until we

146

left home. Licia went first, and as soon as she was settled, she came back and took me. I've always been surprised how she could come back to that house after he died, live there, have her office there, considering what we went through in that place."

"Cheaper than renting," said her husband. "And it was your mom left it to her."

"She left me the furniture and Grandma's jewelry," she said, patting his hand. "It was all fairly divided. Anyhow, when I grew up, I decided to put all that behind me, but Licia couldn't. I said, let others look out for themselves, but Licia wanted to save everyone." The woman dabbed at her eyes again, fussed mildly at herself, and dug into her purse for a fresh tissue. "That's why she came here, to help one of her people."

"What was her profession?" Shirley asked.

"She was a doctor. Oh, not a medical doctor. A Ph.D. In psychology." She said it reverently. "She worked so hard. She had an extensive practice."

Shirley thought the phrase sounded like a quote, perhaps something Alicia herself had said. *I have quite an extensive practice.*

Elaine bubbled on, "She helped so many people! Famous people, even. And now, well, this thing they're telling us makes no sense at all."

"They're certain about the organism?"

"The bug? Oh, yes. We got quite a lecture. The thing was discovered thirty or forty years ago, according to the person who spoke to us. It's not just here either. It's around the world, different places, but it's rare people die of it, because people don't swim in hot springs, mostly, you know, with their heads under, which I cannot figure out to save me. She hated water in her face, around her eyes. Even washing her hair! She wouldn't do it in the shower because she couldn't stand water running around her face."

"She had allergies," Gerald said. He set down his empty cup and eyed the pot meaningfully. Shirley refilled the cup for him. "Lord, did that woman have allergies."

147

"Lots of people have allergies," said Elaine, patting his hand fondly. "With Licia it was mostly dust mites and animal hair. Especially cats. Her whole head would stop up if she was in the same room as a cat."

"She had a cat," her husband said. "You told me."

"That was when we were children." She set down her own cup to fumble with the tissue again. "Daddy always threatened to kill him if she didn't do what he said. Colly was his name, and Daddy did kill him finally. I guess that's what made Licia leave. It was just the last straw. Later she got the allergies."

"What did you say the cat's name was?" asked Shirley. "Colly?" Her lips formed the words Alicia had murmured. Ahmis Macolly. Ma colly. "Did your sister ever say things like . . . she missed Colly?"

The woman nodded, smiling. "She always said that. She'd lean over to pet some cat, and I'd say, Licia, be careful, you'll swell up like a balloon, and she'd say oh, I miss my Colly." Her voice rose in unconscious lament. "She didn't have anyone, not anyone. She couldn't let anybody close to her. No husband, no child. Only her practice. She got so lonely."

Shirley set her cup down, thinking furiously. "Would she let a cat into her house?"

Elaine shook her head firmly. "No, she was a little silly, sometimes, but not that silly. Why?"

Shirley shook her head, not positive, remembering the house, the way she'd seen it that morning. Something there. The cat out along the fence. The muddy marks on the toilet seat. And it had rained the evening before. When she and J.Q. went out to the car, the driveway was still wet.

"She came here to help someone," Elaine Scott cried. "And to have it all end like this. Oh, it's just too sad."

Gerald cleared his throat and returned them to practicalities. "Did she have much with her? Clothes and things?"

Shirley shook her head. "A few clothes. A few paperback books. Did she have a purse? We didn't find one."

"Her black one was in the car with her when she left. It

had a shoulder strap. And what about her briefcase?" Elaine sat forward, eyes wide. "Did you find that? We gave her the briefcase for her birthday. Faux alligator." She said it proudly, as though the stilted phrase actually meant something.

Shirley shook her head again. "No briefcase. Nothing to identify her, as a matter of fact. And the credit-card number we had was wrong. . . ."

"They said that. The sheriff's man said that. Said she came through southern Arizona. She didn't come through southern Arizona. She drove from Barstow over to Flagstaff, and from there to Gallup. I was with her when she marked out the map, which way she was going. She wasn't anywhere near that national forest they talked about."

"You say she had allergies. She must have had medication with her."

"She did. She never went anywhere without it. There was medicine she used every day. Didn't you find it?"

Shirley shook her head. "Was she very cold-blooded?" she asked thoughtfully. "Did she have trouble staying warm?"

They exchanged looks, shrugging slightly. He said, "Not really. Not that I ever noticed. Why?"

"It doesn't matter now," Elaine murmured. "Let's not talk about it anymore." She gulped, almost a sob, stifling it with her cupped hands.

The next question died on Shirley's lips. There was a moment's quiet, filled with sniffles and sips.

Shirley searched for a neutral topic. "Did you find a place to stay in Santa Fe?"

"A motel. I'm afraid it's not very clean."

"Would you like to stay here in the house where your sister was? I can let you stay there tonight, if you like. The next guest doesn't arrive until tomorrow."

They demurred. No. The motel was all right. They didn't want to be in the way. They only wanted to get Alicia's things. They only wanted to make sense of it all.

Elaine asked to use the bathroom. When she was out of

sight, her husband asked, "You think there's something wrong here? You think maybe she didn't get that bug the way they say?"

"I don't know, Mr. Scott. You knew her far better than I ever will."

He nodded sadly. "She was all tied up inside. Like a pressure cooker. Sometimes you'd see her eyes darting, jiggling, just like that little valve on the top of the cooker, like she was ready to explode. Lainy was right about her not having friends. We'd invite her, you know, just family like, go with us to the movies, or out to dinner, but she hardly ever would. She never thought she looked right or had the right clothes, and she was so self-conscious. Only place she ever felt comfortable was behind that desk with her recorder on, or maybe up on a platform, speechifying. Their father, nasty old bastard, you wouldn't believe what he did to those girls. He's the one made Licia so ashamed of herself. Lainy believes that's why her sister was always so thin. Half-starved, punishing herself for things that old bastard did. Or, maybe, just to make herself so unattractive no one else ever would want to."

Shirley's mouth curled in distaste. "I suppose she had a lot of . . . clients who had the same kind of experiences."

"Well"—he stared over Shirley's shoulder—"you know, I'd never say this to Lainy, but Alicia could get a little carried away sometimes. I've never laid a finger on Lainy, not in twenty years married, and I never laid a finger on our kids either. Lainy'll tell you the same. But one time when our daughter Janice was about twelve, she got herself bunged up doing gymnastics at school. She was doing this vault, and she went off the side of the vaulting horse. There were all kinds of witnesses, just how it happened. Well, her aunt Alicia saw the bruises, and she got Janice and Lainy cornered, just positive I was the one who'd bruised her, telling them not to defend me, admit it, get it out in the open. It's like, you know, she was determined to find it everywhere."

"Did you convince her that you hadn't done it?"

"Now you ask, I'm not sure we ever did. Anything wrong in anybody's life, she'd go after the parents, like it was a law of nature or something, especially fathers. I'll tell you the truth, I was always surprised she found so much of it. People who didn't even remember! I asked her one time how come there was so much of it, and she said it was satanism!"

Something clenched in Shirley's chest, and she made an ugly face. "Do you believe that?"

"Well now, I mean, I've been an engineer for almost thirty years. I like proof before I believe something like that. I told Licia that. I said, you've got to have proof, Licia. You can't just go accusing people. She said she could, and she would!" He shook his head, then looked up alertly. "Hush. Don't say anything to Lainy. She won't hear a word against Licia."

He held out his hand to his wife, drawing her to his side with obvious affection, putting his arm around her. "Well now, let's get the belongings, hmm, sweetheart? No point taking up any more of Ms. McClintock's time."

"The suitcase is in the garage," said Shirley, leading the way. Luckily Alberta had put it where it could be spotted at once. Shirley handed it to Mr. Scott; experimentally, he hefted it. Light. His expression said it. Little enough left behind at the end of a life.

"Did you tell the sheriff's men about the purse and briefcase?" Shirley asked. "They should be on the lookout for those."

"They told us about the thief," said Elaine. "Taking her wallet and money and cards. I'm sure he took the other things. We're not going to fret over them. God knows, Licia doesn't need them anymore."

Shirley walked them to their car, still in the middle of the parking area, doors still open. From under the Cherokee, Dog woofed disapprovingly as they got themselves stowed and departed. People who didn't fit neatly into one of Dog's categories were better gone away.

J.Q. came in from the road, bearing the Sunday paper. "You ready for second coffee?"

"Um," she agreed.

"Was that the sister?"

"How did you know?"

"There's a family resemblance. In the eyes. Around the chin. What did she have to say?"

"Alicia Tremple was a psychologist. I get the impression that both girls were incest victims, and that Alicia had divided the whole world into two classes, abusers and victims. If you weren't one, you had to be the other. She was out to find child abuse and satanism in everyone she met. She even accused her own brother-in-law. Her sister is ready to accept that Alicia Tremple died of Naegleria infection and all her things were stolen by Emil. I wish I could accept that explanation."

J.Q. dropped the paper on the table and kicked at the table leg. "Why did I know that was coming? Why did I know the moment the woman knocked on my door that you would make a great mystery of it!"

"It's something nagging at me, bothering me," she said apologetically. She rubbed her forehead wearily. "My mind isn't working right, J.Q. I feel like . . . I don't know. Like I had Alzheimer's or something. There's thoughts in there, words in there, and I know they exist, but I can't find them. I keep seeing her, how she looked that night, and something doesn't fit. Something about her is just . . . dissonant."

"I think you're so sleepy you're having daydreams—daymares maybe."

"No, really. I still know the difference between reality and fantasy. Nothing fits, J.Q. Why did we have a phony address, phone number, credit-card number?"

"I have no idea," he said in a definitely surly tone.

"I don't *know* either, but I get the impression from her brother-in-law that she was a little paranoid. Maybe this whole trip was something very secret or private. That business of saying she'd come to meet a client, then saying no, she didn't know what she was talking about. As though

152

she'd blurted something she wasn't supposed to. She was a zealot. Maybe she and this person were planning something they didn't want people to know about. And maybe the whole thing was a fiction, just a reason to get her out here into a hot spring where she could be dunked. Not once, but twice. She said she'd 'been back to Jemez.' Maybe somebody was making sure she'd been infected!"

"That's farfetched."

"I don't know. Hell, J.Q. All I'm saying is—"

"All you're saying is you want it to be murder."

"Me! I don't want it to be. I just think it might have not been a natural death, that's all."

He fumed. "So. Tell your friend from the sheriff's office all about it. If he thinks there's something in it, he can report it. Leave it up to them. With this Allison business brewing, you've got enough to worry about without this."

She stared beyond him, frowning.

"You won't leave it alone!" he said. "Why?"

"If somebody had a hand in her death, it might have been someone here. It might have been done by someone who's still here."

J.Q. refused to be drawn into supposes, even as a listener. He went down to the bottom pasture and did not return until well into the afternoon, by which time Shirley had decided to keep her suppositions to herself for the time being. She greeted him with wine, cheese, and crackers on the patio, and after a suspicious glance at her face, which she had arranged to display only innocence, he allowed himself to be cosseted. Resolutely Shirley talked only about ranch business.

The Brentwoods and their friends returned about four, leaving their car and going into the Big House without any delay or conversation, even though both Shirley and J.Q. were in plain view inside the open gates.

"They know they've been misled," said J.Q.

"Backs were a little stiff," Shirley admitted.

"When's Xanthy coming back?"

153

"She and Allison were going to visit Stupe Maxwell today. Xanthy said they'd come back tomorrow, just as soon as the Brentwoods left."

"If they leave."

"They have to leave. The house is rented to someone else."

"I suppose." He sounded dissatisfied.

"What is it, J.Q.?"

He squirmed. "You're not the only one who gets itchy. Aunty and Uncle raise the hairs on my neck, that's all." He looked up at the sound of a slammed door. Esther Brentwood came crunching across the driveway to the gate.

"May we borrow a good knife," she called in a dulcet voice. "The ones in the kitchen over there are terribly dull."

J.Q. went to the kitchen and returned with a sharp knife.

"I'll get those sharpened for you," he said, handing it to her.

"No need. We'll be leaving very early."

She smiled, a smile of such horrid guile that Shirley glanced behind herself, wondering who the woman was smiling for. Or at.

As she left, Esther called over her shoulder, "We're so sorry to have missed Allison. Perhaps next time."

J.Q. returned to the table. The door banged again.

"I thought we'd have a fight on our hands," said Shirley.

"I don't think she's given up. She's just got something else on her mind."

Shirley moved uneasily. There had been something quite dreadful in Esther's smile.

"They looked angry when they came back. Fifteen minutes later she's gloating," J.Q. mused. "Wonder what happened in between."

Shirley shook her head, which ached. Two or three hours last night had not been enough sleep. She felt wooden, like a marionette, unable to move on her own.

"Let's have a bite of supper," she said. "Let's get this day over with."

They settled on soup and sandwiches, easy and filling,

without much to clean up afterward. Outside, they could see the Brentwoods and the Evanses putting things in the car. Packing, ready to leave early.

"I'll clean up," J.Q. murmured. "You go back and lie down. You look like you'd been dragged through a knothole feetfirst."

She grinned ruefully, agreeing with him. Her mother had used to say that. You look like you combed your hair with an eggbeater. You look like death warmed over. Who had eggbeaters anymore? With all the forests being destroyed, how much longer would anyone know what a knothole was?

"Thanks," she said, getting herself out of there, back into the quiet of her own quarters. No pill. No help for it. A hot shower first, then a couple of aspirins, then the piled pillows and the book, courting sleep, which proved coy. The hours went by. Clouds sailed across the moon, making an impenetrable darkness outside, a brooding shadow that pushed at the open window. Cats purred and dozed and rose to go out through the recently installed cat door, then returned to purr and doze some more. Dog let herself in through the cat door, something she did only occasionally as it was an uncomfortably tight fit.

"Saw my light on, didn't you?" said Shirley, casting a covert look at the clock. Good Lord, three A.M. and counting. And then four. And later five. Dog, who had slept, curled into a tight ring, woke, stretched, slipped out through the door, and was gone. Shirley yawned. And about time for a few yawns. Now if she could only . . .

She turned out the light and snuggled down, one soft pillow under the recalcitrant knee. She had decided the knee hurt when it was straightened out. If she kept it propped, it shouldn't hurt. The pillow did help. After a few moments of pro forma protest, the muscles seemed to accept the position and stop twitching and screaming.

Quiet. Quiet. Almost sleep.

And then Dog! Her alert, trouble bark, again and again. Shirley sat up, catching her leg in the covers and sending a pang all the way to her ankle. Danger, said Dog. Trouble. Get here fast.

She was up, her robe around her, hand fumbling for the flashlight she always kept in the drawer of the bedside table. Then out, into the patio, through the gate, down the hill toward the pastures. Dog was down there, by the barn, standing by the fence, her strident bark like a trumpet call, again and again, with another sound behind the bark, a thin screaming, a tortured plea.

Shirley stopped beside the fence, flashed the light, saw a huddled little form inside by the water tank, heard the pitiful bleating, went through the gate. One of Isabel's kids. Blood everywhere, and that pitiful bleating. One of its front feet cut off. My God, one of its little feet cut off, and the knife lying there that had done it.

She didn't allow herself any time for thought. She knelt, took up the knife, and slit the little creature's throat, feeling a flash of light along with the gush of hot blood, not sure for the moment she hadn't imagined it, then looking up, blinded, knowing she had not. Dog was in full cry, chasing someone up the hill. Heavy footsteps crunched the gravel, running.

The kid wasn't suffering anymore. It was limp and dead. She looked down at her sodden robe, bloody as a butcher's apron. Poor little beast. Sweet little doe goat. Poor little thing. It couldn't have lived, maimed like that, but poor little thing. She stroked the soft hair, sorry, oh, so sorry, tears falling on her hand. Little horns just showing. Who would do such a thing!

"Shirley! What happened?" J.Q. standing there with a flash of his own, tatty old robe pulled over his pajamas.

She tried to tell him, fumbling it. "I slit its throat," she said. "To stop it suffering. And somebody took my picture while I was doing it."

After that, of course, there was no sleep. Two nights, she told herself fatalistically. Nobody died from missing two nights' sleep. But how many more?

She put her bloody robe in the washer and set it to soak in cold water. She wrapped herself in an old housecoat almost as ratty as J.Q.'s bathrobe and joined him in the kitchen. Too late for cocoa. Too early for coffee. They would have tea.

"It's still pitch-black, and the Brentwoods are gone," said J.Q. "I think you can figure it was one of them."

"I can't see Esther or Lawrence maiming a little animal like that," she said dully. "It isn't in character. Someone had to catch it first. Someone accustomed to animals. Esther and Lawrence don't get dirty."

"They weren't alone. There were other people with them, people we don't know. A lot of people are raised in habits of casual cruelty, Shirley. You know that as well as I do. Fishermen who cut the hind legs off a frog to use as bait and throw the still-living frog into the pond. Ranchers who hot-brand cattle when it's absolutely unnecessary. Down here we've seen drivers go out of their way to hit dogs on the road. Cutting the foot off a kid goat could be small stuff to someone like that."

"Why! Damn it, J.Q., why?"

"I haven't the least idea. It makes no sense at all."

"But you think it was them?"

"They're gone, that's all I know. Maybe their departure is entirely coincidental."

"Maybe this has something to do with Tremple dying."

"That's farfetched. Even if it was murder."

"It wasn't just natural. I know it."

"You'll need to prove it. I don't think the sheriff is going to try."

"Her sister. I need to talk to her sister. Elaine Scott."

"Hasn't she gone back to California?"

"I don't know. They were staying at a motel on Cerrillos Road. I wrote it down. . . ."

"Wait until dawn, at least."

"We could see if they're registered."

Shirley rose wearily and pulled out the desk drawer. She had cleaned it out just a few days ago, but it was already

157

furry with bits and pieces of this and that. Cash-register receipts. Messages. She'd written the name and phone number on a yellow notepad. She found the note crammed into one corner.

"La Quinta Inn," she said, handing him the note. She was too tired to dial the number.

He did so, waiting a long time for someone to answer, waiting a long time after asking the question. He thanked the person and turned to her. "They're still there."

She sighed. "I'll get dressed. Let's be there before they have a chance to leave."

"Their coffee shop opens at six-thirty."

"I'll be ready in ten minutes."

It was enough time for a fast shower, for donning clean clothing, though nothing removed the gravel behind her eyelids, the fur at the base of her tongue. It was enough time for J.Q. to shave. They looked, Shirley thought, dog weary but clean. About the best that could be expected. Darkness still filled the valley. Only along the mountains to the east was there a thin gray line, a bright star pulsing just above it.

"I am so tired," she breathed. "I feel as though I were moving through molasses. Everything's in slow motion. I can't even think fast."

"I know." He yawned widely. "Did you get any sleep at all?"

"I was just drifting off when Dog started." She put her head back against the headrest and closed her eyes. "I wonder how much longer this insomnia is going to last."

"Are you tapering off?"

"I'm doing without."

He shook his head. "You can doze off now, if you want. I'm all right."

"Believe me, J.Q., if I want, I will. I don't think I can keep from it."

Still, she did keep from it, or only just, drifting uneasily in and out of an unrestful vagueness. When the car turned

158

into the parking lot of the motel, she sat up, blinking like an owl. "Now what?"

"Now we find out what room. Now we call them. Ask them to have breakfast with us."

"Right." She took off her glasses and rubbed her eyes. "I'll go get started on some coffee while you're doing that."

The coffee shop was virtually deserted, though all the tables were set and kitchen noises came through the doors behind the counter. J.Q. slipped in through the door and joined her. "Fifteen minutes or so," he said. "They were asleep."

"Why did I want to see them?" she asked the air, then lifted a coffee cup and waved it at a young woman who peered for a moment through the doors, who vanished, then returned, a pot held before her like a chalice, redemption in chrome.

"You didn't say," J.Q. answered.

"Satanism," she murmured, lip deep in the hot brew, not even waiting for her customary milk and sugar.

"Satanism?"

"It sort of came to me. Several things, recently. Him. The sister's husband. He told me Alicia Tremple was into satanism. I don't mean into it herself, but into finding it. Into stumbling across it wherever she turned, as a matter of fact. Like a mushroom hunter, the morning after rain, falling over puffballs and campestris—"

"Presupposing fertile ground."

"I guess she presupposed fertile ground, yes. She isn't alone. Remember when the pope came to Denver? He was fulminating against women who were turning away from the patriarchal religions—"

"Shirley, what are you talking about?"

She rubbed her forehead, trying to bring clarity. "I think I'm talking about beliefs, J.Q. When the pope came to the U.S. he spoke harshly of women who have turned to a sort of neopaganism because they find no freedom inside a patriarchal religion. He accused them of heresy or witchcraft, just as the church did during the days of the Inquisition."

"You sound delirious."

"Del-weary-us. Tired out."

"I mean you're confused. There are two things going on. Allison and Alicia Tremple's death. Neither of them is a religious question that has anything to do with witchcraft."

She squinted, trying to focus. "It's not the witchcraft, J.Q. It's the *accusation* I'm talking about. What I'm trying to say is, when well-known, respected people accuse others of witchcraft, the accusation gives credibility to the idea there really is witchcraft. Just like Joe McCarthy accusing people of being commies, back in the fifties."

"Here they are," said J.Q., hushing her.

Elaine and Gerald stood in the doorway, peering sleepily around the empty room. Shirley beckoned, and they came over.

"What's happened?" Elaine asked.

"Weirdness," Shirley answered shortly. "I'm not sure it has anything to do with what happened to your sister, but it might. Your husband mentioned today . . . yesterday that your sister found a lot of satanism among her clients."

"Oh, she did," breathed Elaine. "She was so distressed by it, too. You know, she never used to think of that, but after all the things about it on TV and the book she read, she started asking her clients, getting them to remember, and you know, over half of them did remember. It took a lot of patience, she said, but she got it out of them."

"Got what?" asked J.Q., lost.

"How they were abused by satanists. How they had to kill babies and animals. How they watched the rituals. You know."

"What book was it that she read?" Shirley asked.

"I'm not sure." Elaine faltered. "There was more than one. She had . . . oh, a lot of books. And it was on TV all the time, you know. I know she had one book, *The New Satanists*, or something like that, and it tells psychologists and social workers and people like that to be aware. Be on the lookout. I remember the pictures. People worshiping goats, sacrificing babies."

Shirley fixed J.Q. with her gaze. "Elaine, have you ever heard of the Salem witch trials?"

"Gracious, no. Do they have them in Oregon, too?"

Shirley pinched her lips together to keep from screaming. "Did your sister think you and she had been abused in that way?"

"Well, she was going to work with me, see if I could remember. I am a little older, so maybe I would."

"But you don't remember now."

"No. I've repressed it."

"You know you've repressed it?"

"Elaine said I had. She said she was sure we were abused by satanists, that our father was a satanist, but we've repressed it."

Gerald said pleadingly, "Elaine. You know, that may just be Alicia's idea."

"She's right, Gerald. Just look at how much of it she's found."

"Among her patients," Shirley said.

"Right."

"And when she'd find it, among her patients, what would she have her patients do about it?"

"Why, they had to confront their parents about it, of course. Make them admit it. Get it out in the open. Go to the law. Get them arrested."

"And if the parents didn't remember?"

"You mean, if they'd repressed it?"

"I mean, if they couldn't remember any such thing."

"That's what I just said. If they repressed it, they had to be helped to remember it."

"It couldn't ever be that it just hadn't happened."

"No," the woman said angrily. "If Alicia said it happened, it had happened. People just didn't remember."

"I see." Shirley smiled and nodded. "May we buy you breakfast?"

"Is that all you wanted?"

"I think so. I needed to know what your sister did, mostly. What kind of . . . practice she had."

"She helped many, many people," said Elaine fervently. "Some famous people. Movie stars. Celebrities!"

"And she never made a mistake."

"Never."

"Not even when she accused Gerald of hurting your daughter."

Gerald flushed deeply. "Here, now."

"Well, well, that was, that was a kind of misunderstanding," Elaine gabbled. "It only happened that one time. And I don't think I want to talk to you anymore. I don't think you take this matter serious enough. For all I know, you could be one of them."

"Them?" asked J.Q. in sudden alarm.

"Them. The ones who do it. Devil worshipers." She rose, staggered, put her arm around her husband's waist, and tottered away. He looked back with an odd expression, spoke a few words to her, and then came back to the table.

"I'm sorry," he murmured, casting a quick look at his wife's retreating back. "She and her sister were very close. So far as Lainy is concerned, the sun rose and set in Alicia."

"She's convinced her sister really found satanism."

He grimaced, biting his lower lip. "That time she accused me, I was really angry. I told Licia she mustn't go on accusing people of that. I told her she couldn't go around saying that about people without proof! And do you know what she said? She said it didn't matter if it was factually true or not, anybody who'd done wrong had done Satan's work, so they were satanists! So, I said, Licia, is anybody who makes a mistake a satanist, and she said yes, if the mistake was evil."

He rubbed his forehead. "I told her . . . I said, Alicia, you need to get some help for yourself. I told her she might be hurting innocent people just like she hurt me. She laughed. She said I was trying to turn her from doing her work. She said she was perfectly all right, thank you, and I'd better watch it because she had her eye on me. I had what she called 'tendencies.' "

"That couldn't have been very comfortable for you," Shirley murmured.

"It almost destroyed our marriage, I'll tell you that. I was angry, and Lainy was defending her sister, and it was a mess! I'm afraid Alicia did a lot of harm, and she knew she was doing it. She'd sit there, in our living room, and she'd tell Lainy about her cases. This one got a divorce. That one got her father arrested. This one got her mother locked up. She knew she was wrecking people's lives. You can't go through all that school, a doctorate even, and not know what you're doing. She was sort of like those serial killers you read about. They keep killing, but it never satisfies them because inside themselves they're killing one person, maybe their mother, over and over. That's Alicia. She kept going after other people's parents because she was killing her father, over and over."

"You mean disgracing him," J.Q. said. "Accusing him. Not killing him. Not murdering him."

"Just as good as," he said heavily. "You accuse somebody of that, you've as good as murdered him."

"Why?" Shirley asked. "Why satanism?"

"Took me a while to figure that out," he said angrily. "I finally did. If people are going to believe you, you've got to have a reason. Accusing people of stuff they never did, never would have thought of! You got to have a reason. People say why? Why would her father do that? And Licia would say, satanism, that's why."

He gave them a quick, apologetic glance and left them.

"Did I hear what I just think I heard?" asked J.Q.

She sighed deeply. "He sees it very clearly. It's what I was trying to tell you, J.Q. Once the atmosphere of credibility is established, everybody breathes it in. I saw a poll the other day that slightly over half the American people believe in witches and satanism and UFOs. Such a convenient belief, too. If you hate someone, accuse him of being an alien, or a worshiper of the devil."

"I'm sorry, dear heart, but if people remember this stuff happening . . ."

She smiled wearily. "Give me enough time and I can make you believe you grew up in Afghanistan, J.Q. It's just like that TV show I was telling you about, where the quack psychologist made the kids remember all kinds of things."

"That's what I don't understand," he said grimly. "How do you create a memory of something that didn't happen?"

"You ask a kid, very sympathetically, if anybody's ever touched him 'down there.' He says no. Then you ask him again. He says no, but now he's worried. Then you ask him again. Now he's really worried. Here's this adult asking a question over and over, it must be because he, the kid, is giving the wrong answer. Finally the kid says yes, because that's what he knows the adult wants to hear, and he thinks that'll end it.

"It doesn't end it, because then you ask him if Freddy touched him down there. And he'll say no, and you ask again, and he'll say no, but you keep asking until he says yes. *Then* you write up your professional notes, and you say, 'Child confirmed that Freddy touched him down there.' Needless to say, you did not make notes of all the times you asked the question and the kid said no. You don't make notes of the fact you've been planting the idea, and the vocabulary, and the concept that it's a good thing to confess to having been molested."

"A good thing!"

"Hell, J.Q., ten minutes ago in this very room you heard Elaine Scott say she believed it would be a good thing for her to remember something she does not remember! Her father did abuse her. She remembers that. She doesn't remember satanism because it didn't happen, but given a few weeks I'll bet her sister would have had her remembering it! Adults don't stand up to continual suggestion any more than kids do. Whenever the patient says no, I don't remember, the so-called therapist acts as though the patient is a liar or not trying hard enough. Whenever the patient says yes, I was molested, the therapist tells him he's brave and wonderful. If a patient actually gets up in court and testifies, the world tells him he's really brave. He gets rewarded when he says yes, and the therapist only writes it down when the patient confirms what's wanted. Naturally the 'therapy notes' will reinforce the diagnosis, and the patient goes through life thinking he did a good thing when what he actually did was send innocent people to jail."

J.Q. sat back, eyebrows raised, forehead crossed with deep wrinkles. "It's hard to believe, Shirley. . . ."

"It's obscene, J.Q. And it's going on all around us. Look at the talk shows. Read the newspaper. There are God knows how many people *remembering* they were abused, twenty or thirty years after the fact. It makes a good excuse for being unhappy. Somebody did something awful to me, so I'm not responsible. And, of course, it's titillating. Never mind that it's false, unscientific, harmful—it sells! We see it on the tube ten times a week, we start to believe nobody's normal but me and thee, and of thee I have my doubts."

"And what does it have to do with what happened last night?"

She took a deep breath. "Last night. Well . . . Once there's an atmosphere of general belief, it's only a short step to malicious accusation. You have an ex-husband you want to get even with? Accuse him of molesting the children. You have an old woman you'd like to get even with? Accuse her of witchcraft. You are unable to provide a motive for any of this? Accuse your enemy of satanism. How is your victim going to disprove it? The pope says it exists; he actually did an exorcism. Psychologists say it exists; they treat patients who were victims. The media says it exists!"

"You're shaking," he observed.

"I'm shaking because I'm about to become a victim, J.Q. Guess it was only a matter of time . . . I must have crossed a bridge before I came to it. I must subconsciously have known it was coming."

"What was coming?"

"Wait until we get home. Let's see if I'm right."

* * *

When they arrived back at Rancho del Valle, Shirley let them into the Big House with her master key and began searching it, room by room, looking at the walls, the furniture, the slickly sealed and waxed flagstone floors. In the front bedroom she stopped, pointing down. "There, J.Q."

He knelt, trying to see whatever she saw. "Candle wax?" He peered more closely. "Scratches. Somebody's cleaned up most of it."

"Somebody's had candles there, against that wall. There's a sooty spot, about four feet up. Look at the picture hanging on the wall—see, here, it doesn't quite fill the space it's supposed to. I think this picture is the one from the other bedroom. They must have tried different stage settings, in the bedroom, in here, then they picked this spot. Why?" She stood back, staring, then answered her own question. "Because from here you can see through the window to the gate, with the sign on it. Rancho del Valle. They wanted to take a photograph that would identify the place, so they set the stage in here, but when they cleaned up, they put the wrong picture back on the wall."

"What does the picture have to—"

"They took it down, whichever one was here, and they hung my goat skull in its place."

"Your goat skull!"

"The one I hung out on the willow tree. Dear Esther and dear Lawrence want evidence of satanism, J.Q. What makes good evidence? Photographs. So they make a kind of altar, with candles, and a goat skull hanging over it. I'll bet that's what they were up to the other evening, when they got back from Chama. Let's see if we can find what they used."

One of the bedside tables from the larger bedroom bore traces of wax.

Shirley said, "So they picked a place from which they could see the front gate, set their stage, and then took photographs, evidence there is satanism going on at this place."

"That's pretty weak!"

"It's only a part. The real evidence is a picture of a robed old woman slitting a kid's throat in the night, in the dark.

166

You show that picture to a jury, they'll think she has to be up to something evil. People don't roam around like that in the dark unless they're up to no good."

"How do they explain being there to take the picture?"

"Oh, they say they heard something. Dog, probably. They saw a procession, maybe. Heard weird singing. How do I know? I'm sure they'll think of something."

"Why?"

"We don't know why, do we? It's the same why we've been hunting all along. All this tells us is how."

"How what?" He looked exasperated. "Slow down."

"What I've been talking about, J.Q.! Witch-hunts! Malicious accusation! That's how the Brentwoods plan to get Allison back to Albany. They need to discredit us. Either she goes to live with them, or they drag us through the mud. Might even get us arrested, if they try hard enough. People down here probably believe in the devil; it's a place where everyone believes three impossible things before breakfast. Let's see what else we can find."

She went on with the search, ending with the trash basket outside the back door, which she dumped out on the bricks. A rumple of paper towels, buried deep, held a dozen candle ends and an equal number of Polaroid sheets, the black part stripped off the developing picture.

"You're my witness," she said angrily.

"How could you possibly have known . . . ?"

"It's a lot of little things. Alberta was fuming about Esther, remember. She said Esther complained about the housekeeping and wanted candles in case the power went out. I found a Luz de Nambe paper sack in the driveway. Why this need for candles? For a romantic dinner à deux? To join a religious procession? What other use is there for candles?"

"One immediately thinks of churches," J.Q. murmured.

"Well, rites at least. In that PBS documentary I saw, the quack therapist questioned the children about satanic rites and symbols. She had a book full of such stuff, including pictures of altars and candles and goats' heads. I couldn't

167

figure out why the Brentwoods came here at all. Not to see Allison. They came to scout us out, to figure out what they might use to discredit us. The satanism bit might have been decided after they got here, after they saw the goat skull hanging on the tree."

"It still sounds like an unbelievable coincidence, Shirley."

"Converging senses of reality are not coincidence. If something appears on the morning news and several people mention it during the course of the day, it isn't coincidence, it's part of what's currently happening. Like copycat crimes. Like TV violence begetting actual violence. There's no coincidence to it."

"Where did you find the sack?"

"Where their car had been parked. Maybe it got kicked under the car and they didn't see it. I threw it away. It's probably still in the trash container outside the kitchen door."

"It's only their word—"

"There are five of them, J.Q. All ready to substantiate one another. The Evanses weren't along just for fun. They were present as witnesses at least, and maybe as something more."

"They couldn't have known you'd slit the kid's throat."

"Of course not. What was already done was bad enough. All they had to do was catch you or me and the kid and the blood and the knife in the same picture. It was our knife. The one Esther borrowed."

"You're building an awful lot on a small foundation."

"It's what I do, J.Q." She said it bleakly, truthfully. Indeed, like crossing bridges before she came to them, it was what she did. "I made my living doing it, for years and years. I'm a natural-born extrapolator."

"You're wrong sometimes."

"Sometimes." She had been, occasionally.

"I wish I knew who the Evanses are."

"Me, too. The reservation was in their name. Assuming they didn't lie, we have an address and phone number for them. I have no contacts in New York who would be useful, but Roger Fetting no doubt does."

"You haven't called him in a while."

"I know. I had hoped never to have to call him again."

Roger Fetting, Shirley's onetime boss at the Bureau in D.C. was delighted to hear from her. "Given up on retirement yet?" he asked. "Thinking of coming back to work?"

"I'm an old woman, Roger. I'm invincibly retired. I've settled, like a monument. I'm up to my hips in grass."

"You wouldn't have called me if you were up to your hips in grass. Something's going on."

"I'm being set up, Roger. There's a person involved whose name, I believe, is Evans. Matthew Evans, perhaps aided and abetted by wife, Roxanne." She read off the address and phone number. "I hear from a third party he's a screenwriter. I have a hunch he's something else as well. I need to know what. And if he is a screenwriter, it might be helpful to know what he's worked on."

"Shirley, are you in trouble?"

"I don't know yet. Not certainly."

"But you think so. You smell it."

"I smell nastiness, Roger."

"That's enough. I'll call you back."

She hung up the phone and then sat looking at it. It was barely eight-thirty. The day was scarcely begun, and she felt like she'd run a marathon.

"Why don't you go back to bed," J.Q. suggested.

"That's the wrong thing to do," she murmured. "The right thing to do is ignore it, go to bed at the usual hour, get up at the usual time, and not give in."

"You've spent your entire life not giving in," he said in an exasperated voice.

"Well, it's too late to change my stripes now. Besides, I'm expecting Xanthy to call."

"They're coming back this morning?"

"She said whenever the Brentwoods left. They've left."

"Maybe Xanthy and Allison stopped at Cedar Rest again."

"I suppose." She yawned gapingly. "What needs doing?"

"I need to dispose of that dead kid."

"I need to run that robe through the washer. The blood should be soaked out by now. Damn them!"

"I know. Assuming it was them."

"Oh, it was them. The knife was from our kitchen, the one Esther borrowed last evening."

"You didn't mention it was missing before."

"I didn't think of it until just now."

He shook his head in disbelief, then stomped out of the kitchen. A few moments later Shirley saw him going by on the way to their burial ground, an arroyo they were filling in with barn sweepings, dead branches, autumn leaves, trash lumber, anything organic that would eventually break down under the thin layer of soil they pushed over it. The body of the little kid would not add much to the accumulation. She doubted it had weighed over twenty pounds. It had been a baby, still nursing. It took a certain kind of cruelty to maim an animal purposefully, cause it pain purposefully. Just as it took a special kind of cruelty to use Allison as a shuttlecock, a mere device, to get something or other. What the something or other was, she still had no idea.

The phone rang. She answered it, hearing a girl's hesitant voice as she identified herself as Zinnia, that is Zinny, Reborn. "My dad said you wanted to ask me something."

Shirley laboriously shifted mental gears and explained about Alicia Tremple. "We need to retrace what she was doing that last day or two. Did she mention anything to you about who she had come to see, or where she was going that evening?"

The girl said "um" and made noises that Shirley identified as gum-chewing sounds. That was all right. Thought was sometimes aided by mastication.

"Um," Zinny said again. "She was going to have dinner with . . . ah, somebody who needed her help, she said. She said she helped people. I mean, when I asked her what she did, she said that's what she did, was help people. I mean, that's what she worked at. I said it must be nice, and she said well, she got paid for it."

"Did she say anything more that might help us identify the person? Male? Female? Old? Young?"

"Um," more masticatory noises. "She was going to help this person do a—what's the word? Like getting in somebody's face?"

"Confrontation?"

"That's it. She was going to help this person confront somebody. Oh, she said, confront the old man. I remember, because I said it didn't sound very nice, and she said it was necessary."

Shirley tapped her front teeth with a pencil, thinking furiously. "When she said the words *old man*, how did they sound?"

"What do you mean?"

"I mean, did they sound like separate words, like an old man, or did they sound like ol' man."

"The way some women talk about their husbands, you mean? Like my ol' man?"

"Exactly."

Shirley could almost hear the head shaking doubtfully. "I don't think so. It didn't sound like anything special. Just old man, like any old man."

Shirley thanked her. It was too early to call the restaurant, to ask Al if he'd learned anything from the wait-people. She was too tired to do anything else. She slumped at the table, her head sagging onto her arms. Maybe she'd rest here, just for a few minutes, and not worry about anything.

Xanthippe, Allison, and Vancie had risen and breakfasted early, intending to pay another visit to Cedar Rest Home before returning to the ranch. Xanthippe was alone in the front seat while the girls whispered behind her. Girl talk. Unfortunately. Xanthippe felt she could have done a great deal to set matters straight, but she had played deaf for two days now and had no intention of putting herself into the situation.

". . . but they live in a garage," said Allison. "A garage, Vancie. That's no place for a baby."

". . . temporary," whispered Vancie. "Until I get a job."

"But what kind of job?" asked Allison, exasperated. "You don't know how to do anything."

"You sound like my mother!" said Vancie, lapsing into sullen silence.

Xanthy could see her face in the rearview mirror, swollen lips, reddened eyes. Not for the first time, she decried the social costs of coeducation. Girls this age ought to be locked up. Boys of any age ought to be locked up. They should not be allowed to mingle except at strictly chaperoned events until they were about twenty-four and had acquired a modicum of good sense!

"There's the home," said Allison, with what sounded suspiciously like relief.

"How come you came back today?" asked Vancie. "Didn't you see him yesterday?"

"He wasn't real . . ." Allison couldn't find a proper word to describe what he hadn't been. He hadn't been what a grandfather should be, that was one thing.

"He wasn't very alert," Xanthippe supplied. "One of the attendants suggested we return this morning. She says he's more alert in the mornings, and all the visitors have confused him recently."

"Who visits him?" Vancie wanted to know. "I thought he didn't have any family."

"Shirley and J.Q. came the other day," Allison said. "And somebody came who wanted to do a TV show, about the Two Stupes, I suppose."

The driveway came up on their right, and Xanthippe turned in beside the dark cedar hedge to a parking spot near the side door. They went through, a small bell pinging to announce their entrance. No one was in the office.

"You want to wait here?" Allison asked Vancie. "You don't need to come in. There's magazines and stuff."

172

Vancie dropped into a chair and began flipping through the magazines. Xanthy and Allison went on down the hall.

"Oh, God," said Allison in a horrified voice.

Xanthippe's head came up. Where the hall widened to make a foyer between the dining hall and large front doors, three people were seated: Esther, Lawrence, and Cheryl Brentwood. Esther and Cheryl were looking through magazines. Lawrence was tapping his fingers impatiently on a folder he held in his lap.

"They've seen us," said Allison in a panicked voice.

"Chin up," instructed Xanthippe. "We're here to visit Sheldon Maxwell, who is related to your father. That's all you know."

Allison gulped deeply and forced her shoulders back. She was into the habit of obeying Xanthippe Minging. So far, obeying Xanthippe Minging had been the right thing to do. It was probably ungrateful to wish for Shirley just now, and J.Q., but she did. Xanthippe was very nice, but she wasn't nearly as solid as they were. Shirley and J.Q. were almost as solid as her horse, Beauregard.

The elder Brentwoods' gaze slipped past, incuriously. Cheryl didn't even look up from the magazine she was perusing. With a sense of profound relief, Xanthy and Allison realized they hadn't been recognized.

"Down this way," murmured Xanthippe, making a left turn where the corridor widened and leading Allison purposefully toward the large front doors.

"Oh, Mrs. Minging," came an eager voice from behind them. "This way."

Jaw set, Xanthy turned. The nice young woman who had greeted them the day before was on duty this morning. Ellen Fleshman, beaming at them. How fortuitous.

"Nice to see you again, Allison," she said, bubbling. "Come meet these other people. I think they must be related to you."

The two were escorted back to the seated trio, where they took part in a stiff exchange.

"Aunt Esther? What are you doing here? And Cheryl." Allison almost made it sound spontaneous.

Ums. Ahs.

"We heard via the grapevine. . . ." said Esther, red-faced, obviously uncomfortable.

"I thought you were supposed to be up at Chama," snarled Cheryl.

"What are you doing here?" demanded Allison.

"We . . . ah . . . understood a man here might be related to you . . . your father. Don't know for sure, of course . . ." said Lawrence stiffly.

"Why do you care if somebody here is related to me?" challenged Allison, being direct. "You haven't been interested in me and you didn't like my father."

Lawrence turned an ugly red. "One wants to be sure family is well cared for. Including even you, my dear. We've heard some disturbing things."

"Which I'm sure you'll want to take up with Allison's attorney," said Xanthy, plunging in.

"Yes," said Allison, throwing herself headlong after Xanthippe. "I guess my attorney had better take care of anything you've heard."

Esther, sneering: "And what's your attorney's name, little miss?"

"Pascal Yesney," Allison said, without a moment's hesitation. "In Santa Fe."

An exchange of glances. A tightening of jaws. Lawrence rose, now holding inconspicuously along his side the folder that had been on his lap. Legal length, Xanthippe noted. Something he'd brought along here? For what reason except to have Sheldon Maxwell look at it, maybe sign it. How very interesting.

"I think we'll delay our business to another time," he murmured, spending one more chilly smile on Allison. "Have a nice visit with your . . . relative."

They went off, out the big front doors, down the front walk, and through the gate in the hedge, across the street where they'd parked.

174

"Is there anyone else in the car?" Xanthippe asked. "Can you see, Allison?"

"A man and a woman. Those other people," she replied. "The Evanses."

A great pushing of chairs and stumble of feet brought them back to their duty. Sheldon Maxwell came out of the dining room on Ellen Fleshman's arm.

"Hello there," he said clearly. "You were here yesterday."

"That's right," Allison replied. "We came to ask you about my father."

He looked confused. Ellen led him to the couch they had occupied during their last visit, and he sagged into it. "Your father? Who was your father?"

"Charles Maxwell," Allison replied.

"Charley," mused the old man. "I told Hardin once I told him a dozen times, that boy's just no good."

"I know," Allison said stoutly. "I just want to know are you my grandpa?"

Confusion overcame him. He looked around, reached out for Ellen's hand. "Me?" he asked in a faltering voice. "Me?"

"Are you my grandpa?"

"Now there," said Ellen, patting Sheldon's hand. "Isn't that interesting. You think he may be your father's father? I guess you never knew him, did you?"

"She never did," said Xanthy, watching Allison's expressionless face. "Or maybe when you were a very little girl, Allison. Before Charles Maxwell and his family left Albuquerque."

"You're Charley's girl?" The old man was following this with a good deal of difficulty, but he was following it. "She's not the TV people."

"No, Mr. Maxwell. The TV people left."

"The people who were here just now?" demanded Xanthy. "What do they have to do with TV?"

It was Ellen who answered. "I understood they needed the rights to some old films of Mr. Maxwell's, his and his

175

brother's. They need the rights to do a TV show. They're going to give him a thousand dollars for the rights. Isn't that right, Mr. Maxwell?"

"Don't want to," he said, his voice slipping into a childish register. "Don't want to sell."

Ellen shook her head. "There now. We've upset him all over again."

Xanthy put her hand on the younger woman's arm. "Ellen, I would suggest most strongly that you not allow Mr. Maxwell to sign anything at all. Particularly anything conveying property that might have been partly his brother's. His brother may have left a will, and if there is such property, this young woman may have an interest in it."

"Well, I wouldn't let him do any such thing, now," Ellen said, affronted. "I didn't know he had any kinfolk. I don't think Mr. Maxwell knew either. He didn't know until those folks told him."

"What did they tell him?"

"That they were responsible for his granddaughter. That they needed the money to provide for her."

Allison opened her mouth, about to wax indignant, when the old man interrupted her.

"But Charley was Hardin's boy," the old man wavered. "Why don't people pay attention. I'm not anybody's grandpa. Charley was Hardin's boy."

6

I⊤ was almost noon when Xanthy and Allison returned home to find Shirley still seated at the kitchen table, head on arms, sound asleep. Xanthy shook her gently.

"Wake up. We have something to tell you."

She came blearily upright, blinking, trying to focus on them. "Lord. What time is it? I have to call—"

"Not right now, dear. Allison, get Shirley a cup of coffee." Xanthy herself found a clean dishcloth, dampened it, and gave it to Shirley to wipe her face and eyes.

"I passed out," Shirley said. "It was a wild night."

"We had a wild morning," offered Allison. "Aunt Esther and Uncle Lawrence were at the nursing home. They were trying to get Great-Uncle Sheldon to sign a paper."

"Great-Uncle!"

Allison said, "That's what Xanthy says he is."

Xanthy nodded. "Charley Maxwell wasn't Sheldon's son. He was Hardin's son."

"But the pharmacist said . . . Oh. He didn't really, did he?"

Xanthy agreed. "The pharmacist said that Charley was Stupe Maxwell's son. But they were both Stupe Maxwell."

"And the Brentwoods were there! Why?"

Xanthy sat down and folded her hands neatly before her, ready to expound.

"It probably has something to do with Evans being a screenwriter. Ellen Fleshman, the woman at the home, told us the Brentwoods wanted to buy Sheldon's rights to the Two Stupes material. I've noticed lately that many of the television movies are quasi-biographical, what some producers no doubt regard as foolproof. If someone is interested in doing a film about the Two Stupes, they would need story rights or rights to the old tapes. Any attempt to get such rights would have begun with the Maxwell brothers in Albuquerque and have led from them to the Brentwoods."

Shirley nodded. It made some sense. Hardin's rights would have gone to Charles, Charles's rights would have gone to Allison. If Allison had money and the Brentwoods had custody of Allison, they'd no doubt be able to siphon off some of it.

Xanthy went on, "The Brentwoods were most unhappy to see me and Allison at the nursing home. I'm positive they counted on keeping the relationship secret."

"They must have visited Sheldon at Cedar Rest before they came here," Shirley remarked. "He was talking about TV people when J.Q. and I were there. Though maybe that was the Evanses."

"Who are the Evanses?" Allison asked.

Xanthy shook her head. "All we really know is what Mrs. Fley told Shirley, that he says he's a screenwriter."

Shirley sipped at the coffee Allison had provided. "Lawrence and Esther must estimate the rights being worth a good deal, or they wouldn't be going to all this trouble."

"It's only worth it if they've got me in their clutches," Allison cried dramatically. "They should know better! I'd never go with them. Never in a million years."

"You sound like a soap-opera heroine," Xanthippe said disapprovingly. "Settle down."

Shirley felt her face sag. Inside, everything dwindled to a bright point of light and vanished, leaving her in darkness.

"Shirley?" Xanthy was beside her. "What is it?"

The sound was there, but not the sight. Shirley took a deep breath. The darkness wavered, grayed, vanished, all at once. She shook her head, testing, being sure the world would be still. "I'm not sure, Xanthy. It's happened a couple of times recently. Sort of a dizzy spell. I think it's just that I'm tired and I'm frazzled, and I keep feeling panicky and breathless and almost passing out."

"You said it had been a wild night? What happened?"

Shirley told them, starting with her meeting with Elaine Scott and continuing into the wee hours of the morning, minimizing it where she could. She couldn't minimize the death of Isabel's kid.

"Isabel's baby," cried Allison, tears on her cheeks. "Oh, that's rotten."

"Cruel and barbaric," said Xanthy. "You're sure of all this, Shirley? You're not . . . well, imagining it?"

Shirley growled, not at all amused. "You mean, am I having drug-induced fancies? I don't think that goes with what I've been taking. No, I'm not imagining it! Ask J.Q. He's about as fanciful as a barn door, and he saw and heard everything I did. I called Roger Fetting and asked him to find out about Evans."

"It's hard to imagine any of the Brentwoods would have maimed the little thing," said Xanthy, with distaste. "They're far too fastidious."

"She is. And the daughter's useless, but he might get dirty once in a while."

Xanthippe shook her head, pursing her lips. "Shirley, quite frankly, dear, I think all this satanism business is quite farfetched and unlikely. Was it talking with Mrs. Scott that gave you this idea?"

Shirley put her head in her hands, closed her eyes, and

179

concentrated on being comprehensible. "You and J.Q. are just too damned reasonable, Xanthy! It seems unlikely to the two of you because you're so rational and skeptical and well educated you don't believe in witches or satanism, and you can't see why anyone else would either. The fact is other people, millions of other people, do believe in those things."

"Surely you're not saying the Brentwoods actually believe you're a witch!"

"Of course not! They know I'm not a real witch. I don't have to be a real witch, so long as they can accuse me of it. If a lot of people believe in witchcraft, the accusation is enough. If enough people believe in UFOs, writers don't really need to be picked up by aliens, the allegation is enough. People can be the center of attention just by claiming it happened. Those ridiculous people in the so-called psychic network know they're not really clairvoyant. It's the carny of the nineties, Xanthy! It's pure snake oil.

"No, the Brentwoods believe in the same thing the psychics and the psychologists and the channelers and talk-show hosts believe in. Money! They're quite willing to pretend I'm a witch if it will get them some."

Her voice was weary, dragging its way into silence. It was hard even to care.

Xanthy patted her shoulder. "Why don't you go back to your room and get some sleep? I'll fix some lunch for Allison and me, and I'll check to be sure Big House is ready for the young men."

"I've got to let Pascal Yesney know about this," Shirley objected. "I've got to tell him what's . . ." She gaped, unable to control the yawn.

"I'll call him and tell him," Xanthy said firmly. "You go. You're going to drop."

Shirley went obediently back to her room, lay down upon the bed. Sleepiness departed as quickly as it had come. She stared at the ceiling, counting the beams left to right, then counting them again right to left. There were fourteen. Between the beams were splits of cedar, laid herringbone fashion. Too many of those to count.

Her knee hurt. She propped it on a pillow. She shut her eyes and resolved to keep them closed, whatever happened. Time went by. She wasn't asleep. Outside in the driveway, Dog barked her people-arriving bark, sotto voce but quite audible, even here at the back of the house. The sound entered through the one window in the hallway, then used the hallway itself as an echo chamber, the noise echoing along to each of the rooms.

Dog was welcoming someone she recognized. Shirley sat up, got up, ran a comb through her hair, and limped out onto the patio. Cally, Rob, and Harry were standing at the gate, talking with Xanthy and J.Q. Shirley went to join the group, ignoring Xanthy's exasperated look.

"We were just telling Mrs. Minging the sad story of Cally's new job," said Rob, offering his hand.

Shirley took it, nodded. "His work is delayed or something?"

"He was due to start work on a movie," said Harry, turning his thin face toward Shirley, with a haunted smile.

Cally nodded. "The star and the director are at loggerheads. There is rumor of the dismissal of the one or the resignation of the other. The director wishes to replace the star because she has gone off somewhere to sulk and can't even be found to negotiate with. People have been looking for her for over a week. Things are at sixes and sevens. Though I've never understood what that means."

"It concerns playing dice," said Xanthy. "A quotation of Swift, I believe."

"Remarkable," said Harry. "A fount of wisdom."

Xanthy said loftily, "Merely a head full of bits and tags. So, you're back for a week?"

"Thereabouts. Rob and I are working our way back to normal." Harry smiled politely, took Rob by the arm, and went off toward the pool. Xanthy and J.Q. went back inside, leaving Shirley leaning on the wall beside Cally.

"Harry's gotten over it, somewhat," said Cally. "He's doing a lot better lately."

"What's Harry gotten over?" Shirley asked, puzzled.

"What we all spend our lives getting over, I should think. Grief. Regret, maybe. Sorrow. Harry's twin brother, Martin, died not long ago. They were very close. Such a useless death. Harry keeps saying it should have been him, and it should have been, he's the one with AIDS. Martin was perfectly healthy. There was absolutely nothing wrong with him. He should have lived for decades."

"What did he die of?"

"Suicide. He and his lover, both."

"Why?"

"Oh, Martin's friend was having all kinds of personal and family difficulties, topped off by a positive HIV test. Martin thought that if his friend had it, he had it. It was the final straw, so far as Martin was concerned. He knew how Harry has suffered, month after month, in and out of the hospital. Martin didn't choose to go through the same thing. So he and his friend got in the car and turned on the engine inside a closed garage."

"Ugly," Shirley said. "But understandable."

"Maybe so, if he'd actually had a positive HIV. The autopsy established that he didn't, it had been a false positive. Harry is suing the lab, much good may it do him. It was one of those fly-by-night setups that pay doctors a kickback on every patient referred to them and then get rich by double-billing the insurance companies."

"I'm sorry."

"It happens."

"Perhaps there'll be a cure in time for Harry."

"I'm not sure there'll ever be a cure. Used to be, ten years ago, we could believe there was a cure just around the corner. That kept a lot of people hoping. Then we got angry; we believed the epidemic was being allowed to happen, that there would be a cure if there were just enough money and effort put into it, and we all got into the whole political and awareness bit, all the way from subtle to outrageous. Now even the activists are beginning to realize it isn't necessarily lack of funding or lack of effort, that people are working very hard and honestly just can't find a cure."

"I've always wondered why strict quarantine wasn't tried," Shirley said. "We've done it before, with other diseases. . . ."

"Well, now, looking back, we should have, of course, but no one would have held still for that at the time. We were all too proud! We were brought up on the wonders and advancements of American science. We didn't realize there was anything science couldn't do. We thought we had a right to live as we liked and the world had an obligation to make it safe."

"An interesting observation, if true," Shirley said thoughtfully.

"Haven't we been taught that? Some mountain climber gets stranded on a cliff, we spend hundreds of thousands rescuing him. Some skier gets lost; some pilot flies his tiny little plane into the side of a mountain where he shouldn't have been in the first place. Foolish people do idiotically dangerous, even deadly things, and we break our necks getting them out of it. It's the same thing here. We thought the world would rescue us, but it hasn't." He frowned, rubbing his temples with his fingers, as though to soothe some suddenly felt pain.

"But you still hope," she said softly.

Cally shook his head. "A lot of people are losing hope; and when they lose hope, they do what Martin and Kevin did and leave people like Harry to grieve over them."

"It's nice of you to keep him company."

He smiled ruefully. "It's not all altruism. We can't start the shoot until the star shows up."

"Who is the star?"

He mentioned a name. "She has a house here, as a matter of fact. In Santa Fe."

"Working with her must be exciting for you."

"It is, rather. She's a wonderful actress, perfectly believable, no matter what she's playing."

"Well, for whatever reason you've come back, we're glad to have you." So much rather have Cally and crew than the Brentwoods, the mysterious Evanses, the strange crazy lady. "Is Alberta finished with the house?"

"She said to give her an hour," Cally replied. "We're going to loll out by the pool." He raised a hand in farewell and went off after the others.

As Shirley came into the kitchen Xanthippe remarked, "I take it you couldn't sleep? We should have left you at the kitchen table."

Shirley shrugged. "It's okay, Xanthy. That hour or so asleep on the kitchen table was better than I've done for a couple of days. Did you call Yesney for me?"

"He wasn't in, but I left a message. His service said he'd be calling in about two."

"Did you notice how awful Harry looks. Cally says he has AIDS."

"He has that haggard look," agreed Xanthy. "I asked, quite thoughtlessly, how he and Rob were able to get additional time off. He said he was on sick leave, and Rob had taken time off to keep him company."

"What do they do?"

"They work for something called Medi-clerk, Inc."

"And what's that?" demanded Shirley.

J.Q. looked at her over the top of his reading glasses. "It's a franchise operation. They provide basic clerical services for physicians and clinics. They do the insurance forms, the patient billings; they do payroll and keep tax records. All the nonmedical clerical work."

"How do you know that?"

"Article about it in the *Journal* a few weeks back." He turned a page. "Hadn't thought about it before, but it's odd. We do seem to be up to our ears in the health-care field, don't we?"

Xanthy gave him a curious look. "Really?"

"Well, seems so. The Tremple woman, and Dr. Fley—"

"She is a doctor!" exclaimed Shirley.

"Was," said J.Q. "Didn't I tell you? No, I guess I didn't. Her husband says she retired a couple of years back. She doesn't call herself a doctor because she doesn't want to hear about people's symptoms. She wasn't in practice, she was an academic, her husband says. But you were right, she was . . . I guess still is an M.D."

"Mrs. Tremple. Dr. Fley. And the gentlemen in Big House," mused Shirley. "How's that for coincidence, J.Q.?"

"Since about half the people in the country work for the health-care system, probably not."

"I had a thought while I was in there trying to sleep," Shirley said. "Coincidentally."

"About what?"

"Alicia Tremple had some paperback books, newly purchased. They were things about Indians—legends, religious beliefs, symbolism. There was a bookmark, one of those cardboard ones with the bookstore name on it. Books of the Southwest. I thought we might run into town and ask if they remember her. On the way back, we could stop at El Nido for lunch. If you haven't had lunch."

"I haven't had lunch, no. I'll need to clean up a little. I'm all over soot."

"What have you been doing?" Xanthy asked, peering at his black-stained hands and arms. "Cleaning out a fireplace?"

"Only in a manner of speaking. I was cleaning that place out front of Ditch House where the crazy lady had her bonfire. Vincente showed no interest in it, so I decided to do it myself."

"She was burning all kinds of things," Shirley remarked dully. "I remember a diary."

"Yeah, the looseleaf rings were there. Lots of metal bits and strips, too."

"She said she was getting rid of her past, or something like that," Shirley commented. "I suggested she use one of the barbecues, and she said that would be the wrong context."

185

"Well, the actual context is a sizable burned spot that I've just reseeded. While I was down at the hardware store, getting the grass seed, I saw Emil going into the Pueblo gambling hall."

"They let him out?"

"According to him, they did. On his own recognizance."

"Who around here recognizes him?" Shirley demanded.

"A lot of people, evidently. About three people spoke to him while he was talking to me."

"I thought she said she picked him up in Albuquerque," Shirley remarked. "The crazy lady. Tanya. Tanya . . . Roth."

"She may have, but he's either been here in the past or he makes friends quickly."

Shirley started to ask something else, but the phone rang in the kitchen.

"That may be your attorney," said Xanthy.

It was. Shirley filled him in on what Xanthy had learned, what she herself had seen, and what she supposed concerning the Brentwoods' motivation.

"Sounds like fiction," said the lawyer.

"Might be," Shirley admitted. "A lot of it is guesswork."

"You really think they're the kind of people who might accuse you of . . . being a nut?"

"Oh, sure," she said with a twinge of discomfort. "Even people who know me quite well sometimes consider me a nut. Not this kind of nut, however."

"You're finding out who this Evans character is?"

"A contact of mine is finding out."

"Contact as in law enforcement. Or contact as in VIP."

"Both," she replied after a moment's consideration.

"I can check Hardin Maxwell's will, if any. This also gives me some additional ammunition I can use to reply to Brentwood's suit. This friend of yours, she's pretty sure the Brentwoods were surprised to see Allison at the hospital? Unpleasantly surprised, that is?"

"Xanthippe Minging is quite sure they were unpleasantly surprised. They left immediately, without mentioning the paper they wanted signed. If the young woman who works there hadn't mentioned it to Xanthippe, we wouldn't have known."

"Since you and the girl both know what he's up to, you're less vulnerable than you would have been otherwise."

"Well, if blackmail was in their minds, they can disabuse themselves of that notion."

"And you're prepared for these strange allegations you think they're going to make?"

"Quite prepared, Mr. Yesney."

"Pasc, please. All right. That's enough to go on for now."

When Shirley went back outside, Xanthy told her that J.Q. had gone to clean up. He'd be ready in a few moments. "Though I think you'd be better off getting some sleep."

"Oh, I think so, too," Shirley said angrily. "Shall I go back on the little blue pills, Xanthy? I always slept very well on the little blue pills!"

Xanthy shook her head, dismayed. "Of course not. You're really doing very well. It's just, I worry about you."

Shirley growled and muttered, sufficiently worried about herself not to need additional worrying. "Where's Allison? I haven't seen her since you two got back."

"She and Vancie are exchanging confidences. They had several long talks over the weekend. I must say, Shirley, Allison has a very good head. She's wasting it on Vancie, however. The girl is incapable of seeing beyond her infatuation with this thoroughly irresponsible-sounding boy."

"You eavesdropped?"

"I did not. I did not sneak about. I merely pretended more interest in my driving or reading than was actually the case."

"What's the story?"

"Vancie's mother is working one full-time and one part-time job trying to support herself and her two children. Though her husband was an unregenerate womanizer— Vancie admits as much, though not in those words—Vancie

187

believes Mom should not have thrown him out. Because Mom threw him out, all of what followed is Mom's fault."

"Naturally. Tell me, has Vancie ever heard of AIDS? She obviously never heard of contraception!"

"Vancie needs a mature male in her life, she says, quoting her high-school counselor as though everything uttered by said counselor were a prescription, not an opinion. So she took up with a dropout, Tommy, who's mature by virtue of being eighteen instead of fifteen. Vancie is now determined to have his baby. She sees no reason she should not live with him and his three friends in the garage they are currently inhabiting."

"Three male friends?"

"So it seems. They sleep on the floor. They do not cook, preferring to live on fast foods, which they get by begging, or by a little thievery. At least one of them is on drugs, though Vancie claims her boyfriend is not."

"Allison got this out of her?"

"Oh, this and a lot more. She did a marvelous job of eliciting information. Vancie knows the facts, but she can't see the implications. Fact is meaningless to her. She's lost in a romantic haze."

"Must have been no fun for you," Shirley said in an apologetic voice. "I'm sorry you were saddled with it."

"It's more or less old stuff, so far as I'm concerned," Xanthy replied. "Even though we had a very fine student body at Crepmier, there would occasionally be the odd precocious boy or girl, set on sex at an early age and impossible to dissuade." She sighed. "Speak of the devil."

Shirley turned, to see Allison and Vancie approaching across the parking area.

Xanthy ducked for the kitchen door. Shirley stayed where she was. Allison's face was set, her jaw determined.

"Shirley, can we talk to you?"

It was obviously not Vancie's idea. She was looking everywhere except at Shirley.

"About what?" Shirley asked.

"Vancie is pregnant. She wants to have the baby and live

with her boyfriend." Allison threw a glance in Vancie's direction, then plowed on, telling Shirley a little of what she had just heard from Xanthy. "And I keep telling her she's crazy. Will you tell her?"

Shirley turned away with a sigh, gesturing at the girls to come along. They sat at the patio table, the umbrella turned to give them a spot of shade. Shirley examined the face across from her: Vancie set in concrete. Adamantine Vancie.

Well, why not?

"I don't see any reason she shouldn't marry him and live with him if she really wants to," said Shirley.

Vancie's head came up, eyes glittering.

"But since she's too young to marry without her family's consent, I think she will have to prove to her family that she's thought it through."

"You see!" cried Vancie. "I told you!"

"Right." Shirley nodded. "My guess is, you just haven't focused on the details yet, Vancie. Maybe I can help you with that."

Allison looked at her as though betrayed.

"Really, Allison. We just need to help Vancie focus on the details so she can demonstrate to her family that she knows what she's doing. Now, let's take an example: Suppose you're ready to bring the baby home from the hospital. As I understand the situation, you're going to be living in a garage with four other people, so you have to plan carefully. Where will the baby sleep?"

Vancie focused her eyes and said, "Uh . . . in a crib."

"Fine. That's good. Now, where will you get the crib?"

"I'll buy it," the girl said.

"Where will you get the money to buy it?"

"I'll get a job."

"That's good. That's the place to start. That's something your mother needs to know, that you intend to support yourself and your baby. At your age, you'll be working for around four dollars per hour, that's a hundred sixty a week, full-time."

"That's a lot," said Vancie. "That's plenty."

"Oh, yes. Lots of people live on less than that. They're very poor, but they manage. Being poor is hard. You have to be very brave to live in poverty. You may decide you can't afford a crib, not even a used one. In that case, the baby can sleep in a cardboard box. Now, because you're pregnant, you'll need good food. Is there a kitchen in the garage where you'll be living? No? Well, that makes it harder, because you'll have to buy prepared food. What really makes it hard, you'll probably have to buy food for five people, for you and Tommy and the other three guys, because you'll be the only one working. Food for five people will take most of your paycheck—"

"I'm not feeding them," said Vancie.

"Well, I know you won't want to. But they're Tommy's friends, and if you're living there, you'll almost have to."

"I'll eat at home. At Mom's."

Shirley shook her head thoughtfully. "That's not fair, Vancie. It's not fair to expect your mom to feed you or another child if you're not living there. She's worked hard to provide for you. If you're making your own decisions now, then you have to live by them. You can't do it sort of halfway."

Vancie frowned. Shirley sailed on, taking no notice.

"Then there's medical expenses. Have you thought about the doctor bills, when the baby comes? And the prenatal care? You'll need three or four thousand dollars, just to get the baby born. How many weeks' wages is that?"

"That's more than twenty weeks' wages, right there," Allison offered.

"How had you planned to pay the doctor, Vancie?"

"There's a clinic," she mumbled. "You don't have to pay if you don't have any money."

"But if you do have money, you have to pay, right. And you said you were going to get a job?"

"Well, then, I won't get a job," she snapped.

"Then you won't have money to buy food for yourself and Tommy."

Vancie looked away. "I'll get welfare."

Shirley shook her head. "I don't think they'll give it to you if you live like that, in a garage, with four men. I think at your age, they'll put you in a home with some other girls who have babies. So if you want to live with Tommy, you'll have to work. And that brings up another detail, what are you going to do with the baby while you're working?"

"He . . . Tommy can baby-sit."

"Well, if he agrees to that. There are three other people there, however. How are they going to feel about this? They may not be willing to have a baby there twenty-four hours a day. Babies cry a lot, sometimes all night, and it gets some men really uptight. You read about it all the time, some male friend of the mother kills the baby because it wouldn't stop crying, and then they lock up both him and the mother for child neglect. Even if Tommy will baby-sit every day, he'll be tired of it at night. He'll want to go out with his friends, so you'll have to figure on staying alone with the baby every night. Or maybe he could get a night job? Have you talked about his getting a job?"

Vancie stared through her, two tiny wrinkles between her eyes. "He tried. He couldn't find anything he liked."

"Well, so you'll have to work all day, then take care of the baby at night while Tommy has a little social life."

For the first time Vancie looked vaguely concerned. "I could ask my mom to baby-sit. . . ."

"It wouldn't be fair to ask your mom to do that, not when she works all day, not when she's had such a hard time providing for herself and you kids. No, I think your moving out will be nice for her, it'll take the pressure off. For the first time in a long time she'll have a little money and time of her own, won't she? She and your brother can have a few things they couldn't have before. Your getting out of the house and supporting yourself is going to make life a lot easier for her. It'll be a hard adjustment, but you're young. Young people can work all day and stay up with babies all night and hardly notice it."

191

Vancie seemed mesmerized, deep in consideration of some obviously new idea.

Shirley nodded. "Now, there's a lot we haven't even mentioned yet. We need to figure out every detail, so no matter what questions your mother asks, you'll have an answer for her. It's not going to be any fun for you, I'm afraid. . . ."

Vancie flushed again, brick red. "That's what he said!"

"Who? Tommy said that? Well, he's right. It's not going to be any fun for you at all, but if it's what you want, then it's what you should do. All it takes is concentration and determination and years and years of really hard work. Washing diapers, for instance."

"I'll use disposable diapers!"

"A hundred and fifty dollars a month," said Allison, almost gleefully. A warning glance from Shirley made her change her tone to one of pure sweetness. "I know, because some people I baby-sat for up in Columbine complained about paying that much every month for diapers."

Shirley said, "Things are so darned expensive! Think of that! A fourth of your pay, just for diapers."

"Shirley, are you ready to go?" asked J.Q.

She turned, blinked. He was standing there, clean shirt, clean jeans, ready to depart.

"Of course, J.Q." She got up, wavering for a moment as she bent the steel knee back and forth, trying to make it feel like flesh. "You and Vancie discuss it, Allison. The more details you figure out, the better."

She stalked off, J.Q. trailing along. When she glanced over her shoulder, he was trying not to laugh.

"Don't you dare," she told him. "We're working very hard to plan Vancie's life."

"You've put Allison up to something."

"Consideration of detail, J.Q. That's all. It isn't the big things that crack us and break us. It's the little ones. It's the diapers and the all-night crying and the no TV and the sleeping on the floor. Nature, in order to assure propagation of the species, has provided us with a sexual urge that's strongest among those least able to resist it. When we're that age, we can take a mate, get ourselves pregnant, have a baby, all in a rosy haze of unsee."

"Hormonal, of course," he remarked.

"Of course. Only old age or cynicism can outwit it. Maybe Allison is cynical enough to do it for Vancie."

"I wouldn't count on it."

"I never would, J.Q."

On the ride into town Shirley thought back to the books Alicia Tremple had left in Frog House. While she could remember only one title, all the covers had been distinctive enough that she thought she could pick them off a shelf.

This proved to be the case when they arrived upstairs at Books of the Southwest. While J.Q. wandered happily among history and biography, Shirley went to the area labeled MYSTICISM AND SPIRITUALITY, picked out three books, and spread them on the cashier's counter.

"A woman named Alicia Tremple died here in Santa Fe last week. Several days before, she came in here and picked out copies of these three books. We're trying to reconstruct her last few days. Where she went, who she was with."

The young woman toyed with the braid that dangled across one shoulder, a very decorative plait, twined with leather thongs and turquoise beads, plumed with a feather at the end. "What did she look like?"

"Thin to the point of emaciation. Black hair. Probably in a high-collared, long-sleeved dress."

"I do remember her. She was here with her mother."

"Her ... I'm sorry. Her mother died many years ago."

"Really." The young woman became thoughtful. "I just assumed, I guess. It was a woman old enough to be her mother. No, come to think of it, it would not have been her mother, because she—the older one—was asking the thin one about her work. She said, 'It sounds fascinating.' A mother wouldn't say that, would she? *My* mother wouldn't. A mother would say, 'Why do you put up with that?' or 'If you'll take my advice ...' "

193

"Did she buy anything? The older woman?"

"I can't remember. I do remember the thin one buying copies of these paperbacks. They're not the good ones."

"Not good ones?"

"Not scholarly ones. These are fringy stuff. Books about Indian spirituality and symbolism, written by gushy Anglos. Oh, she also bought a set of cards, like tarot cards, with Indian symbols on them, all mixed up, some Pueblo symbols and some Plains Indian and some northwestern—Kwakiutl or Aleut—with a guide to tell you how to tell your fortune the Indian way. Never mind that Native Americans do not tell fortunes. They were the kind of books the nuts go for."

"I might be one of them," said Shirley.

"No, you're not. You don't have the manner. But the black-haired lady did. She homed right in on what I call the junk shelf. I don't even like carrying the stuff, but we have to. We like to specialize in the authoritative books, anthropology and history and religion. We buy very carefully. But some people see the ad, they think southwestern means chewing peyote and sitting around naked, banging on drums. We have to carry some books like that, or we wouldn't make the rent. Actually, that kind of thing belongs in the crystal shops. Where Shirley MacLaine goes."

"People really sit around naked, banging drums?" asked J.Q.

She laughed. "The other day one tourist woman went out to Tesuque and took all her clothes off so she could lie on the ground and commune with Indian spirits, never mind that Indian spirits wouldn't commune with a naked person because nakedness isn't respectful. A couple of the pueblos are thinking of shutting the tourists out completely. People don't know how to behave. Foreigners, particularly. The Taos people say the French and Germans are the worst."

"They've had more practice than the rest of us," said Shirley. "They've had hundreds of years to perfect an absolutely insular rudeness. The Germans consider their interest to be in everyone's interest, and the French consider their culture to be so superior that no other is worthy of consideration."

"Well, the people who live at Taos pueblo are sick of the tourists invading their homes and taking pictures without permission and tramping around on their burial grounds."

Shirley brought them back to the subject at hand. "So, you sold her these books, and a set of tarot cards with . . . ah, Native American motifs."

"Right, and then she and the older woman left."

"When was this, do you have any idea?"

The young woman went to a card file and flipped through it. "Spirits, spirits ancestral, spirits of the earth, here it is. Spirit deck. The last set of those cards I sold came off inventory last—let me see, what day—Tuesday a week ago."

"What time of day?"

"The two women were here about noon. I remember, because when they left, I did, too. I was starved. I put the sign out, the one that says back in a minute, and I went over to the plaza to pick up something for lunch."

"You were here alone?"

"I was that day. My partner was sick."

Shirley thanked her by adding a Smithsonian volume about southwestern Indians to J.Q.'s selections, and they strolled back to the car for the drive to Tesuque. "Tesuque the village," Shirley specified. "Not Tesuque the pueblo. We will not invade the privacy of Tesuque the pueblo."

"Do you suppose that was true, about the naked lady?" J.Q. asked.

"I'm sure it was. Seems to me there was something in the paper about it. Also about the tourists at Taos, the ones who can't or won't read the notices about no photography and then get upset when the pueblo authorities confiscate their film. I know how irritating photographers can be. We had that German lady staying in the Little House, a month or so ago, remember her?"

"Frau Schmidt."

"That wasn't her name, but it should have been. She

came onto the patio, even though it says private on the gate, and started snapshotting me. I told her to stop it. She wanted to know why not. I said because I didn't like it. She was dumbfounded that anything she wanted to do might be subject to someone else's approval."

"You were being obstreperous, as usual," muttered J.Q.

She nodded. "My obstreperosity is purely personal, but the pueblos are in an ambiguous situation. They need the tourist dollars, but they want to maintain their cultures and observe their religions. The two aims are not always congruent."

"Gambling may give them a way out. They'll take a lot of money from the Hispanics and Anglos through bingo and electronic poker, enough that they won't need other income, and that'll let them put the pueblos off limits. Poetic justice. Anglo and Hispanic greed turned to Native American advantage for a change. Whoops. Here's the turnoff."

J.Q. pulled the car to the right, and they went away from the highway, down into the village gently set into the bosque along the Tesuque River, under a generous umbrella of old cottonwoods and pines that sheltered one general store cum restaurant, and one restaurant cum nothing else at all.

Shirley spotted their previous informant the moment they went through the door. "Al, wasn't it?"

"Still is," he said. "You're the lady who wanted to know about the woman who died."

"I am."

"I did find out that Jake served them, and he's filling in for someone, so he's here early today. I'll see if I can break him loose for a minute."

"Or, give us a table where he can wait on us," suggested Shirley. "We haven't had lunch yet."

He glanced at his watch. "If we hurry, I can get you in under the wire." He led the way back through the bar, into the dining room, where he seated them at a table set for four before approaching a mustached waiter. He indicated their table, and the waiter came over.

196

"I'm Jake," he said as he handed them menus. "If you want lunch, let me get the order in right away."

They ordered. Steamed mussels. J.Q. asked for a glass of wine. Shirley passed. She felt too delicately poised to unsettle anything.

The mussels arrived, impossibly plump and delicious. "They're good, aren't they?" Jake asked, moving an ashtray to make room for an empty bowl. "Here's a bowl for the shells. They're ranch mussels. We don't buy the wild kind anymore. The wild kind, there's too much pollution. Back in a minute."

Shirley nodded at Jake's back, for the moment feeling peaceful and well cared for. She hadn't had seafood so good in a very long time. All the current worries could be set aside for a moment.

But only for a moment. Jake was back, sliding into the seat opposite Shirley.

"Al said you wanted to know about the skinny lady? She was here for dinner a week ago. Tuesday night. I remember her. She sat right over there." He indicated a corner table. "She wanted some aspirin, for her headache. She was with a young woman, I thought maybe her daughter, but then maybe not. They looked something alike, though."

"What did they eat?"

"Not much. She ordered the grilled marinated chicken breast with the sweet-red-pepper sauce. Ate maybe two bites. The younger woman had chicken enchiladas, and she didn't eat much either. They were talking about something upsetting. Mouths all pinched up. You know. Like they tasted something sour."

Shirley nodded. "You didn't see them leave? Didn't notice the car?"

"From in here? I don't see anything until it's time to go home. There aren't any windows, and the smoke's so thick sometimes you can cut it."

It was true. Some walls were painted with a semblance of arched windows, but they were only decorative.

"And you didn't hear what they were talking about?"

"Only about her headache. She said she'd taken some aspirin an hour or two before, but it hadn't helped. She wanted more. I got her some from the bar, but those didn't help either. She just pushed her plate away, and as soon as the other woman finished her coffee, they left."

"Credit card?" suggested J.Q.

"Cash," he replied. "The younger woman gave me a fifty. They didn't have any drinks, their bill was only twenty something, so it was a nice tip. She didn't wait, just put the money on the table and they went."

Shirley thanked him, and he departed, returning from time to time to refill glasses and take away the empty plates.

"So, where are we?" J.Q. wanted to know as they started for home.

"Alicia Tremple was out by the mailboxes at ten in the morning. Somebody old enough to be her mother picked her up and took her to the bookshop, maybe had lunch with her, then returned her to the ranch, where Reborn picked her up a little later. He dropped her in Tesuque, where she had supper with someone young enough to be her daughter. How old was she? Tremple?"

"What did her driver's license say?"

"She was forty-six."

"So the morning person was sixty to seventy-something; the evening person was twenty to thirty-something."

"Takes in a lot of ground," he murmured.

"How did she get home?"

"Presumably her supper companion dropped her at the ranch."

"Let's ask when we get back. Let's see if anyone noticed. Both the Fleys and the Stevenses were there last Tuesday."

"So were the men in Big House."

"The men couldn't have seen her. Harry and Rob drove out about ten; the others were already in town. They didn't get back until the following morning."

"There's the crazy lady."

198

"She's gone. Moved over to Peñasco."

"We could probably find her."

"We will if we have to. There was something about her. I kept getting a feeling that she was playing games, you know."

J.Q. was watching the truck behind them in his rearview mirror. It was less than one car length from their bumper. He turned on the hazard lights. "Well, you said that, days ago. You said she was playing at voluntary poverty, or something."

"That's right. I did. The guy isn't getting off our bumper."

"I'm slowing down."

The car behind stayed behind, mindlessly, as they crawled along at thirty-five. "It's a woman," said J.Q.

Shirley turned around to get a better look. "She's nursing a baby."

"She's what?" J.Q. pulled over. The woman behind almost followed them, then abruptly swerved into traffic once more.

A semi screamed by, horn blaring.

The car with the nursing mother at the wheel wavered into an exit farther down the road and departed. J.Q. wiped his face on his sleeve. "Every time I think I've seen everything . . ."

"There were two children standing up in the backseat," Shirley remarked.

"Just waiting to be statistics." He started the car again. "What were we talking about?"

"The crazy lady. Tanya Roth. About how she was playing. J.Q., do you suppose Emil is still at the pueblo gambling place?"

"We can stop if you like."

"Do. Just for a minute."

They found a place outside the door and went inside, down the hall past several offices, and into the hall proper. It was a no-frills establishment, catering to the lowest com-

199

mon denominator of gambling public, rows on rows of machines, most of them in use.

"Over there," said J.Q., elbowing Shirley slightly. "In the corner."

It was Emil, sitting slumped before a lighted console, punching buttons with one hand, the other gripping the top of a bottle-shaped brown bag. Shirley and J.Q. edged up behind him.

"I'm usin' this one," said Emil.

"We just wanted to ask a couple of questions," Shirley said soothingly.

He turned, recognized her, and attempted a snarl. "Whatta you want."

"Remember the woman you were with at my place?"

"Sure. Tanya. What about her."

"Would you tell us where you met her?"

"Right here. Met her right here by this same little old machine. Said she was . . . on the run. That's what she said, on the run."

"From what?"

"Didn' ask. She didn' say. Jus' said she needed com-company for a few days. Said she'd pay me jus' to keep her com-company."

"Did she pay you?"

Emil thought about it, his eyes actually focusing. "Couple days. No. More'n that. Almos' a week. Then she got shitty. No more money. Fine. Fine with me. Who needs it?"

"Where are you getting money now?"

His eyes wavered. "Who you think . . . you are? Huh?"

"That's all right," said J.Q. "She just thought maybe she could help."

"You need somethin' did?" he asked, slyness creeping into his voice, into his eyes. "I do good rock work. Plaster, I do that. Stucco."

"Only one thing right now," Shirley said. "I need some information. It won't matter to you what the answer is; it only matters to me. When you took the wallet from the car, was there a briefcase in there?" She fished in her jacket pocket, holding out a crumpled twenty. "The truth. That's all I'll pay for."

He stared, started to say something, shook his head, then blurted, "It wasn't there. I'd've took it if it'd been there, but it wasn't there."

She handed him the twenty. He grabbed it, crushing it up small in his hand.

"You want anything did, you let me know."

"Maybe later on. Can I find you here, if I need something done?"

"Here. Right. Or ask him, over there." He jerked his chin at the impassive man behind the counter. "He knows me."

"Emil ... what's your last name?" Shirley asked.

"Not AY-meel. She called me AY-meel. Name's Emilio Hawktell. That man. He's my uncle."

They went back to the car in silence. Only when they were almost at the driveway to the ranch did Shirley say, "He's a native. He never knew her until she got here."

"Obviously not."

"So all that business about saving him from himself was a story. A role she was playing. Why?"

"She needed him for something?"

"What? What was he good for?"

"Making off with Alicia's billfold, for one thing. Giving us a suspect."

They were approaching the ranch. J.Q. turned into the side road.

Shirley asked plaintively, "But a suspect for what? Killing her? He didn't even know her. She wasn't killed in a robbery. He only took her wallet. I believe that. And she died slowly. She had her brain eaten out!"

The words set up a terrible resonance. Shirley gasped, held on to the door handle, let the dimness pass.

The car was stopped. J.Q. was leaning forward, his hand on her knee. "What?" he urged. "What is it?"

"J.Q., it's ... I don't know. Maybe it's withdrawal symptoms. Maybe it's clairvoyance, crossing bridges before I get to them. It's fortune-telling. It's ... not thinking very clearly."

"About what, love?"

"About eating people's brains out, J.Q. About poetic justice. Let's go home. If I don't sleep, I'm going to die."

Xanthippe met them in the parking area. "Roger Fetting wants you to call him immediately."

Shirley sagged into a kitchen chair and punched in the number, leaning her head on her fist while it rang. Behind her she could feel Xanthy's questioning glance, J.Q.'s shrug, hear them murmuring together. They didn't know what was the matter with her. She didn't know what was the matter with her.

"Shirley," Roger greeted her, when she had gone through the usual obstacle course of secretaries and assistants. "I've got your information. About Evans? He's ex-military, ex-mercenary. He isn't a screenwriter, but he has been a script consultant. He did some consulting work on a couple of *Rambo*-type pictures. His money is said to come from drugs, but he's never been indicted. He isn't married, but he sometimes travels with an—oh, I guess you'd call her an adventuress. She calls herself his wife, sometimes. The word is that lately he's gone back to being a mercenary, doing detail work for movie producers, cleaning up problems."

"What kind of problems, Roger?"

"Oh, somebody acting in a movie gets harassed and it interferes with the shooting schedule, Mr. Evans fixes it so the harassment stops. Some actor needs drugs to get up for the role, Mr. Evans supplies them. Whatever's needed. He's a fixer. The so-called fixing hasn't always been nonviolent. You get my meaning?"

"Thank you, Roger," she said in a voice that didn't sound like her own.

"Are you all right?"

"Tired. That's all. Just tired."

"You want me to send you some help?"

"We'll manage."

"I'm as close as the phone."

"I know, Rog. Thanks. Really."

She hung up.

"We'll manage what?" asked J.Q.

She repeated what she'd heard.

"Shirley," Xanthippe said plaintively. "What did Mr. Fetting mean by 'not always nonviolent.' "

"In this case, he meant that if Evans thought he could get somewhere by faking photographs or maiming a little animal, he'd do it."

"He may have meant worse than that," said J.Q.

"I know," Shirley said, keeping the phone propped on her shoulder while she reached for the Albuquerque phone book. *Nursing Homes. Cedar Rest.* She punched, squinting to make her eyes focus.

"May I speak with Ellen Fleshman, please."

She turned, facing the others, who were poised, she thought, like a bunch of cats ready to leap at a mouse. "Where's Allison?" she asked Xanthy.

"The two girls are in Allison's room. They're listening to cassettes."

"Ellen? Hello. This is Shirley McClintock, the woman who was talking with Sheldon Maxwell. Right. How is he?"

She listened, her face stony. "When did that happen?" And listened again.

"Thank you, Ellen. I'll check back with you."

She hung up. "He had a bad fall. Hit his head on something. They don't know how badly he's hurt, or whether he'll recover. Damn it, J.Q. We've got to get into his house."

"You didn't get an answer to your letter .... No, of course you didn't. There hasn't been time. We can try the housekeeper."

"You try, J.Q. I'm not functioning." She gave him the chair by the phone and sank onto another one at the table.

"What would you hope to find at his house?" Xanthy asked apprehensively.

"Photo albums, movie scripts, the manuscript of an auto-biography, the tapes of those early TV shows, Xanthy. I don't know."

Xanthy brushed crumbs into a cupped hand. "I had a friend who sold a book to a producer. They took an option on it for three years, and they only paid my friend fifteen hundred a year. Then, when they decided to make the movie, she only got thirty thousand. That doesn't seem to me to be enough money to warrant . . . well, these strong-arm tactics. If it were millions, maybe, but it may be only a few dollars."

"I don't know," Shirley whispered into her cupped hands. "Xanthy, I don't know."

J.Q. had reached someone at the Maxwell house and was carrying on a muffled conversation. When he hung up, he turned and gave them a bleak look. "Somebody else had the same idea. They broke in and trashed the place. The housekeeper says the police have been there."

"Lovely," said Shirley, inexpressibly weary. "And the Brentwoods will have been publicly elsewhere. In fact, they probably flew back to Albany this morning."

"Do you think it was Evans?" Xanthippe asked.

"Probably," J.Q. answered. "Shall we call the Albuquerque police?"

"We have to, don't we?" Shirley said. "We know of a possible motive, so we have to. You do it, J.Q. At the moment I'm no good to anyone. I'm going to lie down." She suited her action to the words, though slowly, as though moving through thick grass or deep water. Wading through life, she told herself solemnly. Here she was, wading through life, with a bedroom on the opposite shore.

She reached it at last. The Baron was asleep on her pillow. She pushed him out of the way and fell onto the cover, turning to pull it half over her, her head in the warm spot where the Baron had been.

Behind her, in the kitchen, J.Q. and Xanthy looked helplessly at one another.

"She'll be all right," he said.

"Do you think . . . Allison? Is she in any danger?"

"You think Evans assaulted old Maxwell?"

"It's possible, isn't it? If we could just figure out what it is they want."

"Lawrence Brentwood knows what they want. And he knows we know he knows."

Xanthy laughed painfully. "He went back to Albany."

"Best place to be. Where he can't be questioned. Not easily, at any rate."

"What do we do now?"

"Damned if I know, Xanthippe. Definitely, damned if I know."

A sound wakened her. Persistent, plaintive, a shrill peeping that would not let her rest. She opened her eyes reluctantly.

Dim. Must be dusk. She turned on her light, looked at her watch. Six-thirty. Couldn't be dusk, not this early.

She struggled out of bed, got to the window, thrust the drapes aside, momentarily confused because she didn't remember closing them. The stretch of lawn beyond the back patio was speckled with poultry, guinea hens pecking at the grass, moving erratically between the long shadows that stretched from the house toward the west. There, a glitter of glass betrayed the existence of the town upon the mesa top.

It obviously wasn't evening. The sun was coming up behind her! It was morning. She had slept for . . . what? Fourteen or fifteen hours?

Her stomach clenched, and she was abruptly conscious of hunger. She'd had lunch, but that was a day ago. Turning her head experimentally, she tried to find the woolliness she'd become used to. Nothing. Taking a step, she waited for the wading sensation. Nothing. She blinked, experimenting with dizziness. Still nothing. Legs were legs and eyes were eyes and both seemed to be up to doing the day's work.

The peeping came again. Guinea chicks, half a dozen of them, tiny fluffy balls, rolling along among the adults' feet.

She watched while they and the adults ran around the corner and out of sight.

Not bothering to dress, she belted her robe around her and went to the kitchen. Coffee. And eggs. And maybe an English muffin or two. The morning was clear as crystal. The day was bright. Yesterday's impenetrable mysteries seemed simple things. Yesterday's threats seemed laughable. The odor of brewing coffee was all the soothing anyone needed.

J.Q. found her there an hour later, a notepad under her hand as she wrote rapid sentences.

"J.Q. Glad you're up. Don't you have a friend or acquaintance or somebody who works at *Variety*?"

"The movie paper? I know a man who works there."

"Can you get hold of him and ask him if he knows about a new movie or TV series based on two brothers who are comics."

J.Q.'s jaw dropped. "Where did you get that idea?"

"Something Xanthy said about money. She said there wasn't all that much money in selling a story to the movies. Not usually, at any rate, though I'm sure there are exceptions. So why would anyone go to all this trouble to get rights to the Two Stupes material? They would do so to protect a large investment that had already been made, right? So, if a producer has already spent a mint making a film or, more likely, filming a series, and has only now found out he doesn't have rights to the story, he might be fairly urgent about it, right?"

"Right." He filled a cup and dropped into the chair across from her. "You think that's what happened."

"I think it may have. Probably some legal eagle in the main office suddenly realized they had no release from the heirs or assigns, or some such thing. So they went looking, found the Brentwoods, and whoever was assigned the task—Evans, most likely—ended up making common cause with dear Lawrence and family. They tried a two-pronged attack, one prong aimed at old Sheldon and the other at

Allison. Because of the kind of people they are, they were not straightforward. They tried to blindside us."

"Why trash Sheldon's house?"

"Probably to find something with his signature on it. I don't imagine forgery is beyond Mr. Evans. Or beyond someone he knows. They'll predate a release, forge a signature, and who's going to argue with them? An old man who can't remember stuff?"

"You think they went after him?"

"Possibly. Though he may just have fallen. Old people do." She smiled mirthlessly. "Even some not so old people do. At any rate, we'll know soon enough. They've either given up or they're going on with it. If they go on with it, we'll hear from them."

"What else have you got on the pad there?"

"The story of who killed Alicia Tremple. And why."

"You're joking."

"I don't joke about things like this, J.Q. I'm just ashamed of myself that it took so long."

WHILE J.Q. WAS feeding the animals, Shirley made a couple of phone calls. When he came back from the barn, she asked him to take a little walk with her.

"Where are we going?" J.Q. wanted to know.

"We're going to peek through the window of Frog House," she said.

"Who were you talking to, just now?"

"I called Gerald Scott. The Scotts are still here in town, and there were a couple of things I wanted to know."

"Like?"

"I wanted to find out what Alicia Tremple's financial situation was, and ask about her housekeeper, and find out about her medicine, and a few more questions about Alicia's personality. I also called Cedar Rest. Sheldon Maxwell is feeling better this morning."

"I'm glad to hear that. Why are we going to peer through windows?"

"To see what we can't see, J.Q."

She went into the house first, turned on the bathroom light, then led J.Q. to a position out beside the fence.

"That big bush blocks the window," objected J.Q. "I can't see anything."

"Neither can I," she admitted. "If someone were dyeing her hair in the basin at night, would you be able to see that?"

"Not unless I got right up against the window."

"Let's try."

They tried, accordingly, only to come away with various wounds. "What the hell is that?" snarled J.Q., balefully regarding the shrubbery.

"Xanthy says it's a firethorn, a pyracantha. Like the one by the front wall that's always stabbing me. Even when I get as close to the window as I can, I can only see the ceiling. There's a half curtain inside that hides everything up to about five feet."

"Why do we care?"

"The crazy lady said the woman in Frog House dyed her hair black. She said she saw her. I said, the window is on the other side, and she explained she was out walking. I think she wasn't out walking."

"How did she know, then?"

"If, in fact, she did know, it was because she was in there, inside the house. Do you remember where you put the junk from the fire? The one the crazy lady set?"

"Over in the dump."

"That'll be our next stop."

They walked, accordingly, down the drive, through a gate, across a field, and down into a small arroyo that fed, a few hundred feet farther along, into a much larger one. The near end of the small arroyo had been filled and graded over. The next section was partly filled with barn cleanings, broken branches, and brush.

"Bottom," said J.Q. laconically, easing himself down the steep side. "What do you want?"

"The trash. Whatever you dumped."

He muttered, fished a pair of work gloves out of his jacket pocket, and started rooting about in the trash, placing his finds in a pile on a flat place level with his head. Shirley wandered over where she could peer down at these.

"Is there any paper or cardboard?"

"This," he said, reaching up to hand her a cardboard piece, charred around the edges, shiny, white on one side, a coyote's ear and eye pictured on the other. "There's two or three more."

The others were more burned, less clear. Shirley thought she made out a wing on one of them, a buffalo head on the other. She offered her hand to J.Q., who came struggling up out of the arroyo, one hand full of scraps and shards. She took them from him. Several thin strips of metal about twelve inches long and less than a quarter inch wide. A brass latch, partly melted. A scrap of what appeared to be alligator skin but was probably, Shirley thought, sniffing it, plastic. The rings and spine of a small looseleaf book.

"You know what these are?" Shirley asked, waving the strips.

"Should I?"

"In suspended files, these are the metal pieces that go through the top of the file folders. This"—she waved the coyote picture—"is probably part of a deck of cards. Alicia Tremple bought the cards at Southwest Books the day before she died."

"Same deck?"

"Can't prove that," she admitted. "Same type of card, that's all. The scrap of plastic is probably from the outside of a briefcase. Faux, as Elaine would say, alligator."

"You're saying the crazy lady sat out in front of her house and burned Alicia Tremple's briefcase?"

"Not so damned crazy, J.Q. She couldn't use the fireplace, it was too smoky even for her, so she sat right out there in the full glare of the noonday sun and burned the briefcase—having previously, no doubt, bashed it to pieces—knowing we'd be more interested in her behavior than in what she was burning. She also burned what was in the case."

"Which was?"

"Complete file folders. Records, perhaps, of several of Alicia Tremple's clients. Records, certainly, of her most recent client, or patient. The one she came here to help."

"Why burn them?"

"To destroy them, of course. To get rid of them. To disestablish them. Now no one can prove they ever existed."

"Wouldn't Tremple have copies? Back home in California?"

"I doubt it. I think it likely that any copies, references, log entries, appointment books were destroyed at about the time Alicia Tremple was. When I called her home number, her sister was there. Her sister was there because the police had been called—the cleaning lady had called them; the house and office had been broken into. Elaine said the house was messed up, the office was untouched. I doubt it. I think the office was carefully gleaned through and the house was then messed up to account for the break-in."

"But the cleaning lady called the hospital. . . ."

"No. Someone who feigned little or no English called the hospital. Someone who wanted to know how sick Mrs. Tremple was. Alicia Tremple's housekeeper speaks perfect English."

"Now how in the hell—"

"I asked Gerald Scott this morning. Alicia's housekeeper had been with her for ten years. She's second-generation Scandinavian; Gerald says her English is better than his."

"You're saying the crazy lady killed her?"

Shirley shook her head doubtfully. "I'm not ready to say that, J.Q. But I'll bet the crazy lady had dinner with her the night she got so sick."

"Now, how do you get to that conclusion?"

"When we went to the restaurant in Tesuque, we were seated at one of Jake's tables, so we could talk to him, and it was in the smoking section. Normally I'd have objected, but since we were there to see Jake, I suffered in silence. Whoever sat there a week ago sat there by choice. We've had only one fanatic smoker among us."

"And all this leads where, exactly?"

211

"I think the crazy lady became sufficiently intimate with Alicia to visit her in the house and, probably, drive her to Jemez Springs. She either saw her dyeing her hair or heard her mention doing so. I think the crazy lady met her for dinner. I think the crazy lady, feigning an accent, called the hospital to find out how sick she really was."

"Is that all?"

"No. I think if we go to Peñasco, we won't find hide nor hair of her. I think she's long gone."

"Why did Tremple come here?"

"She said it, on the ride to the hospital. 'I came to see a client.' Then she denied it because it was supposed to be a secret."

"You don't know how Tremple was killed. If she was killed."

"I think I do. Yes."

He took off the dirty gloves and slapped them idly against his thigh. "So what are you going to do now?"

"I have no proof. And I'm not positive what the reason was. And . . ."

"And?"

"And in the absence of anything else that must be done, I've decided to have a dinner party."

His jaw dropped. "Shirley? Are you out of your head?"

"I used to give dinner parties," she said loftily. "Rather good ones. In Washington. Small, of course. Our house wasn't huge. But the food was always delicious."

"It was?"

"I had a good caterer."

"Who's coming to this party?"

"Oh, you and Xanthy and I. Plus Mr. and Mrs. Stevens, and Cally, Harry, and Rob, and Dr. and Mr. Fley. The dining table seats ten easily."

"When?"

"Tonight. It's the Stevenses' and Fleys' last night. They've been enjoyable guests. And I've managed to find a caterer who will produce a meal on short notice."

"My, my, haven't we been busy," he said. "You're feeling a lot better, aren't you?"

"I suppose. It's hard to remember how I've been feeling. A lot of it's very foggy."

"It's good to have you back," he said, reaching a tentative finger toward her cheek, stroking it. "I've missed you. So has Xanthy."

"You might have said something sooner," she said with some asperity. "How was I to know?"

"How were we?" he asked. "We're none of us getting any younger, Shirley. Derelictions come with age. Some of them may be pathology; others may be merely wear and tear. Not nice to reproach people for wear and tear, and how are we to know which is which?"

"True," she said, staring at her shoes. "Bring that trash along, J.Q. We might use it as Exhibit A."

The cateress and her assistant arrived at three and chased everyone out of the kitchen. Vancie and Allison were given the task of assisting Alberta in cleaning the public part of the house, Allison to keep Vancie company, Vancie to get a taste of housekeeping, which her uncle said she did little enough of. Ostensibly it was the other way around and Vancie was company for Allison.

"How far did you get yesterday?" Shirley asked Allison, when they encountered one another going in opposite directions in the corridor. "Is Vancie being enlightened?"

"I think what I said yesterday sort of got to her," Allison whispered. "She said if it didn't work, she could go home to her mom, and I told her her mom didn't have to take her or her baby. I read about that in the paper last week. Her mom can go into court and have her declared a ward of the state. I told her that."

"And?"

"And it scared her. She's not so sure about living in the garage anymore. I told her it would be like in Tibet, where one woman marries several brothers and has to look after all of them. She'll end up doing laundry and cooking for all

213

four of them, and she doesn't even like doing it for herself."

"Interesting."

"Anyhow, we're doing what you said. Thinking of details. I keep thinking of new ones. Like just getting places. She doesn't have a car, and her boyfriend doesn't have a car. So if the baby gets sick, how does she get him to the doctor? There's no phone in the garage. How does she even call the doctor? Stuff like that."

"Does Vancie tell you anything about her aunt and uncle—her aunt, particularly? Why she's so unhappy?"

"Mrs. Stevens?" Allison made a face. "Yes. She does."

"Could you tell me what she's said?"

Allison made the face again. "Mrs. Stevens was having a lot of trouble at work. So Mr. Stevens suggested she go to a counselor, you know, somebody who could tell her how to handle it. Well, so this counselor told her her problem started when she was a kid and she was abused. She told Mrs. Stevens she had to go to her dad and tell him off before she can tell her supervisor off."

With a sinking feeling, Shirley allowed as how she could believe it.

"So, anyhow, Mrs. Stevens's father—he was seventy, I guess. So she went to have it out with him."

"But then her father died," said Shirley.

"Right. And then he died, almost right off. And Mr. Stevens, he tells Mrs. Stevens if her father was going to die, he was going to die, because he had this heart thing for a long time, because he was in a real bad accident a long time ago, when Mrs. Stevens was just a baby. Mrs. Stevens knew he had scars all over, but she didn't know about the heart thing. She says now there were a lot of things she didn't know about him. And no matter what anybody says, she thinks she's responsible for his dying."

"I see," said Shirley reflectively. "That's very helpful, Allison. Can you and Vancie entertain one another while we're having dinner tonight?"

"Oh, sure. That lady in the kitchen said she'd fix us a tray, and we can have our own party."

Shirley started to leave and was stopped.

"Shirley. I just . . . you know, all that stuff we're telling Vancie, they're things I needed to think about, too."

Shirley felt herself paling. "You're not . . ."

"Pregnant?" Allison giggled. "Don't be funny! You are being funny, aren't you?"

"Of course," Shirley said, swallowing deeply. "Just teasing."

"No, I mean this whole business about having a boyfriend and wanting to live with him and stuff. J.Q.'s very smart, those rules he made up. You know. No sex before eighteen? I think it's too bad we have to worry about it when we're my age. Vancie's age. It would be better if we didn't even think about it until a lot later."

Shirley hugged her, astonished, as she so often was where Allison was concerned. "Allison, I lucked out the day I met you!"

And she was off. They were to have cocktails first, with several hot hors d'oeuvres. Then wine with dinner. J.Q. was not satisfied with anything they had, so he and Shirley had to drive over to Kokoman's and pick something out.

She arrived back just in time to shower and get herself into a skirt for the first time in . . . well, months. A skirt was appropriate for tonight. Skirts were disarming. Feminine. She glared at herself in the mirror, daring femininity to make any appearance whatsoever. What the hell. A little makeup. A bit of lipstick. Earrings. A touch of mascara? She drew the line at a touch of mascara.

The guests arrived at six-thirty from their various houses. It was the first time she'd used the cavernous living room for anything, but with discreet lighting and a few drinks, it seemed less forbidding. Hot crab puffs. Tiny filled chilis. The obligatory salsa and chips. One could not entertain anywhere within fifty miles of Santa Fe without serving salsa and chips. A pitcher of margaritas, white wine, red wine, plus a serve-yourself bar with a few well-chosen bottles. All very nice. Mr. Stevens looking prosperous in well-cut Western wear. Mr. Fley looking retired, in loose shirt and huaraches. Dr. Fley in her usual grandmotherly garb; Mrs. Stevens in skirt and embroidered blouse, something from Yucatán, Shirley thought. The three young men from California looking interchangeable, all tanned, all in similar shirts, trousers, and loafers. Harry looked a little better than when she'd seen him last. A bit more rested.

There was one extra seat at the table. "One of our guests couldn't make it," said Shirley, with a smile. The cateress offered to clear the place, but Shirley shook her head. Leave it, she said.

J.Q. gave Xanthy a long look. Now what was this woman up to? Xanthy shrugged.

First course, sopa limón. Lemon-flavored chicken soup, with floating slices of avocado and toasted tortilla strips as croutons. Second course, salad of marinated vegetables. Baby beets, baby carrots, asparagus spears, all banded with slices of red pepper. Entrée: rack of lamb with blue potatoes (Peru, originally, said the cateress, now grown at high altitudes in Colorado) and some deep-fried squash blossoms. Dessert to follow. Raspberries and cream.

Coffee. Decaf. Everyone mellow.

Shirley tapped her wineglass with a spoon.

"I hope this dinner has been pleasant for you," she said. "Though I've had an ulterior motive for inviting you. I have a story I think you should all hear. Something disturbing that I think has affected some of you as much as it has me."

Silence at the table. A few puzzled looks. One or two, perhaps, apprehensive.

"Some rather unpleasant people are attempting to extort something from me by threatening to accuse me of child abuse, neglect, or perhaps witchcraft."

More puzzled looks.

"Some of you may have seen a show on PBS about child-abuse accusations that resulted in life sentences for some people who in all probability are totally innocent.

You're all well-educated people. You know what witch-hunts are. You know how they work. You know they begin with an accusation, often of a completely innocent person.

"We had a guest staying in Frog House who seems to have been responsible for a number of such accusations. Her name was Alicia Tremple. According to her sister and brother-in-law, she found evidence of abuse and satanism everywhere she looked. She found it in her own sister's marriage. She found it in women who came to her for help with problems totally unrelated to childhood abuse. She found it in homosexuals who came to her needing affirmation of their essential worth as individuals. She found it everywhere around her, and she was determined to root it out."

"Look," Mr. Fley interrupted, "I'm sure this is all very interesting, but—"

"Don't interrupt, dear," said Mrs. Fley. "I find this fascinating."

He subsided unwillingly, with a piercing look at his wife.

Shirley went on. "She was a psychologist. Her usual way of working was first to allege abuse, then to make her patients 'remember' such abuse, then to insist on her patients confronting and accusing their parents, blaming their parents for whatever was wrong with them. Some of Alicia's patients were in their middle thirties or forties. Their parents were not young. Hearing such accusations is difficult for anyone. It is particularly difficult for people in their later years. I know how I would feel if a child of mine accused me of satanism or abusing him or her in any way, much less sexually. I would feel despair."

"As well you might," said Dr. Fley crisply. "Aside from the pain and the feeling of betrayal, there is the social taint. Such accusations are so very hard to disprove."

"Except sometimes," cried Mrs. Stevens. "Sometimes there is proof. Sometimes the things you remember turn out not to be true!"

"Ree," her husband said in a worried voice, putting his hand on her shoulder. "Ree . . ."

"Can one ever be sure they are not true," murmured Shirley.

Ree Stevens shook off her husband's hand. "Sometimes it's certain! Like, she makes you remember someone doing something . . . you really remember it, only later you find out—"

Mrs. Fley interrupted. "An example of what Mrs. Stevens means is that sometimes a patient is encouraged to remember explicit details of the abuser's sexual organ. Counselors of the kind you mention often encourage the memory of anatomical detail. They dig for it almost salaciously, for anatomical detail is what they are most horrified at. Think how the patient would feel if she found out later her accused parent had lost his sexual organs after begetting her but before she was born, because of a terrible accident. Think of the trauma of learning that what she had been encouraged to remember could not be true."

"That would be quite awful," Shirley agreed.

The older woman nodded slowly. "Tragic, and unnecessary. Innocent people die because of tragic and unnecessary mistakes."

"Yes. They do. Your grandson was one who did, I believe."

Mrs. Fley cleared her throat, and there were tears in her eyes as she said, "He was a victim, yes."

"And his lover." Shirley switched her gaze to Harry's intent face. "He, too, was a victim."

"My brother, Martin," whispered Harry. "Oh, yes."

Shirley murmured, "Three families with tragic losses. Three victims. I believe there was at least one other victim, one associated with our absent guest."

"Who?" asked Cally. "Who's your absent guest?"

"I don't know, Cally. However, we can make certain inferences about her.

"When I spoke to Alicia's brother-in-law, I asked him if Alicia had a lucrative practice. He said no, not particularly. Her office and home were in the house she'd inherited, she made enough to get by, but she was more interested in root-

218

ing out evil than in making a lot of money. Nonetheless, while Alicia Tremple was here, she looked at real estate. Real estate is expensive in Santa Fe, but this trip was supposed to result in real money for her."

"Did he know from whom?" asked Dr. Fley.

"No. Alicia was closemouthed about it. All she told her sister was that her new client was paying her well for her help. During the time Alicia was here, we had a guest who gave the impression of having wealth. The woman in Ditch House. Our absent guest. Who talked of poverty but drove a new Mercedes all-terrain vehicle."

"It could have been borrowed," said Dr. Fley. "It could have been rented. The impression of wealth may have been false."

Shirley nodded. "That's true. It might have been borrowed. We're in one of the nation's bastions of conspicuous consumption. More celebrities to the inch than anywhere outside of Hollywood. Unfortunately, I didn't get the license number of that Mercedes."

J.Q. said, "You said you thought she was playing a part."

"I think she was. And she played it extremely well. I doubt I'd recognize her if I saw her on the street. The glasses, the turban, the manner! They could have been as phony as the travels in India. Take off the disguise, return the vehicle wherever she got it, who's to know?" She stopped, sipped at her wineglass, looking at the faces before her, all carefully blank. She smiled grimly and went on.

"I believe our absent guest was the one who made Alicia Tremple's reservation. Tremple asked Allison if there was a weekly rate. If she'd made the reservation herself, she'd have known there was a weekly rate. It's likely someone else made all the arrangements for her. The reservation was made with a misappropriated credit-card number, the confirmation letter was sent to an Arizona hotel, and the phone number was out of service. Also, while we were taking her to the hospital, someone removed all her ID."

"That seems unnecessarily complicated," said Cally, puzzled.

"The removal of ID provided enough time for someone in California to go through Tremple's office and remove all references to our absent guest. And, probably, to certain other clients as well."

"You're saying she had a confederate?" asked Dr. Fley, her eyes narrowed.

"A coconspirator." Shirley said, staring into the slitted eyes. "Oh, yes. At least one."

The doctor laughed. "You spin a good story, Ms. McClintock. But it's just a story. The woman died of a microbial infection she caught in a hot spring. Tragic. But perfectly natural."

"Impossible," said Shirley. "Sorry, but impossible."

"Why?" There was some anger in the tone, a hint of frost.

"When I spoke with Alicia Tremple's sister and brother-in-law, I got a picture of a woman who was seriously repressed. A woman who hated herself. A woman with low self-esteem who was obsessive about her personal appearance. Though it was a rainy, muggy night when we drove her to the hospital, she wore a high-necked, long-sleeved dress and stockings. Her brother-in-law told me that she never went in the water. Never once, all the years he had known her. Never in all the time her sister had known her."

"She was so skinny," said J.Q.

"Indeed she was. Her brother-in-law told me why. After her mother died, her father used to abuse her, calling her old skin and bones. He used to hold her head in the toilet until she would consent to have sex with him. She was ashamed of her body. She never undressed except in a locked bathroom. She dyed her hair to change her appearance. She could not bear water in her face."

"How did you get onto that?" Dr. Fley asked, almost in a snarl.

"When I went through her things, there was no swimming suit. A young woman might have bathed nude in a hot spring, but a woman of that age? A woman, as her sister said, self-conscious about her appearance?"

"Even if she'd been all alone?" Harry asked plaintively. "Some of the springs are in quite remote areas. There might have been no one else around."

Shirley said, "It wouldn't have mattered to Alicia Tremple. In the backyard pool at her sister's house, with trees all around, she would not go in the water. She always undressed and bathed behind a closed shower curtain. So I was told this morning. She didn't get the microorganism in a hot spring."

"Then how did she get it?" Cally, head cocked, intrigued.

"I was told she always carried medicine for her allergies. I didn't find any medicine in the house. Agreed that our absent guest's acquaintance, Emil, might have burglarized the house, but why in hell would he steal medicine? Alicia Tremple was allergic to cats, but there was a muddy footprint on her toilet seat. I've seen footprints like that in my bathroom when it rains. The cats normally drink out of the pond, but when it's wet out, they drink out of the toilet. So she had a cat in her house. On our trip to the hospital she said, 'It came in the house.' Her sister says she wouldn't let a cat in, and that implies someone put it there. Alicia no doubt found him there and put him out, but the hair was already in the house, the dander was in the air."

Mrs. Fley objected, "But you can't say definitely that—"

Shirley clenched her teeth. "I can only say definitely what I know. I know there were muddy footprints on the toilet seat. I know it rained that night. I know the cats drink out of the toilet when there's no other water available."

A long silence fell.

Harry broke it, clearing his throat, two hectic patches of red on his cheeks. "There's a story you might like to hear."

"By all means," Shirley said, sitting back and again picking up her wineglass.

J.Q. got up and filled the glasses all around. Mr. Fley put his hand atop his glass, his face set in angry lines. Mr. Stevens was puzzled; he whispered to J.Q., who simply shook his head.

"There was once this really nice woman," said Harry.

221

"She was well-known in her field and had a lot of friends. She had a daughter she adored, but she grieved over the daughter quite a lot because the daughter was born unhappy. Under an evil star, the mother said. No matter what Mother did for her, the daughter was miserable. She was diagnosed as having a particular kind of depression."

"It might have been attention deficit disorder," said Dr. Fley. "People who have it can't attend to life. They can't concentrate, can't achieve. They hate people, they blame other people, they put things off. They're miserable, all the time. The people who love them are miserable. Some doctors have learned recently that it can be treated."

"It could have been that," said Harry. He fell silent, stirring his coffee.

"What happened to her?" asked Xanthy.

"Well, the mother was determined to do everything for her daughter that she could. She read, and she researched, and she found out about this disorder and located a doctor who could diagnose it and who'd had success treating it. The daughter was sent to the doctor, and put on a certain medication, and she was better! She was actually almost happy!"

"A happy ending?" asked Shirley.

"Well, it would have been. Except that the daughter went to a lecture by a psychologist who didn't believe in medication, didn't believe in 'chemicals.' The psychologist convinced the daughter she'd be better off with counseling. The daughter was suggestible, so she quit taking her medication and went to the psychologist, and the psychologist convinced her she was depressed because she'd been abused in childhood."

"So she accused her mother?" J.Q. asked.

"I imagine she did, don't you?" said Dr. Fley angrily. "Accused her mother, and her stepfather. She may even have tried to kill her stepfather when he denied it. He did deny it, of course, because he'd never abused her. He'd never done anything of the kind."

Cally was staring at Harry with a strange expression:

222

partly horror, partly pity. Rob was peering into his glass, listening, but remote from all this.

"The mother had good friends among the police. They managed to keep the attack quiet, but the daughter ended up in a mental hospital," said Harry sadly. "They don't know if they can bring her out of this one."

"I imagine her mother was at her wit's end," murmured Shirley. "In this story you're telling me."

"Oh"—Harry nodded—"in the story she would have been at her wit's end. Of course, it's only a story."

Shirley smiled at him. "If I were writing a story, I'd plot it this way. Harry, here, would be very despondent over his brother's death. He would blame the psychologist. He would look up her billings in his computer at work, finding the names of other of her patients. He would call some of them, or more likely, their next of kin."

"Next of kin would be good," said Rob, in a tone of surprise. "They'd be listed, of course."

Harry said in a heavy voice, "It would surprise one to find how many of them had been hurt. Husbands and wives. Parents. Stepparents. Even grandparents."

"Of course he wouldn't need to locate many others," Shirley said. "He would need someone who could access Alicia Tremple's own medical records and come up with a method of revenge. A doctor, particularly a parasitologist, would be an interesting addition. That'd be you, Dr. Fley. I made some calls today. You are a parasitologist, aren't you? A nice touch, though unnecessary. Any physician would have done. And once the method had been decided, then they would need someone who works in a lab, with access to cultures of microorganisms and skill in maintaining them. That'd be you, Mrs. Stevens. They'd need one more person, to provide other details. Our absent guest, who would play the part of the well-to-do client. The one who would bring Alicia Tremple to Santa Fe. She would make the reservation, using a real but unauthorized credit-card number—provided by you, I think, Harry. Your records no doubt have such information available—credit-card numbers and discontinued phone numbers.

"By doing this, our absent guest would lay a false back trail for Alicia Tremple, one that led through Arizona and southern New Mexico, past many hot springs. This was all well researched, well thought out. Detailed though the research was, however, it didn't allow for the fact that Alicia Tremple was so repressed she would never have bathed in a hot spring, no matter how convenient."

From someone in the room a sigh, perhaps of disappointment.

"Alicia Tremple had not met our absent guest before she arrived here. They did meet shortly afterward, for it was she, our absent guest, who needed access to Frog House so she could provide the infective agent."

"How would she do that?" asked Mrs. Fley.

"Oh—in an inhaler, I think. Alicia always had one with her, according to her brother-in-law. He described the bottle to me. We didn't find one in her house, but the imprint of a typically shaped inhaler bottle remained on the radiator cover, set there by a wet and soapy hand. A silly place to leave an inhaler, on a hot radiator, unless it is necessary to keep the organism alive. Perhaps the infective agent needed heat?"

An indrawn breath. Shirley's eyes were fixed on her own knotted hands. She didn't look up to see who had gasped. It didn't matter.

"Someone broke off the thermostat control in Frog House, so the radiator stayed on from the time the medicine was set there until Alicia Tremple used it, and perhaps between usages. Someone sent Alicia to Jemez Springs, or took her there, laying more false trail. Someone took Alicia to town, an older woman, someone who could assess the progress of the disease, I should imagine. They went to a bookstore, and something purchased there turned up later in refuse left by our absent guest. Someone arranged to meet Alicia for dinner, the night she died. A younger woman, perhaps our absent guest herself. That woman brought her back here, to the ranch, to play out the final stages of the drama.

"Someone watched while Alicia was taken to the hospital. When she had gone, someone went into her house to remove everything that might be incriminating or identifying, and that same person put temptation in the way of a weak man to provide an explanation for the removal. A scapegoat, if you will.

"What, exactly, was Alicia Tremple supposed to do here in Santa Fe? It could only be the thing she did constantly—to find an abuser, accuse an abuser, confront an abuser."

"A father, perhaps," said Harry. "A father who didn't exist."

"That would work well. Alicia was flattered to be asked to come to Santa Fe to help this well-to-do person. She understood the necessity of keeping it quiet. Perhaps the secrecy of it even gratified her own sense of drama and importance. Even better, she had been offered generous payment, generous enough that she had at least thought about buying expensive real estate.

"When our absent guest first contacted Alicia Tremple, who did she say had referred her? Your grandson, Dr. Fley? Your brother, Harry? Alicia didn't know either of you. Had you made the referral, Mrs. Stevens? Alicia did know you, but you never saw her while you were here, did you?"

"You're mistaken. I never knew her," said Mrs. Stevens, tight-lipped. "I never met the woman."

"Of course not. This is only a story. And there's another character in it, a minor one we haven't mentioned yet. In addition to the scapegoat thief we had here, we also had a thief in California, one who ransacked Alicia Tremple's house in order to cover up an office break-in. I should think Alicia's records have been thoroughly sorted through. What's left there will not connect to any of you, will it?"

"Of course not," said Dr. Fley. "None of us knew her. None of us knew anyone who knew her."

Shaken heads. None of them. Of course.

225

Shirley mused, "Of course there are the records at Mediclerk, Inc."

"Oh, they wouldn't tell you a thing," said Rob, staring into Harry's face. "I'll bet nobody there is on record as being her patient or being related to any patient she had."

Harry smiled. "I'm quite sure of that because I'm in charge of programming. I know what's in the files."

"Of course. You would be."

"Very interesting," said Dr. Fley. "This story time. I understand this used to be the custom in some good gentlemen's clubs. A delicious dinner, then storytelling around the fire. But we don't have a fire."

"In the living room." Shirley smiled. "Now it's cool enough for a fire."

She had laid the fire that afternoon, after spending a fretful half hour trying to figure out the damper. There were liqueurs and brandies on the table.

"There's something I don't understand about your story," said J.Q., when they were seated. "The grandson character died because he thought he had AIDS, didn't he?"

"Oh, we can work out that detail," said Harry. "He was told he was HIV positive. In any good laboratory, positive results require very careful follow-up, including more elaborate tests, but cheapy labs don't bother with careful follow-up. They just say, positive and the hell with you."

"Cheapy labs?"

"Laboratories that make their money billing Medicaid," said Dr. Fley. "Laboratories without quality control or professional standards. Laboratories that bid for the business. Laboratories that pay kickbacks to doctors who do business with them."

"In our business, we get to know who they are," said Harry. "They have a reputation, you know?"

Dr. Fley said, "One could allege such a laboratory was used in this case—since it's only a story."

"One could," said Shirley.

"One might say that the practitioner who accepts a kickback for using such a laboratory is as guilty as the lab it-

226

self. When a practitioner does not really care about the people she treats, when they are only a means to an end, she does not care that she risks their lives."

"Oh, I understand. A person set upon rooting out demons is not interested in bodily ills. Only the demon interests her. As during the Inquisition, when rooting out heresy took precedence over every other consideration."

Silence fell. They looked into the fire, some sipping, some merely sitting. Mr. Fley stared at his wife with a particularly intent expression, as though he did not know her. Mr. Stevens patted his wife's knee while she stared past him, into the shadowy corners of the room.

"She was an incest victim," Shirley murmured. "She was obsessed, but only because of what she had suffered. She spent her days slaying demons, and they were all the same demon. Surely she should have been pitied."

"We should pity all serial killers," said Dr. Fley, rising. "I pity mad dogs as well. But I do not let them run among my children, not if I can help it." She put her hand on her husband's shoulder. "Time we go back to our house and get packed. It's been a pleasant vacation, Shirley. I intend to tell all our friends about you. I know they'll enjoy this lovely place as much as we have, though it has a hostess who's a bit more perspicacious than counted on, one might say."

Shirley shook them both by the hand and let them go. Dr. Fley's hand was warm, callused, firm. Mr. Fley's hand was limp and cold.

Mr. Stevens's grasp was warm, though a bit tentative. "I don't know what to think about tonight. It's like those murder-mystery tours, isn't it. Not what I expected, I'll tell you. Not sure I liked it, either, though Ree seemed to get right into it."

Mrs. Stevens said quietly, "Good-bye," without looking at her husband.

Rob slipped out without a word while Harry made their farewells. "That was quite an exercise. Fun to do it as theater sometime, wouldn't it be? I'll have to tell Marsh about it."

"Marsh?"

"My friend in California. He couldn't come with us this time. He had some things to attend to. He's a writer, actually. This is exactly the kind of thing that interests him. Conspiracy theories. Just when one thinks they're passé, here comes some other application. Remarkable."

And he, too, was gone.

Cally lingered, his face drawn. "How much of that was . . . ?"

"How much was what?" she asked gently.

"How much do you believe?"

"All of it," she said. "Every jot and tittle."

"Good Lord." He sighed. "I had no idea. . . ."

"I know you didn't, Cally. You and Mr. Stevens and poor Mr. Fley were along for the ride. As were Rob and I."

"The Fley woman was right, wasn't she? Tremple was a killer. She killed people as surely as if she'd shot them with a gun."

"Yes," Shirley admitted. "She did. Obsession plus superstition yields inquisition, and inquisitions kill a lot of people."

"Couldn't someone have stopped her?"

Shirley frowned. "How? She was entitled to her opinion. Ph.D.s aren't immune from spouting nonsense. And as I understand it, the whole field of psychiatry is divided on this 'delayed memory' question. My gut tells me it will turn out to be a witch-hunt, just like in old Salem. Hysteria, suggestion, mob psychology . . ."

"Like lynch mobs," Cally said. "Like the House Un-American Activities Committee, accusing and accusing. Killing people. Ruining their lives. I know people in Hollywood who still talk about that." He turned his troubled face on her. "Is there something we should do? Something we can do?"

"What?" she asked softly. "You want to get sued for

slander? You want to get yourself tied up in court for the next several years? With what outcome?"

"But people just shouldn't . . ."

"Cally, people just shouldn't. That's what we make law for, to protect us. What do people do when the law can do nothing?"

They stared at one another, mutually troubled and as mutually impotent. He went away wordlessly. Out in the kitchen the clattering had ceased. The cateress peeked in, then came in when she saw they were alone.

"Beautiful dinner," said Shirley. "Very nice. Your check is in an envelope on top of the refrigerator."

"They did seem to enjoy it, didn't they?" She shook hands and left, humming, pleased with herself.

"Who was your absent guest?" J.Q. asked.

"I don't know who she really was, J.Q. But Mrs. Fley knows. And Harry knows. And probably Mrs. Stevens knows."

"They didn't eat like people troubled by conscience."

"They weren't troubled by conscience. None of them did anything illegal."

"Nothing worth reporting to the police?"

"What do I say? That I think Dr. Fley researched Naegleria fowlerii? That I think Mrs. Stevens may have grown some in the laboratory? That I think Harry or Rob may have erased some computer records? That I think Rob's friend Marsh broke into a house in California? None of it's provable. None of it's even . . . sensible. The one person who did something murderous wasn't here. I did what I could do, working with what we had." She frowned, still troubled. "There is one thing I might have done differently. I might have ordered a cold supper tonight."

"And why is that?" asked J.Q.

"Revenge is a dish better served up cold," she quoted. "And I hope never to taste one served any colder than this was."

* * *

229

Contrary to their previously stated plans, the young men in Big House packed up and left the following morning, Rob and Harry in one direction, Cally in another. With no pangs of conscience at all, Shirley charged them for the full stay, which they paid without demur. Three of the houses were empty. Quite frankly she hoped it would stay that way for a while, though a glance at the calendar disabused her of this notion. By Friday they would be full once more. Families with children. Families with dogs. The German family was leaving, but another group was coming on the same day. So much for peace and quiet.

J.Q.'s friend who worked for *Variety* had referred J.Q.'s question to someone else, and that person called on Wednesday night to say there was indeed a TV series in production with almost a dozen episodes completed. It was called *The Stupe Brothers,* and the producer was so-and-so.

Shirley called Pasc Yesney and put him in touch with so-and-so. Any rights belonging to Allison should be negotiated by him.

"I'm confident she owns fifty percent," he said. "I picked up a copy of the will. Hardin left all property of which he was possessed to his son. Sheldon has half rights on the Two Stupes, of course. Anything Charles owned would have passed to his daughter because his wife died so shortly after he did, though I don't find that anything was done on her behalf at the time."

"Back then it didn't matter a bit, Pasc. At that time Allison's inheritance consisted of two cardboard boxes the mortgage company turned over to me on her behalf. They were what was left in the house after everything was repossessed and we'd given the clothes to the Salvation Army."

"What's in the boxes?"

"I've only looked in one of them. Junk. Those prescription medicine bottles I showed you."

"Better look in the other one. I'd prefer not to have any surprises."

The other box yielded some photographs and the tapes

Allison remembered seeing when she was a little girl. The Two Stupes, in glorious black-and-white.

Rights to Sheldon's share were subsequently negotiated by the board of Cedar Rest. Pasc Yesney got enough for Allison so that she could plan on going to college pretty much wherever she liked.

"I called Mr. Brentwood," Pasc told Shirley, when everything had been wrapped up. "I asked him if he thought he had any claim. He snorted and snuffled about family honor and the possibility of a preexisting contract, but when I said the very existence of such a contract might involve him in a criminal prosecution, he decided he didn't have one after all. I asked for his friend's address, Mr. Evans. He said Mr. Evans wasn't his friend. That he hardly knew the man. That in any case, the Evanses had moved away."

"You think we've heard the end of it?" asked Shirley. "I wish I had those photographs."

"There's nothing in it for them," he replied. "There wasn't, not from the moment you found out what they were up to. Must've smarted some, but I think he'll swallow it and pretend it never happened."

Which is what, more or less, Shirley conveyed to Allison.

"I knew it was going to be all right," Allison said. "I just knew it was. They're such . . . blundery people. Sort of like Vancie. All full of words and no sense."

"Are you going to hear from Vancie, do you think?"

"I don't think so. She doesn't remember stuff very well. I talked and talked, but I'll bet she forgets it all when she gets back to Tommy. Until she's lived in that garage for a while, she won't remember what we talked about. By then it'll be too late." She reached out and grabbed Shirley's hand, held it tightly between her own. "I think about that baby. The one she's going to have."

"I think about it, too, Allison."

"I look at Vancie and see that anybody can have a baby. But it's going to take more than just having it to be a mother. More than just begetting it, like J.Q. says. If Vancie

231

and her boyfriend cared anything about the baby, they'd be out getting jobs, finding a decent place to live. She isn't thinking about that at all."

"I know, Allison."

"She says all the words, you know? My flesh and blood, she says. Tommy's child, she says. Those words don't mean anything! I was flesh and blood, too, and that wasn't the important thing. I guess I know. It's what people plan to do before they ever get a baby! Even birds build nests first! It's carefulness. Uncle Lawrence and Aunt Esther, they don't know that. The judges don't know that. I wish they could all get it straight!"

"I wish they could, too. I've always wished they could."

A month passed, and another. Allison was in school. Xanthy was busy with bulb catalogs, checking the packages she was receiving almost daily and making copious notes. Summer was over, and with it the crowded season. Now the guests were fewer and more relaxed, less determined to pack a year's enjoyments into two weeks. Summer had been mostly families with children. Now many of the guests were retired, enjoying the golden foliage and the splendor of winy air and a cloudless sky.

"As should we," said J.Q., with the air of one making a pronouncement. "I am taking you into town. We shall walk Canyon Road, view art, and have tapas at El Farol."

"Shall we indeed?" she asked. "Just you and me, J.Q.?"

"Xanthy has kindly offered to phone-sit. I think you deserve a break."

"I think so, too." She was inordinately pleased with the idea. They had done nothing silly and spur of the moment for a very long time. She even put on her best boots for the occasion, and her best hat, the one with the silver band.

They walked, in company with other strollers. They stopped and had coffee. They went into galleries and stood there, looking pontifical. They were approached by gallery owners who talked knowledgeably of art as investment, art as demonstration of shared humanity, art as craftsmanship and appreciation for tradition, everything but art as a way of making a living.

"They're all in it altruistically," said Shirley. "Not one of them is in it for the money, have you noticed?"

He had. Nonetheless, he had seen things he liked. He wondered about a certain bronze. Wouldn't it sit well in the patio of the main house?

Bemused by consideration of this possibility, Shirley was led into El Farol and provided with a glass of wine and several small plates of things. She munched, sipped, let her eyes explore the place, fastening, with a shock of recognition, upon a figure seated against the far wall.

"My God," she muttered, sotto voce, "isn't that . . .?"

And it was, unmistakably. Sitting there eating, just like a normal person, a presence known to most of the English-speaking world. A real celebrity. Shirley peered covertly, beneath her lashes, amused to find within herself that quality of curious interest, that gawking quality she had often decried in others. The face was lively, unmistakable, fully disclosed by hair knotted high. When she ordered from the menu, she held it a little close. Perhaps she was near sighted.

Resolutely Shirley turned her attention back to J.Q., who was watching her with a half smile.

"Cute little gesture she has there," he said softly. "That way she runs her finger down her ear."

Shirley glanced again, seeing it. The hand sneaking up, almost without volition, touching the ear, running down it to the jaw, and on to the chin.

"Some people do it to stop smoking," said J.Q. "I looked into it when I quit cigarettes. You have something put in the ear, like a staple. Whenever you get the urge to smoke, you feel of it, move to the mouth, think of that, and it breaks the chain of habit. At least so I'm told. Maybe she's trying to quit."

The woman across the room was looking at them. Almost staring. Shirley met her eyes. The little gesture again,

233

and then the lifted glass. She was toasting them, a tiny smile barely bowing her lips, her face serene, untroubled.

Shirley almost lifted her glass in acknowledgment. Instead she let her eyes drift past, then wiped her lips firmly and pushed back her chair.

"Time to go home, J.Q. I'm having all kinds of fanciful ideas. Must be the wine."

"Must be," he agreed, rising. "Oh, absolutely, must be."

The Shirley McClintock series

by Anthony and Edgar Awards nominee

B. J. Oliphant

Published by Fawcett Books.
Available in your local bookstore.

Call toll free 1-800-733-3000 to order by phone and use your major credit card. Or use this coupon to order by mail.

__DEAD IN THE SCRUB	449-14653-7	**$4.95**
__DEATH AND THE DELINQUENT	449-14718-5	**$4.50**
__DESERVEDLY DEAD	449-14717-7	**$3.99**
__THE UNEXPECTED CORPSE	449-14674-X	**$4.99**

Name_____

Address_____

City_____State_____Zip _____

Please send me the FAWCETT BOOKS I have checked above.

I am enclosing $_____
   plus
Postage & handling* $_____
Sales tax (where applicable) $_____
Total amount enclosed $_____

*Add $2 for the first book and 50¢ for each additional book.

Send check or money order (no cash or CODs) to:
Fawcett Mail Sales, 400 Hahn Road, Westminster, MD 21157.

Prices and numbers subject to change without notice.
Valid in the U.S. only.
All orders subject to availability.   OLIPHANT